The Flower of the Family

The Flower of the Family

(Cover photograph by Mrs. Sharon White: "A beautiful lake in Vermont, near Mrs. White's home.")

The Flower of the Family

The Legacy of Home Press Classic Edition

by Mrs. Elizabeth Prentiss

"Though I have a rooting here,
Which holds me downward, yet in my desire
To that which is above me I aspire;
And all my best affections I profess
To Him that is the Sun of Righteousness."
—Wither

The Flower of the Family

The text from the current edition was carefully transcribed and lightly edited from the 1883 edition, originally published by:
Anson D. F. Randolph and Company, New York

Any additional images or text that has been added includes their source.

All Scripture Quotations are from the King James Bible.

Copyright 1854: by Mrs. Elizabeth Payson Prentiss (1818 – 1878) (Wife)
Copyright 1883: by George L. Prentiss (1816 – 1903) (Husband)

Current edition:
Copyright 2022 by Mrs. Sharon White and The Legacy of Home Press:
For supplementary material; format; cover design; and light editing of text.

ISBN Number: 978-1-956616-08-8

The Legacy of Home Press
    Vermont - U.S.A.

Foreword

THIS book is part of a series we are republishing by Mrs. Elizabeth Prentiss.

A beautiful feature of her work is the reference to Scripture without stating the exact location of the verses. Bible passages occur in her writings, just as they must have been spoken in normal conversation. I have left them just as they were in the original edition and hope you will search out the passages using a "Strong's Concordance." You will be blessed!

You may also notice a handful of uncommon words. I have found the 1828 edition of Noah Webster's dictionary to be a great help in finding just what she meant in her expressions.

Her stories are bright, wholesome, and delightful. Her words encourage and instruct. You will be cheered along on the path to Heaven.

A couple of years ago, I visited the town of Dorset, Vermont and saw the beautiful home owned by the Prentiss family. It is a lovely place!

I have taken photographs of the scenery around Vermont, of views Mrs. Prentiss may have seen while she was living here, and used them as covers for the books. I hope you enjoy them.

Mrs. Sharon White
- The Legacy of Home Press -
Vermont, 2022.

The Flower of the Family

Portrait of Mrs. Elizabeth Prentiss: From the 1882 edition of "The Life and Letters of Elizabeth Prentiss."

The Flower of the Family

Contents

Foreword   5

Portrait of the Author   6

Introductory Notes:

    I
Note to the 1883 edition, by her husband, George Prentiss
    11
    II
Review from 1877   12

The Flower of the Family

    Chapter 1
    Comfortable Troubles   13

    Chapter 2
    Trouble Bearing Fruit   19

    Chapter 3
    Homely Discipline   24

    Chapter 4
    Arthur   29

    Chapter 5
    Baby Number Two   35

    Chapter 6
    Sorrow at Night, Joy in the Morning   48

Chapter 7
The Uncle's Visit   56

Chapter 8
New Scenes and New Friends   67

Chapter 9
A Glimpse at "Society"   75

Chapter 10
The Sixteenth Birthday   84

Chapter 11
Good Intentions, If Not Good Works   92

Chapter 12
The Consequences of a Prescription   100

Chapter 13
The Storm Before the Calm   108

Chapter 14
Cases of Conscience   119

Chapter 15
The Sea-Side   125

Chapter 16
Life at School   133

Chapter 17
The Holidays   144

Chapter 18
Lucy in Trouble   153

Chapter 19
A Visit from Miss Prigott, and What it Led To   163

Chapter 20
Every Life has its Romance   173

The Flower of the Family

Chapter 21 A Not Agreeable Surprise	181
Chapter 22 Shows the Clouds Dispersing	187
Chapter 23 A Resolve	194
Chapter 24 A Relief	201
Chapter 25 A Shadow	208
Chapter 26 The Broken Circle	214
Chapter 27 A New Home	221
Daily Food for Christians	229

The Flower of the Family

*If on our daily course our mind
Be set to hallow all we find,
New treasures still, of countless price,
God will provide for sacrifice.*

*Old friends, old scenes will lovelier be,
As more of heaven in each we see;
Some softening gleam of love and prayer
Shall dawn on every cross and care.*

*We need not bid, for cloister'd cell,
Our neighbor and our work farewell,
Nor strive to wind ourselves too high,
For sinful man beneath the sky.*

*The trivial round, the common task,
Would furnish all we ought to ask:
Room to deny ourselves; a road
To bring us daily nearer God.*

—Keble

Note to the 1883 Edition

I.

WITH THE EXCEPTION of "Stepping Heavenward," no one of Mrs. Prentiss' larger books has had so wide a circulation, both at home and abroad, as "The Flower of the Family."

A French translation, entitled "La Fleur de la Famille," has passed through five or six editions. It was also translated into German under the title, "Die Perle der Familie." In both languages it received the warmest praise. The work depicts a marked type of the family life of thirty years ago, which is becoming rare in our own day; and on this account, as well as for its intrinsic merits, deserves to be reprinted. Its aim cannot be better expressed than in the following extract from a letter of Mrs. Prentiss to a friend, written soon after its publication in 1854:

"I long to have it doing good. I never had such desires about anything in my life: and I never sat down to write without first praying that I might not be suffered to write anything that would do harm, and that, on the contrary, I might be taught to say what would do good. And it has been a great comfort to me that every word of praise I have ever received from others concerning it has been "it will do good," and this I have had from, so many sources that, amid much trial and sickness ever since its publication, I have had rays of sunshine creeping in now and then to cheer and sustain me."

Numberless testimonies to its usefulness continued to cheer her to the end of her days,

- G. L. P.

New York, September 1883.

Review from 1877

II.

THE FOLLOWING is a review of "The Flower of the Family," taken from the original publisher, Anson D. F. Randolph and Company. It was gleaned from the back pages of one of her other books, published in 1877:

"It aims to exact trivial home duty, by showing how such duty performed in the fear of God and the love of Christ may lead upward and onward through present self-denial, to the highest usefulness, peace and joy.

Published more than seventeen years ago, it has continued to hold its place among the foremost books of its class. It is free from the objection which characterize too many of the modern story books prepared for the young. It is full of interest, without being sensational, and the standard of duty which it sets up is within the possible reach of all."

At the time of publication, this book was suggested for girls from 12 to 16 years of age. However, the present publisher believes it would also be much appreciated by women of any age.

The Flower of the Family

CHAPTER 1

Comfortable Troubles

"THE BABY is crying, Lucy; won't you come down and take him a few minutes?" said a voice from the foot of the stairs.

Lucy sighed heavily, and threw down upon the table before her, with a gesture of impatience, a book on which she had been intent.

"He's always crying, I do believe," she said to herself, as, casting a farewell glance at books and papers, she went slowly down to soothe the cries, from which her sensitive ear shrank as from the sound of a trumpet.

"I'm sorry to interrupt you, dear," said her mother, "but baby will not be still any longer, and here are my hands in the bread. Just take him up a minute, and I will soon be ready for him."

Lucy took the child, and as his cries of discontent gave place to a smile of delight, she put down the ungracious feeling that struggled for the victory, and kissed his round, rosy cheek, more than once.

"I can't help loving you, though you *are* such a little torment," she said. "People call children troublesome comforts; I don't wonder, I'm sure."

"*I* call them comfortable troubles," returned her mother, glancing fondly upon them both. "One must have trouble in some shape, and this is the best of all."

"Yes, I suppose so," said Lucy; "but we have a great many other troubles, besides."

"What, for instance?" asked the mother, whose energies were not all concentrated upon the bread.

The Flower of the Family

"Oh dear! There are plenty of them, if it comes to that," replied Lucy. "In the first place, you and father have to work so hard."

"Well?"

"And we are so poor; and the boys are so noisy; and I can't go to school; and a new baby comes so often; and it tires me when I think it will always be so."

The mother sighed, and kneaded the dough with a wearied hand.

"Yes, it is all true," said she. "It is all true. I wish I could shield you from these troubles, my child; but I cannot. By and by, as the children get older—then—but I don't know, I can't see far ahead myself."

"As fast as the children get older, some more keep coming," said Lucy, despondingly.

"Yes, I know," said her mother; "but they'll get over that by and by; and you shall have more time to study than you've had lately. Rebecca shall stay home and help me."

"*That* won't do," returned Lucy. She walked to the window, and stood looking out, in gloomy silence.

Her mother finished her work in silence equally profound, took off the clean checked apron in which it had been performed, and approaching the window, offered to take the child.

"Now, dear," said she.

But the child, pleased with its new position, hung back, smiling, and clasping its little arms closer around Lucy's neck.

"How the little fellow loves you," cried her mother. "It's such a pity he isn't fond of Rebecca. I wonder, by the way, where the child is, and Hatty too. It's high time they were all here."

"It's half-past five," said Lucy, "and they ought to be home, I'm sure. But this is always the way! Just because I want to study."

"You can study now," said her mother gently, and taking the baby from her.

"No, I can't; it's time to get tea," returned Lucy. "And it's Rebecca's week to get tea. But she's taken herself off, nobody knows where."

Ungracious in word, but not in deed, Lucy went now and filled the tea-kettle, and arranged the fire.

The Flower of the Family

"I wouldn't do that, dear," said her mother. "If Rebecca finds she can depend on you to do her work for her, there'll be no end to the trouble."

"But father will be in, next news, wanting his supper. Besides, I see the boys coming up the road, and they'll be hungry too."

She hurried about, cutting bread, skimming milk, and arranging plates and knives with neatness and precision.

"She's worth a dozen of Rebecca," thought her mother. "Where can that child be? It's too bad! Now, baby, you *must* sit in the cradle awhile and let mother help sister Lucy."

She seated the child snugly amid pillows, gave him a tin plate and pewter spoon for his amusement, and hastened to relieve Lucy. Baby began forthwith to raise a noise suited to his peculiar taste, by means of a series of irregular thumps of the spoon upon the plate. While he pursued this pastime with great energy, the boys rushed in from school.

"There you go!" shouted John to his books, as he threw them down, "and good enough for you, you old plagues! Is supper ready? I hope so, for I'm as hungry as three bears."

"One bear will do," said his mother, smiling, and patting his shoulders. "But where are the girls?"

"Why Rebecca is creeping along on the road somewhere. She'll get here by midnight, I dare say. And Hatty had to stay in. She blotted her writing-book, and then went and got angry about it, and so she's got to stay in till she's learned a chapter in the Bible."

"Why, Rebecca!" said her mother, as this young lady came leisurely in: "where have you been?"

"Why, nowhere, mother: I came straight home from school."

"But you should have been home in time to get tea. Here's Lucy has had to do it for you."

"I came as fast as I could, mother," said Rebecca. "Susan Turner and I, we came along together. I couldn't come running up the hill as the boys did. And Lucy needn't have went and got tea. She knew I was coming."

"Needn't have *went*!" said John; "let's hear you parse that, do!"

"I wish I could shake you and Lucy up together," said her mother, as she contrasted Lucy's hurried, rather excited step, with Rebecca's slow pace. "It would improve you both. But run

The Flower of the Family

now, and call father. Tell him tea is on the table. And come here, all of you, and wash your faces," she added, as the boys prepared themselves for an onset upon the table. But at this auspicious moment, the baby's energetic spoon flew up with great force upon his fair, high forehead, instead of the plate at which the blow was aimed.

Down fell spoon and plate, and up went shout after shout of baby-terror and pain. Everybody ran to see what was the matter; everybody tried to catch up and appease the poor little victim; yet somehow it was in Lucy's arms that he was borne off; and it was Lucy's hand that bathed the aching head, and Lucy's voice that, now melted into the tones of tenderest love and pity, finally soothed and hushed those grievous cries.

"Oh, what a bump there is on his forehead!" said Rebecca, who, as usual, arrived at the scene too late to offer anything more than an exclamation of horror.

"I'll keep him while you are at supper, mother," said Lucy now quite lost to farther thought of self, in sympathy for the child. "He'll soon get over it. I'll take him out of doors."

She went out, kissing him as she went along, and as soon as they reached the open air, found herself repaid by the brilliant smile that lighted up the tears with which the blue eyes were brimful.

"There ought to be a rainbow somewhere," said she, holding the baby up to the window, where he could be seen, and pointing out his tears and smiles; "for it rains and shines at the same time."

"You're the rainbow yourself," said her father, giving her one of his own rare, precious smiles.

Lucy turned quickly away, with a blush of shame upon her cheek that no reproof could have burned there.

"He didn't hear me fretting when mother called me," thought she. "He doesn't know how cross and selfish I was. If he had, he wouldn't have called me a rainbow. He'd have called me a thunder-cloud!"

And the "thunder-cloud" relieved itself of a few large, heavy drops, and grew lighter. She went in to supper, giving the baby to her mother. They had all risen from the table, and as she

The Flower of the Family

seated herself, she perceived that not a morsel of bread remained for her.

"I should think somebody might have cut a slice of bread for me," thought she. "But it's always the way. Nobody cares whether I eat or not."

At this moment her brother Arthur came running up to her, bearing a huge loaf of bread in his arms.

"It's for you," said he. "I got it all myself. And I picked a few strawberries for you, on the way to school."

"Why didn't you give them to mother?" asked she.

"Oh, I did give her half," said he.

"But why did not you give her all?" she asked, knowing well the reason, yet wanting to hear it still.

He only looked up, however, and smiled. Yet the smile answered and cheered her, and again she felt humbled and reproved.

"Oh! I do wish I was good!" thought she.

She finished her supper in silence, and then helped her mother get the little ones off to bed.

In the midst of their labors, Hatty came running in, tired, flushed, and out of breath.

"Oh dear!" cried she, "have you all done supper? It's too bad! I hate to eat all by myself! I should think somebody might have waited for me. Where's the milk? Oh! here it is. Where's mother? Mother, mother! I need a new pair of shoes. There's a hole in the side of one of mine, and the heels are all worn out, so that little stones get in and half kill me."

"You've only had them a month," said Rebecca, reproachfully.

"Well, what of that?" retorted Hatty.

"Nothing; only if we are all going to have a new pair of shoes every month, I wonder where the money is to come from."

"Who said you were all to have a new pair?" asked Hatty, laughing, and pouring down milk as fast as possible. "If I went creeping along like a snail, as you do, maybe my shoes would last longer; but I'd as lief die as go crawling about in that style. How cross Miss Wheeler was this afternoon! Well! I don't care. I feel as well as ever, now that I've had my supper; and I had the comfort of keeping her in, at any rate. And now I'm going down to Mary Johnson's."

The Flower of the Family

She caught up her bonnet, and was hurrying away, when her mother detained her.

"Have you finished those stockings, dear?" she asked.

"No, mother, not quite; I'll finish them to-morrow. I'm going to Mary Johnson's now."

"I'm afraid Arthur won't fare very well in your hands," said her mother.

Hatty wavered a little between Mary Johnson and Arthur. "To-morrow is Saturday," said she, "and I shall have time to see to all his things then." And, satisfied with her mother's half consent, away she flew.

"Lucy, dear, hadn't you better go too?" asked her mother.

"I thought I would study a little now," she answered.

"Oh, run out and get rested, first; you have had no rest to-day."

"It rests me to study," said Lucy.

"Just to please me!" urged her mother.

Lucy took down her bonnet, and stood holding it in her hand a moment irresolutely; then slowly left the house, and turned her steps towards a neighboring grove, among whose shadows she was soon lost to her mother's anxious eye.

"She has not gone with Hatty, after all," thought she. Her hopeful heart was heavy with care this night, and she looked down with a troubled face upon the baby who lay half asleep in her arms. He opened his eyes, and seemed to catch the shadow from hers, for he curled up his lip with a pitiful, grieved expression, very touching to behold. She reassured him with a smile, and began to sing,

"There is a land of pure delight."

The baby lay quiet, and soon fell asleep, and the heavy heart lay quiet too, for there was comfort for it in that good old hymn.

CHAPTER 2

Trouble Bearing Fruit

Lucy sauntered listlessly along, and at last threw herself down upon the ground, at the foot of a tree. It was a lovely, quiet evening; the crickets hummed cheerfully around her, and the fresh, pure air was as full of life and cheer as they.

"I wish I was good!" said she. "I wish I was a Christian! I wish I could help being fretful and selfish. Oh! I do wish I *could* be a Christian! But it's no use. The more I try to be good, the worse I am. I do hate so to sew and to work; and I do love so to read and to study! Mother says the children are growing older; but so am I growing older, and not learning anything, hardly. But it is wicked to fret about it, I know. Oh! I do wish I was a Christian!"

Silent as was the energetic desire, Lucy started as she heard an approaching footstep, as if detected in some guilty act.

It was her father. He sat down by her side, and for a little time both were silent. At last he said:

"Your mother has been telling me that you are greatly interrupted and hindered in your studies. She feels troubled about it, and so do I. But we must try to keep up our courage, and hope for brighter days."

"If mother could spare me, I should like to go away somewhere to school," returned Lucy. "There is a good school at H__ , and it would not cost much."

"Mother would spare you," he answered kindly; "but, my dear child, why not go to school here? Why leave home? Is it already distasteful to you?"

"No, indeed, father; but Miss Wheeler says there's no use in my coming to her any longer. She says," she added, coloring, "I've learned all she can teach in a village school."

The Flower of the Family

"You should have told me that," he answered.

"There was no need, at first: mother thought she could manage it so as to give me time to study at home, and I thought it was going to be so nice. But she has to interrupt me. She cannot help it. And so I don't learn anything at all."

"Rebecca will soon leave school," said her father. "Let me see! She's two years older than you, isn't she?"

"She's nearly that; but you know she got behindhand by her long sickness. That's the reason I know more than she does."

"That's one reason," he answered, smiling.

"Well, father, when she leaves school, if you and mother could spare me to go to H__ , I would be very industrious, and I would wear very simple clothes, and very soon I could keep school myself."

"Dear child," said he, "I certainly will not refuse to consider the question, at least." He rose and walked slowly homeward. Lucy sat still, with a beating heart. She was full of that hunger and thirst after knowledge that would not be appeased, and, for the moment, it almost consumed her. She did not see the big drops on her father's brow, as he revolved her proposal in his mind, nor hear the sighs that had forced them there.

"Mother," said he, as he entered the house, "Lucy says she has learned all Miss Wheeler can teach her."

"Yes," she answered, quietly, "I know it. Miss Wheeler told me so herself."

"But you did not tell me."

"You had cares enough already."

"Could we possibly send her to H__ , do you think?"

The mother cast her eye about the room.

"Is there anything we could sell?" thought she.

"You can't spare us," said the old chairs, as her eye fell upon them. "There are too few of us now."

"Where will you eat your dinner; how will you do your ironing, if I go?" asked the pine table.

"I must stay and rock the baby!" cried the cradle, now appealed to. "I've rocked all your babies for you, patiently; yes, I rocked you when you were a baby yourself. And now, would you turn me away?"

She sighed a little; then her patient heart took courage, and her imagination ran into her bedroom, and looked in all her drawers to see what was there.

"Dear me!" it said, "what is there worth looking at here? Old, patched shirts; baby-frocks and aprons, faded and worn; that collar you've had ever since the flood; nobody would take the gift of them. And, for pity's sake, what would you do without them?"

"You don't think of any way in which it could be done?" said the father, at last.

"No, not just yet. But perhaps I shall in time," she said, determined to look at the bright side of the case.

"If it were not for that debt, there'd be something to hope for," said he.

"Yes, that debt! But one must have trouble. If we had not that, we should have something else."

"A pleasant view of life!" he said, bitterly.

"You are not well to-night," she said.

"I should be well enough if I could see that child satisfied," he returned.

Unobserved by her parents, for it was now quite dark, Lucy had entered the room, and heard the last few sentences.

"A debt!" thought she. "How dreadful! No wonder father looks so careworn, and works so hard! And I have been worrying him about school!" She crept noiselessly away to her own room, until her father assembled the family for evening worship. As she knelt with the rest, and listened to his prayer, she understood the secret care and sorrow veiled amid its petitions. As she bid him good-night, she whispered,

"Father, I think I won't go away to school. I can get a good deal of time to study if I am careful; and it's just as well."

He kissed her more than once, not deceived by these generous words, but willing to gratify her for the time by seeming so.

"Well, we will let it rest for the present," he said; "and, oh! my precious child, remember it matters little how wise he is who has not learned Christ!"

"I know it! I know it!" she cried bitterly to herself. She lingered near him after the other children had retired.

The Flower of the Family

"I do not mean to depreciate human wisdom," he said; "only I would place so far above earthly, all heavenly good."

"I do not remember the time when I did not place goodness first," she answered timidly.

"And isn't it time this feeling should bear fruit?" he asked very tenderly.

"Oh, father! Hasn't it borne any fruit?" she asked, now bursting into tears.

"Do not misunderstand me, darling," he said, "I was only trying to lead you to say just what you have said. We have watched you too long, and with too much solicitude, not to perceive that old things were passing away and all things becoming new, and I thought you would feel better to open your heart to us."

"Yes, father, I wish I could. But it was only a few hours ago, when mother called me from my books, I felt irritated; and after that, I said to myself, 'There's no use! I am not a Christian! Christians don't feel so!'"

"I wish that were true, my dear Lucy. But it is not. Christians do feel so. But they do not *allow* themselves in sin. They watch and pray, and struggle against it."

"But it does not do any good for me to do that," said Lucy, sadly. "I go right away and do wrong the moment I have resolved never to yield to temptation again."

"Then go right back to your Saviour and tell Him all about it; and beg Him to give you true and hearty sorrow for and abhorrence of it."

"I have, a great many times; but it's no use."

"And yet you have been growing, meanwhile, more patient, more gentle, every day. Your mother has observed it, and so have I. You may depend upon it, God never hears a prayer, however poor and imperfect, without answering it."

Lucy felt cheered and encouraged by this assurance. She had long been groping about in the dark, wrapped in a reserve painful to both her parents and herself; and now the ice was broken. She would gladly have opened her heart more fully, but this was needless. One glance had sufficed to show to her father that the struggle against sin and the pursuit after God had begun; and he felt that he could safely leave her in His hands who giveth the victory through our Lord Jesus Christ. He made her kneel once more by his side, while, in a few solemn words, he gave himself and her to God, to be His, and only His, forever, and then retired for the night. Lucy returned to her room, greatly cheered and comforted. Many months ago she had begun to hope that God had made her His child; but she had found little satisfaction in serving Him so long as she felt doubtful as to her acceptance with Him. The tendency to despond, to which in other respects she was prone, assailed her here disastrously. And as yet she lacked that clear, distinct view of Christ as *all in all* without which, even if there is religious life, there can be neither peace nor progress.

"Now I will *go on*, with God's help," she thought, and from that hour she never faltered.

CHAPTER 3

Homely Discipline

IN LUCY'S INFANCY, her mother used often to say, "This child will make something, either good or bad; I don't know which." For even when a very little girl, she gave evidence of a proud, sensitive, and moody temper, hard to understand and hard to control. Great strength and tenderness of the affections adorned the wayward childhood, which else would have been all root and branch, and no flower. Her delight was to wander by herself in lonely places; to sit musing and dreaming away the hours other children spend in play; and to venture into and court danger and mystery. No stranger could have met the child in her wanderings, or seen her sitting thoughtfully by the fireside, or watched the grave face she wore at church on Sundays, without marking and holding her in long remembrance. Oftentimes, when the serious face was lifted to her mother's, she saw in it a depth and intensity that made her tremble. "Will she grow up a good child?" used to be the question; but as years advanced, it oftener was, "Will she be a happy one?" One cannot say what she would have become, had the solitary childhood passed into the solitary girlhood, wherein the busy mind could have reveled on and consumed itself.

But as years passed, other children were added to the family; the inner life of this sensitive being received many a shock, and the delicate taste was wounded at a thousand points. The mother had not now time to ask, "How shall I train her?" Domestic care took her in hand; set her down to hard, homely tasks; forced her from the unreal into the actual; and tampered with every morbid fancy and poetic longing. For many years she brooded over and repined at this lot, and strove to disentangle herself from the cares and duties in which she was involved. But in time this discipline accomplished for her that which prosperity never has wrought, and the morbid soil on which it was exercised bore fruit both rich and rare. The sunshine lies upon the mountain-top all day, and lingers there latest and longest at eventide. Yet is the valley green and fertile, and the mountain-top barren and unfruitful.

On the morning after the conversation with her father, Lucy rose early, and opening her window, enjoyed for a few minutes the pure fresh air. The stillness of this early hour, broken only by the songs of cheerful birds, went down into her very heart. She would gladly have dreamed away hours in contemplation of the scene before her, but life called her to something besides dreams. It called with a shrill, boyish voice, "Lucy! Lucy Grant! Mother says, won't you come down and wash my face, and Tom's face, and all our faces?"

She ran down and performed those necessary acts with so much more than ordinary gentleness and patience, that the children were quite docile under the operation.

"I wish you'd always wash me," said Tom. "Rebecca is so slow, and she does bear on so! And Hatty doesn't half wash me, she's always in such a hurry."

"Shall I take the baby, mother?" she asked pleasantly.

"You may, dear, a few minutes, and I'll see about breakfast. Baby's getting more teeth, I think. He was very restless all night."

"I mean to have him to-night, then," said Lucy.

"Oh no, that won't do. I can't have you deprived of sleep."

Lucy took the baby, smoothed down his little rumpled night-gown, and went to the door-step, where she seated herself and tried to read from a book drawn hastily from her pocket. The baby hailed the appearance of the book with a cry of pleasure, and made a sudden descent upon it with a speed that well-nigh threw him from Lucy's arms.

She held her book at arm's-length, still trying to read, till baby, tired of reaching forth his hands in pursuit of it, began to cry. Lucy felt irritated. "Why couldn't you let me have a little peace?" she said, returning the book to her pocket and beginning to walk up and down with the child.

The Flower of the Family

It was a warm, damp morning: the baby was a great, heavy fellow, and full of that incessant motion young people of his age see fit to keep up. Now he twisted himself this way and now that; at this moment he bent backward, and she saved him from a fall by a desperate grasp at his feet; the next, he threw himself half over her shoulder, climbing over her face as if its features were made for his special benefit and pleasure. Lucy felt weary, and out of sympathy with his life and spirits, and was afraid, besides that, she had been very impatient, if not angry, about her book. "Oh, God! Help me to be patient!" she whispered; and again, and again, and yet again, as she continued her walk, she repeated the words, till patience came.

At that moment, Rebecca came out to look for them.

"Give him to me now," said she; "your arms must ache, I am sure. Besides, mother wants you."

Lucy went in, and found breakfast nearly ready.

"Hatty has not come down, though I've called her twice," said her mother. "Just run up and tell her to come directly, will you, dear?"

Lucy went, and found Hatty standing in her nightdress before the little glass, arranging her hair.

"Mother says she has called you twice, Hatty," said she.

"Well, I can't help it. I'm hurrying as fast as I can. What does she want, do you know?"

"Breakfast is nearly ready, and the table isn't set."

"Oh, is that all? Well, you set it for me just this once. I'll do as much for you some time."

She curled and re-curled her hair at her leisure, until she was startled by her mother's voice.

"Hatty, do you know Lucy is setting the table?" she asked.

"Yes, mother, she said she would just this once. Setting a table is no great hardship, is it?" she asked, fancying her mother looked displeased.

"No, dear, that in itself is no hardship. But all our happiness depends on regularity and method, and I wish very much you would attend to your own share of the work, and not so often throw it off on Lucy."

"Well, I will next time, mother," said Hatty, "and I'll hurry down now."

The Flower of the Family

Not until breakfast was on the table, however did she make her appearance, and then she came in, looking so fresh, so smiling, so pretty, that not one of the family felt like frowning on her.

"We must take her as we find her," thought her mother; and found her very beautiful and charming.

This day, being Saturday, was as full of care and labor as it could hold. The baby would have one at least devoted solely to his pleasure, and would not have thought the united attentions of the whole family out of place, under the circumstances. The children had a half holiday, and were playing about the house with all conceivable clamor; there were Sunday garments to be got in order; there was the usual Saturday baking: Lucy had not one moment of leisure. Never in her life had she so longed for a few hours for reflection. Once or twice, in the course of the day, she caught a kind sympathizing glance from her father's eye; more than once or twice a loving word, warm from her mother's heart, had put life into her own. So the day wore on, as days will, till it had worn itself into twilight, and its heat and labor were past and gone. Her father stood in the open door, and she went to him.

"This has been a busy day," he said.

"Very busy," she answered. "And, father—"

"Well, dear."

"How *can* I be a Christian when there is so much to do?"

He did not answer her for a moment, but seemed looking for something in the little garden before them. Presently he said:

"Do you see that vine climbing up there by the wall? It lays hold of the stones and sticks for support, and makes them help it. Just so you must make your daily tasks and cares help you. Take fast hold of them and climb up by their means."

"That would be very hard."

"Yes, I know it. But it is the only way. And God will help you."

"Instead of being a help, they have been a hindrance all day," said Lucy.

"That is owing to your not looking at them in their true light. You may be sure of one thing: God Himself has placed you in your present circumstances, and it is He who appoints for you your daily task. Now, is it possible to conceive that a Being of so much wisdom and goodness would place you amid duties whose tendency is to draw you away from, rather than towards Himself?"

Lucy sighed; she felt a little puzzled, and did not quite understand what her father was saying.

"Reflect upon it as you have leisure," he said, "and pray over it, and by degrees you will understand it."

He bade her good-night, and she went up to her own little room. Very little indeed it was, and poorly furnished; yet within its friendly seclusion she had sought and found God. And as she now knelt and communed with Him, what mattered it whether the walls that enclosed that blessed spot were low and whitewashed, or high and lofty and adorned with tapestries?

CHAPTER 4

Arthur

SOME MONTHS LATER, as Lucy one afternoon entered her room, she was startled to hear the sound of suppressed, but very bitter weeping. She stopped and listened: it came from Arthur's room, which adjoined her own. She went and knocked gently at the door, but he made no answer, only the sound of the weeping ceased, and there was a great silence. Lucy lingered, perplexed and anxious, about the door. "It must be something very bad indeed to make *him* cry!" thought she. "Boys do not cry at every little thing, as girls do!"

She went down, hoping to learn the cause of Arthur's grief without betraying him.

"Do you know where Arthur is?" she inquired of Hatty.

"I heard him singing in his room just now," returned Hatty.

"Singing! Yes, a sad kind of singing! Even crying sounds cheerful to Hatty, she is always in such good spirits herself," thought Lucy.

"And speaking of Arthur reminds me that he hasn't a whole stocking to his name, and it's getting cold for bare feet I declare, I forgot all about them."

"I am glad you don't have the care of my things," said Rebecca.

"And I am glad you haven't the care of mine," retorted Hatty. "They would never be done, I'm sure. Now you shall see how soon I'll have those stockings done. While you are saying 'Jack Robinson,' I'll darn every hole in them."

"I a'n't going to say 'Jack Robinson,'" said Rebecca. "And it isn't my fault if I am slow. I was made so."

"Then I'd go back and be made faster," said Hatty.

Rebecca was silent. Hatty's tone had been unkind.

The Flower of the Family

"Rebecca is slow to take offence," said Lucy. "I wish I had half her patience."

Rebecca looked up gratefully at Lucy, and Hatty felt reproached by the look.

"Dear me!" she cried; "I'm always hurting somebody's feelings; and yet there's nobody in the world whom I would hurt on purpose. Why, I wouldn't kill a fly, if I could help it. Come, have we made up?" she cried, dropping from her lap stockings, balls of yarn, thimble and scissors, and kneeling down before Rebecca.

Who would resist the beautiful young face as it now looked up, half penitent, half saucy, into Rebecca's? Not that good, patient sister, at least. They kissed each other, and were friends again; and Hatty forgot in two minutes that she had offended, repented, and been forgiven. She resumed her work, and admired the fair ringlets that, falling around her shoulders as she leaned over her stockings, lay upon her lap, caught in her scissors, and played all manner of pretty caprices.

"Mary Johnson says my hair is lovely," said she.

"Yes, it is," said Rebecca.

"But it isn't equal to Lucy's," pursued Hatty.

"Nobody has such beautiful hair as she, unless it is the angels."

"Angels!" said Rebecca. "Do angels have hair? Are not you thinking of mermaids?"

Down again fell Hatty's work, her balls, and her scissors.

"Mermaids!" cried she, convulsed with laughter.

"Oh! Becky, you'll kill me yet!"

Both Lucy and Rebecca laughed too, for Hatty's mirth was good-humored this time, and infectious.

"These poor stockings will never be done at this rate," said Lucy at last. "Come, let me do them."

She soon finished them, and this done, ventured again to Arthur's door.

"Arthur," she cried from the outside, "here are your stockings."

He opened the door a little way, reaching forth his hand to take them.

"Mayn't I come in?" said she.

He allowed her to enter, and she seated herself, with her usual tact, where she could not see his face, and made some cheerful remark about his books, which, few as they were, had been arranged neatly on shelves of his own manufacture. He made no answer.

At last he asked abruptly, "Lucy, how soon do boys get old enough to earn money?"

"I don't know," she answered. "Some boys begin very soon."

"As young as I am?"

"Oh dear, no; I guess not. Why, do you want money?"

"Not for myself."

He was silent again. Lucy knew him too well to press him to speak, so she was silent too.

"Don't they take boys of my age into stores?" he asked at last.

"Yes, I believe they do, but they don't pay much. It would take all you could earn, and more, too, for your board and clothes."

"How do you know? Are you sure?"

"Yes, I am sure. I heard Mr. Johnson say so. He thought of sending Josiah to New York or somewhere, and he made inquiries about it. He told father so one day."

"I wish I was out of the way, at any rate," he said, gloomily.

"Out of the way! Why, Arthur! What can you mean?"

"Nothing; only I wish I *was* out of the way."

"I used to wish so once," said Lucy; "but it wasn't right. We are just where God has put us, and it is a pleasant place, after all."

"Do you call it pleasant to be as poor as we are?"

"*God* has made us poor," she answered, with a tone that said, "And so I call it pleasant."

"Yes," said Arthur, seriously, "it is right, I know, but it's very hard. You see, I never knew till today— though I suppose you've known it this long time— that father is in debt; and thinking about it has made me wish I could do something for him instead of idling round here."

"I'm sorry you've found that out," said Lucy. "I have only known it myself a few months, but somehow it seems as if I had grown old fast since then."

"It has made me feel just so," cried Arthur. "I am going to leave school if father will let me, and help him, and I've made up my mind not to go to college."

The Flower of the Family

"Not go to college!" cried Lucy in dismay. "Oh! Arthur, father has always said you should go, and you've been talking of it ever since you were a little bit of a boy."

"Then there's the less need of my talking about it now."

"Father will be sorry to know this," said Lucy. "All that keeps him up is his love for us, and if he knows we are thwarted in any of our great wishes, it wears upon him sadly."

"Well, I've made up my mind what *my* duty is," replied Arthur. "I sha'n't go to college. I shall stay and help father."

"You *shall* go!" cried Lucy. "I am strong and well. I am older than you; I can earn money somehow, and I will."

Arthur smiled, and shook his head.

"At any rate, don't say anything yet to father. I do not believe it is a very large debt; and we're all growing older; and before long you'll see me teaching school, and money will be as plenty as blackberries."

Half believing herself, and having quite cheered him, Lucy was about leaving the room.

"I must go down and see about tea now," she said.

"There's always something for you to see about," he answered, half detaining her. "You might allow yourself time to breathe, I should think."

An impatient, restless feeling gnawed at Lucy's heart, as she detached herself from his grasp, and went down.

It said, "Yes, you've always something to see about except your own business. It is too bad!"

But something else exclaimed, "Your own business! Have you really any of your own?"

"No; I am not my own!" she answered, "and I am glad that I am not. I am glad that there is a God, and that I am His child, and that I haven't anything to do but just to obey Him."

The restless feeling vanished for the time, and she went cheerfully about her work, "doing it as unto God."

Her father, who had come in tired, and not inclined to talk, sat watching her.

At length he said, "What are you thinking of now, darling?"

She stopped and smiled, as she answered, "Only of some lines that keep running in my head all the time, about:

The Flower of the Family

*'Serving with careful Martha's hands
And loving Mary's heart.'"*

He was touched by the tone in which she spoke for he knew how distasteful all domestic labor was to her.

"It is homely discipline," thought he, "but its results are just as beautiful."

He closed his eyes, and leaned back in his chair. They all fancied him asleep, but his thoughts were very busy; and when the children began to whisper among themselves, "Father's asleep; don't let us make a noise," he astonished them by rising and going out to the favorite seat on the door-step.

It was now Lucy's turn to watch him, and after a while she ventured to go out and whisper, "Is anything the matter, father?"

"No, dear, no," he answered. "I was only thinking how much discipline it takes to make us meet for God's kingdom, and that you are having your share!"

She looked at him in surprise. "Why, father! Nothing very bad happens to me! Nothing special, I'm sure!" She felt ashamed to have her petty trials called "discipline."

"Your trials, such as they are," he answered, "suffice as such, just as truly as great afflictions and misfortunes could. God can sanctify the small as well as the great events of our lives."

"But, father, I am not unhappy or discontented. I enjoy a *great deal*." She was thinking of her little room upstairs, and of the true peace she had so often found there.

"But you could not always say that," he answered. "This is the fruit of years of gentle but constant chastening."

Lucy was silent. She felt herself almost blush with shame.

"I understand you, Lucy," he went on. "I know what it is to have one's tastes thwarted and put aside as yours have been. I know what it is to long for solitude, and be forced into a crowd; to thirst for knowledge, and to be consumed by that thirst."

He had touched the soft spots now. Sigh after sigh, suppressed, and yet very heavy, attested it, as Lucy stood behind and out of his sight.

"Oh, father," she said at last, "don't let us think of it!"

The Flower of the Family

"Nay, let us rather walk boldly up to the truth, and look it in the face," he answered. "You will find your burden easier to bear when you have learned exactly what it is, who has appointed it, and who is to help carry it. I shall have to tell you, I cannot send you away to school. I see no reason to think I ever can."

"Oh, I had given that all up long ago!" cried Lucy. "And I never even think of it now, excepting when—"

She stopped; for at that moment she remembered her late interview with Arthur, and her promise that she should teach school, and so help him through college.

"Well, I don t feel anxious about it, at all events," she said.

"It is hard to be obliged to deny you, my dear child, a wish so rational. I little thought, when you were a mere baby on my knee, and I fostered in you the desire you even then showed for knowledge, that the time would come when I should have to extinguish it."

"You can't extinguish it," said Lucy. "But you can help me to be cheerful and even happy; and that is better. Oh, father! I feel so grateful to you for teaching me to love God!"

"I trust He has taught you that Himself," he answered. "And with it, I am sure He will give you everything else you need. I rejoice that I can trust Him for that. It is my only comfort."

CHAPTER 5

Baby Number Two

As time passed, Lucy's cares and labors increased. Just as the baby had got upon his feet, and was making himself the terror of the household, by pulling burning sticks of wood from the fire, for toys, and climbing up the sides of the well to throw therein whatever else he could lay his hands on, there came another young gentleman upon the stage.

"Well, sir!" cried Hatty, as she came with her hair half-fixed to greet the new-comer; "you're a fine young man, a'n't you? Don't you know we needed a great many things more than we needed you?"

She kissed him, as she spoke, with her cold face, and he began to cry.

"What are you crying for?" she continued. "Do you suppose we've got anything to give you? No, indeed! You've come to a poor place, sir!"

"He shall have a warm welcome, at any rate," said Lucy, taking him tenderly in her arms. Her mother looked up, with a quick, grateful smile.

"Dear child," she whispered, "can you really give him that?"

"Yes, indeed, mother, and more too." She went with the child to the kitchen fire, and let the little ones take a peep at the small pink face. On seeing his place thus usurped by Baby Number Two, Baby Number One relieved his feelings by a fearful shout of displeasure, and began pulling at Lucy's dress, still farther to attract her attention.

"Do take him away, somebody," said Lucy, trembling for her new charge.

The Flower of the Family

"He won't let me, I know," said Rebecca. "You have weaned him from us all by taking so much care of him."

This was true. Of late, Lucy had been mother to him as well as sister.

"Well, then, you must dress the baby," said Lucy, offering to relinquish her low seat by the fire.

Rebecca shrank back in terror.

"Oh I couldn't dress it," said she; "I never did such a thing in my life."

"I know that," returned Lucy, "but somebody must do it, and if you can't amuse Horace, I don't see what I shall do. Arthur dear, couldn't you take Horace out on your sled awhile?"

"Yes, indeed, if it isn't too cold."

"If he is wrapped up nicely, I don't believe it will hurt him," said Lucy. "Come, Hatty, you see to it, will you?"

Hatty proceeded to the task with her usual precipitation, and in a few minutes off they went.

Lucy now gently removed the blanket from the new baby, and prepared to array him in the little worn garments that had already done so much service. But at this moment Arthur rushed in with Horace in his arms, screaming as only Horace could.

"He fell right off the sled the moment I began to pull," said Arthur.

"Why, Hatty! Did you suppose such a child would do anything else?" said Lucy. "You should have fastened him on somehow."

"I told him to hold on tight," said Hatty. "The fact is, seeing him by the side of the new baby made him seem like such a big boy, that I forgot he was so young."

"You might put him in a large basket," said Arthur, "and tie the basket on."

"Sure enough!" cried Hatty, who was now quite in her element. The little boys stood around and admired, while Hatty arranged Horace nicely in the basket, out of which his head peeped like that of a bird from its nest. The little face was covered with smiles and tears; the little hands held fast to the sides of the basket; the little air was one a small king might have put on.

"Let mother see him," said Lucy, looking with delight at the happy result of Arthur's suggestion. The children lifted the basket, and bore it in triumph to their mother, who from her bed

The Flower of the Family

in the adjoining room had watched the little group, longing to be among them.

"I great boy now; not baby now," said Horace to his mother, peering over the top of the basket, and pointing with one little white finger to the infant in Lucy's lap. He went off, well satisfied with himself and his new-found dignity, and the younger children went too. Lucy had now quiet and leisure for the baby.

Rebecca and Hatty stood by, and handed pins, and aired tiny clothes, and gave advice, but the difficulties of the task were all Lucy's. She grew anxious and heated, as she pursued it amid the cries of the child.

"I'm afraid it makes you fairly ache to see how awkward I am," she called out to her mother.

But the weary mother had fallen into placid sleep.

"That's nice," said Lucy; "I was afraid I should worry her. Well, girls! We get along pretty well as nurses, don't we?" She looked with pleasure on the little creature that now lay, with closed eyes, upon her lap.

"He's a noble fellow," said she.

"Yes, now he's dressed, he looks like folks," said Rebecca; an announcement hailed by Hatty with as hearty laughter as she dared venture under the circumstances.

Their father now came gently from their mother's room, closing the door behind him.

"Mother is sleeping now," he said. "On the whole, I think we make pretty good nurses. I never knew her sleep so soon, before."

Lucy remembered, with a pang, that she had been very ungracious on the advent of Horace; and felt thankful that she could make some atonement for it by present devotion.

"A nurse would have been a great expense," said she, "and we shall get along nicely, I know."

"I wish this fellow would open his eyes, and let us see what color they are," said Hatty.

"We mustn't expect too much from him," replied Lucy, who already felt a sort of maternal pride in him. "But I must make some gruel for mother now, so who'll take him?"

The Flower of the Family

"Oh, let me make mother's gruel," said Rebecca, quite briskly for her.

"Let me take the baby; do!" said Hatty. "I haven't had him yet."

Lucy relinquished her charge, and went out to look for the children. She came back immediately.

"I don't see anything of them," said she. "I wish I had charged Arthur not to go far. Father, could you go up the road, and see if they're coming?"

"I would, dear, but there are the cattle to fodder. It ought to have been done long ago. I wouldn't worry about those boys. They're safe enough, I'll warrant."

He looked tired and abstracted. He had been up all night, and many painful thoughts had stirred in his heart. For this was the tenth child, and he had hardly the wherewithal for the nine. He went hastily out, and Lucy stood a moment, looking after him. She knew pretty well what troubled him, and longed to take that weight off his mind.

"It seems strange," thought she, "that just Arthur and I should have found out about that dreadful debt. I don't believe any of the others would have cared as we do. Rebecca never worries about anything; and Hatty can't realize that there is any occasion to 'borrow trouble,' as she always calls it. But Arthur! He doesn't seem like the same boy. Sometimes I think he doesn't eat half he wants, so as to save. But there'd be no use in asking him." She took down her shawl and hood, and went out to look for him.

"*Now* shall you find any time to study?" asked something within, as her thoughts went back to the baby.

"I don't know," she answered, a little sadly. "But it's no matter if I don't." A few great tears gathered in her eyes, saying it *was* a deal of matter; and she felt like throwing herself right down there in the snow to cry. But that would never do! She walked on quickly; the cool morning air invigorated and cheered her.

"We shall get along somehow," she said— and then she smiled, as she remembered hearing of somebody who had said he was afraid he never should "*get through*" being asked if he ever heard of any one's "sticking by the way!" "Yes, we shall get along; Rebecca seems to brighten up, lately; and Hatty grows older every day. To be sure, she's not to be depended upon. I

The Flower of the Family

hope she won't jump up while I'm gone and let the baby fall off her lap as she does her work and books."

The fear of this not at all unlikely contingency made her quicken her steps; and she hastened on, looking anxiously up the road, till a sudden turn brought the party full into view. They were still at a distance, but she saw in a moment that something was the matter. Several men occupied the middle of the road; they were lifting something; at first she thought it was Horace and his basket; but as she flew panting on, she saw that it was Arthur.

As she came forward, Horace stretched forth his arms, and the other children all broke forth together in incoherent details. "Arthur," and "a wicked naughty man," and "frightened to death," was all she could catch in the confusion, till she came up with the men in whose arms Arthur now lay, pale and quite senseless.

"Been run over," said one of them, in answer to the question of her terrified face.

"Is he hurt much?" she forced herself to ask.

"Don' no," said the man. "Maybe he a'n't. He's kind o' stunded now. We'll have a hand-sled here in a minute, and fetch him home. There'll be the doctor along, too."

Lucy took Horace from his basket, wherein he had not ceased to scream and kick ever since the accident, and turned homeward. She had presence of mind enough left in this great terror to know that her mother must not be alarmed.

"Stay with him, John," she said to the eldest boy, and turned away. The other children followed, crying, after her. She never knew how she got home with that heavy boy in her arms, but it seemed as if the winds took her up and carried her there. She opened the door and stepped softly in. On one side was the great kitchen; on the other the best room, used only on special occasions, now shut up, dark and cold. She opened the shutters, and then stepped back into the kitchen.

"Is mother asleep still?" she asked.

"No; she's awake, and has got the baby," said Hatty.

"Come out here, both of you," she whispered, retiring into the entry. "Rebecca, will you help me bring down Arthur's bed?" she said. "And, Hatty, you make a fire in the north room. And, Tom,

The Flower of the Family

you'll stay and watch mother; that's a good boy— and don't tell her anything has happened."

There was authority in the trembling voice and in the pale young face. Mechanically they all obeyed her. "Oh, what *is* the matter?" cried Hatty as they hurried lightly up the stairs together.

"Something has happened to Arthur; I don't know what exactly; but I'm sure he's hurt a good deal; and we must get a bed ready for him, where we can take care of him without worrying mother. She would hear every sound overhead."

They had arranged the bed on the floor, near the fire Rebecca had speedily kindled, when Arthur was brought in.

"Don't speak loud, please," said Lucy to the men; "mother is sick."

She knelt down by the still insensible boy.

"Where is he hurt?" she asked.

"On the head, I guess," said one of the men. They withdrew to a window, where they whispered among themselves.

Lucy lifted the hair that had fallen over Arthur's forehead, and saw the dark purple bruise that disfigured it.

"Will the doctor be here soon?" she asked again.

"Well, not so very soon," they answered. "The fact is, he's gone five miles to see old Mrs. Lovejoy who was took with a fit."

"*I* must do something, then," said Lucy, desperately.

"Could a leech be got anywhere? And I wish father would come."

"What is it she says? " asked one of the men. "Is it a blood-sucker she wants? There's a plenty of 'em handy by. But I never hearn of drawing out a feller's blood to bring him to life, when he's as far dead as that boy."

"I should like to try," said Lucy, hesitatingly, her confidence in herself wavering, as this cold water was thrown upon it.

The leeches were brought; great repulsive-looking things, fresh from a neighboring pond. Lucy had not time, or rather she *would not let* herself have time, to feel disgust, as she applied, with a trembling hand, one of them to Arthur's temple. In a few minutes the greedy creature had so far done its work that Arthur's eyes slowly opened, and his lips murmured the word "Horace."

"He's not hurt," said Lucy, instantly comprehending the anxiety the words expressed. "Nobody is hurt but yourself, and you are getting better."

"Here's the doctor at last," said one of the men, in a relieved tone. "Though it's my opinion that girl's as good, any day."

The doctor examined Arthur carefully, encouraged the flow of blood, called for ice, and turned everybody, save Lucy, out of the room.

"How's that young one in there?" he asked, indicating with his thumb the direction he wished to designate.

"Very well, I believe," she answered. "Oh, why can't he tell me how much Arthur is hurt?" she thought.

"Who put on that leech?" asked the doctor.

"I did, sir. Was it right?"

"First-rate," he answered. "What time did you get up this morning?"

"I didn't go to bed at all last night, sir."

"No, I thought you didn't. And here you stand, looking like a ghost. Now, you go and lie down; I'll stay with the boy. I shall apply the ice when the blood has flowed a little longer, and sha'n't need any help."

"I can't go till I know how much he's hurt," said she, gathering courage from her very fears.

"Then you won't go this day," he answered. "How can I tell how much he's hurt?"

"Do you think any of his bones are broken?" she asked.

"No, they're not," said Arthur, once more opening his eyes.

"That's right, my fine fellow," said the doctor, "And now, Miss Lucy, off with you."

Lucy went, for she knew not how her mother had fared all this time. She found Rebecca engaged in a sharp conflict with Horace, whom she was vainly trying to get to sleep.

"Give him a great piece of gingerbread," said Lucy, hurrying on to her mother's room. And between eating his gingerbread, and hugging it up, and calling it his horse, Horace soon fell asleep, and there was a lull in the tempest for two hours.

"I'm thankful you've come, dear," said her mother, as Lucy entered; "the baby keeps crying, and I thought I heard a great

The Flower of the Family

talking and running; and began to think something had happened. But I'm always too anxious."

"I was busy, or I would have come sooner," said Lucy. She dared not trust herself to say any thing more, but went on quietly to make both mother and child more comfortable. As soon as possible, she went in pursuit of Hatty, who had not been seen since Arthur had been brought in.

"I shouldn't wonder if she has gone for father," said Tom. "May I get up now?"

Lucy looked at him, not understanding the question.

"You told me to stay and watch mother," said Tom, "and I've been sitting here ever since."

"You are a dear, good boy," cried Lucy, stopping to kiss the round cheek that blushed at these words of praise.

"I mean always to be a good boy after this," he said.

Lucy now stole into Arthur's room. The doctor was preparing to go. He gave Lucy a few directions; promised to look in again towards night, and went his way. Lucy longed to sit down by Arthur's side, and tell him how she loved him, and how it almost had broken her heart to see him lie there so lifeless and motionless; and how she was sure it *would* quite break if he should be very sick, and— but no, she could not think of that. The doctor had, above all things, directed quiet for Arthur, and she would not indulge herself with a word. She only knelt down and kissed the dear, pale face, and then went to choose, from among the children, one to sit in the sickroom. Hatty had come in after a fruitless search for her father, and begged hard to be allowed this privilege.

"I am afraid you'll talk," said Lucy.

"No, I won't; I won't speak a word; I'll sit just so. Look!"

Hatty tried to compose her face as Lucy looked at her, but it wouldn't do. She burst out into hysterical weeping, all the more violent from long suppression.

"You're all tired out, poor child," said Lucy: and she led her upstairs and made her lie down, when she soon cried herself to sleep.

Everything seemed to fail Lucy. Her father could not be found; Hatty was laid up, useless; her mother helpless in bed: she felt herself needed everywhere at once. The little boys reminded her,

The Flower of the Family

too, that there had been no dinner cooked, and that father would be hungry when he came in.

"I wish I could think so," she said, and told Tom that he had been so very good, she must let him go and sit by Arthur a little while. Tom was more than thankful; he came and threw his arms around her, and almost choked her with embraces.

"Mother," said she, looking pleasantly in at the door of the bedroom, after Tom had gone, "you can't think how good the children are— Tom especially."

"That comforts me," returned her mother. "I was afraid they would be troublesome. As for Tom, nobody has appeared to appreciate him. He wants encouragement, poor boy."

Mr. Grant now came in to dinner. He had been at a distance from the house all the morning, and had not heard of the accident.

He went in to look at the baby a minute, and to speak a few kind words to his wife.

"The children are as good and quiet as possible," she said, in answer to his question, "and I can't help thinking, as I lie here, how thankful we ought to be that we have such comfort in them. As for this baby, I'm sure we've never had so fine a child before. I shouldn't wonder if he proved the staff of our old age."

Grave as he always was, and unused to mirth, Mr. Grant was moved by this speech to a peal of laughter that called every child within hearing, to the door of the bedroom.

"The idea of discovering signs of a brilliant intellect in a creature not twenty-four hours old! Oh, you mothers! Your last baby is always a wonder!" he cried.

Mrs. Grant laughed too, and looked fondly down upon the small head upon her arm.

"You'll see I am right this time," she said.

Poor Lucy, unused as she was to seeing her father in anything like a joyous mood, dreaded disturbing him now with the news of Arthur. Yet she knew he would miss the dear boy from the table, and that there would be no use in delaying the intelligence. She took him aside, therefore, and told it as gently as she could.

The old careworn expression that for a moment had been gone from his face, came back and settled itself down again like a

The Flower of the Family

great cloud. But he said not a word, and went straight to Arthur's side.

Lucy watched him as he stood there, and as her eye became accustomed to the darkness, she perceived that Hatty occupied a seat in a distant corner, where she was crying quietly.

"I thought you were upstairs and asleep," she whispered.

"I did sleep a little while," said Hatty, "but I had such a terrible dream, it woke me up, and I came down."

Their father now drew Lucy from the room.

"Give the children their dinner," he said: "don't wait for me."

"Oh, father, do try to eat a little," said Lucy, "just to please us."

"I am going to see Dr. White, and see what he thinks of Arthur," he answered.

"But he will be coming in soon," urged Lucy; "and it is getting late, and you were up all night. Do, dear father!"

He let her lead him to the table, and as he sat opposite her, he observed for the first time how pale she looked.

"I don't know what will become of you," he said. "You look already worn out."

"Oh, no, father. I was only frightened at first, Arthur looked so very pale. I thought once he was dead. And mother being sick, and you not at home—"

"She put a leech on Arthur, her own self," said Tom.

"A leech!" said her father; "who told you to do that?"

"Nobody, father, but I thought I must do something; and it seemed to me I had read somewhere that ought to be done."

"Everything comes at once," he answered despondingly.

"Oh, I was thinking what a mercy it wasn't haying-time!" said Lucy. And now she had the comfort of seeing him smile.

When the doctor came at night, he seemed not quite pleased with Arthur's appearance, Lucy thought.

"Have you all been running in and out, crying and talking to him?" he asked.

Lucy assured him the room had been quiet

"What are the plans for the night?" he continued.

"Lucy must not be up, at all events," said her father.

"By no means," said the doctor. "I was going to say that one of the young men who so unfortunately ran over Arthur has been anxiously inquiring about him; and he proposes spending the

The Flower of the Family

night by his side. He has been used to sickness; and, in fact, would suit me better than any stupid woman you could call in; this night, at least."

Dr. White always had things his own way; and though not one of the family liked to relinquish the care of Arthur to a stranger, no one dared object. Indeed, it was necessary they all should have rest.

Lucy had learned, from her mother's example, not to tease a physician with questions. But she knew Dr. White well, and felt sure, from his manner, that he was anxious about Arthur. He always assumed a jocose, careless tone when his feelings were stirred; and Arthur had been his favorite for years. As he left the room with her father, her heart sank within her. Venturing to take one of Arthur's hands gently in her own, she was startled to find it hot and dry; and amid the darkness of the room, she fancied she could detect an unnatural glow upon his cheek. The tears fell upon the hand she held, but Arthur did not heed them, or in any way notice her. She thought if he would speak to her once more, and say he loved her, she could lie right down and die with joy. But as for years she had had no time for dreams, so she had now no time for grief; but, taking the great weight with her wherever she went, she returned to the family. She found Rebecca patiently submitting to the caprices of Horace, who had made up his mind not to go to bed until Lucy came to undress him. She took him, sending Rebecca to take Hatty's place in the sick-room, and sat down with him in a low chair, when he willingly yielded himself to her pleasure.

"Has Horace had his supper?" she asked.

"No, no," said the child.

"Why, he's had a *lot* of supper," said Tom. "I saw Rebecca give it to him with my own eyes."

"He's so sleepy he doesn't know what he's saying," said Lucy, and she drew him up tenderly in her arms, and carried him for a good-night kiss to his mother. In a sleepy voice he repeated to her as he glanced down at the baby by her side:

"I big boy now!"

Lucy took him up to her own little room, and made him comfortable in bed. She was in the habit of singing him to sleep, for he was still only a baby, his own opinion to the contrary

The Flower of the Family

notwithstanding. But now, when she began to sing her voice trembled, and was choked with tears.

"This won't do," she said to herself; and rising up from the bed where she had thrown herself by the side of Horace, she clenched her hands almost fiercely together, and forced back her tears with a resolution that never failed when demanded. And after this, stir as they might in her heart, there were no tears in her eyes. Horace was soon soothed into sleep by the hymn she now calmly sang to him, and then she went down to get tea ready, for it was quite late. She found Dr. White had not gone; he had been paying Arthur another visit, and had promised to stay to tea.

"I haven't heard yet how this accident happened," said Mr. Grant.

"Why, Arthur was going up the road with one of the family in a basket on a sled; Miss Hatty, I suppose," said the doctor, mischievously; "and two young men, strangers here, came behind in a sleigh, and their horses, taking fright at the basket and its contents, became unmanageable. Arthur had time to run out of the way himself, but one of the children stood stupidly still, right in the way of the horses. Arthur flew back and caught the child, but was somehow knocked down himself."

"They were silly horses," said Tom. "*I* wasn't afraid of the basket a bit."

The doctor laughed. "Your mind isn't in a very lively state to-night," said he. "I guess it wants to go to bed."

"No, it doesn't," said Tom. "I a'n't a going to bed at all to-night. I'm going to sit up and take care of Arthur."

Dr. White laughed again; Lucy wished he wouldn't; and she hurried Tom, nervously, off to get wood for the fire.

This long day came to an end at last. The children were all in bed; her mother made comfortable for the night, and her father went with Lucy to take a last look at Arthur.

The young man who had offered his services for the night, sat by the bedside, and a single sentence from his lips assured them that the dear boy was in good hands.

"Such a voice comes from a kind heart," whispered Mr. Grant, as he bade Lucy good-night. "We may feel easy, I think. And now, darling, do try to get some sleep."

And poor Lucy went up to her room silently and prayed; but did not sleep.

CHAPTER 6

Sorrow at Night, Joy in the Morning

ARTHUR HAD A RESTLESS NIGHT, and could not sleep. He had magnified, in his own mind, the trouble his injury was making in the family, at a time when everybody seemed fully occupied, until it seemed like a mountain, over which his thoughts could not climb. When his father opened the door and looked in at day break, he was tossing about from side to side, and it needed no physician's eye to perceive that he was becoming seriously ill. After exchanging a few words with the young man, Mr. Grant thanked him and relieved him of his charge at the bedside.

"His mind wanders at times," whispered the stranger, as he took leave. "He seems to think you are going to be dragged to jail for debt."

A flush almost as dark as that on Arthur's face passed over that of the unhappy father; and marking it, without seeming to do so, the young man withdrew, with delicacy. Immediately afterwards, Lucy stole in. Her disappointed look as she approached the bed, showed her father that she read the case, as he had done.

"Is any one else up?" he asked.

"Hatty is; she'll be down directly. How is mother?"

"She had a good night, and is asleep still. When Hatty comes, let her sit here; I want to speak to you."

He went out, and when Lucy joined him, he asked abruptly:

"Who told Arthur I was going to jail for debt?"

"Nobody, father, that I know of. I don't know who told him there *was* any debt."

"But you are sure he knew there was one?"

"Yes, he knew it; but he hasn't known it long."

"I thought I knew what trouble meant," said her father, "but it seems I did not know the first letter of its alphabet. And so he told you, you say?"

"I knew it before," replied Lucy. "I've known it a good while now. And oh, dear father, I did want so to tell you how sorry Arthur and I were for you, and how willing we felt to work, or do anything that would relieve you!"

He folded her in his arms and laid his hand solemnly upon her head, as if calling down blessings upon it. At this moment Lucy heard the voice of Horace.

"I must go, or Horace will wake mother," said she; and so began another day of domestic care and duty.

As she went from task to task, she felt, as she never had done before, the difference between the earthly and the heavenly love. These cares kept her from Arthur's side, where she so longed to be, but they could not separate her from God. Doing everything for His sake and in His fear, she could continually look up to and commune with Him. And with the deep sorrow, there was peace in her heart.

Arthur became worse from hour to hour, and Dr. White attended him with almost parental devotion.

Kind neighbors came to lighten and share the household labors, and the young men of the village came at the close of a hard day, to watch all night by the sick boy. Even those stranger-gentlemen refused to go whence they came, until they could be assured of his safety. It became impossible, with so many coming and going, to keep Arthur's mother in ignorance of his illness. From that hour she ceased improving, and the poor baby pined and moaned in concert with her. Those were hard, hard days. They never knew how they lived through them. They did not see the Hand that was underneath them, or they would not have wondered at passing safely through seas of fire. But Arthur was not yet to be snatched away. After many weeks of severe illness he began slowly to amend, and the pressure of anxiety was lifted from their hearts. They had yet, however, a difficult task before them. The little wasted form seemed almost lifeless as soon as the fever left him; and to an inexperienced eye, he looked more alarmingly ill than when flushed in the height of his disease. Lucy proved a good nurse. She understood Arthur's wishes before they were spoken, and nobody could feed him so well, or sing so soothingly, or read to him the little he could bear to hear.

"Well!" said Hatty, one day, "I *thought* you would get well. I never believed you would go and die, and leave all of us."

"I might do a worse thing," said Arthur.

"A worse thing than die!" cried Hatty. "Oh! Arthur."

"I thought when I was knocked down that day that I was hurt very much. I only had a minute to think. But I was not frightened."

"No, you were always so good," said Hatty.

"It wasn't that," said Arthur. "It was because *Christ* is so good," he added, after a pause.

Hatty colored, and made some trifling answer; and when, some hours later, they missed her, she was crying upstairs. But she came down in as lively a mood as ever, soon after; for only the surface of her merry heart had yet been touched.

Arthur's sickness had disarranged all household business, and after his recovery, the care of the baby, and the accumulated sewing of many weeks, occupied them all, incessantly. Rebecca left school "for good," as she called it; but, as usual, Lucy stood foremost in the ranks, and made herself useful at every point. At the same time, the old thirst for knowledge had received an impulse. Arthur's illness had left him delicate; she felt sure he could make no farmer, for lack of physical strength; he *must* have an education. She tried to rise earlier and to sit up later, but very little was accomplished in these fragments of time. Her health began to suffer.

"Lucy, was that you coughing all last night?" her mother asked one morning.

"I coughed some," said Lucy.

"She coughs every night," said Arthur.

The father and mother interchanged anxious glances.

His said, "Just as my sister did, who died at her age."

Hers said, "I know it," and there was silence for a time.

"Have you paid Dr. White's bill yet?" asked Lucy at last.

"No," said her father, "not yet. He hasn't sent it."

"It will come to-morrow," said Lucy; "it always does on New-Year's Day."

She had a vague hope that the mention of a bill would deter her father from calling in Dr. White for her cough, as his face said he intended doing. But she was mistaken. The next day the doctor came, and she found herself fairly in his hands. He prepared medicine for her, with directions for its use; then turning to Mrs. Grant, he said,

"And here's medicine for you too."

"For me? Why, I am not sick," she said, looking at the paper he placed in her hand. It was a check for fifty dollars.

"You haven't done joking yet?" she said smiling, and offering to return it.

"It's no joke, I assure you," he returned. "The case is just this: One of those youngsters who ran over Arthur wrote me, not long ago, that he has come of age and into his property, and inquires what is the damage? I wrote him, why, fifty dollars; and back it comes, with my lord's compliments and regrets, and is sure it ought to be more, and wishes I had said a hundred, and so on and so on."

"I sha'n't keep it," said Mrs. Grant.

"Yes you shall keep it. What else would you do with it, pray?"

"Return it to Mr._ what did you say his name was?"

"I didn't say his name was 'Mr.' anything. And you don't know where he lives, either."

"I can find out."

"No, you can't; and you shouldn't, if you could. I tell you it's no use," he said, rising and seizing his hat; "the fellow has gone abroad. Besides, what is fifty dollars to him? If you were not all of you so high in the instep, I should have made it a hundred. It would have been poor payment for all you have suffered: and the upshot of the matter is, I wash my hands of it." He was hurrying off, but came back again. "As for this child," he said, laying his hand on Lucy's head, and making the sweet face look up into his own, "she must go away somewhere, and rest a while. The cough's not so bad now; I've cured worse; but I can't promise what it won't run into if she goes on toiling as she has done. And say to your father, my dear, that he needn't look very sharp for my bill this year. It won't come. I don't need money." And this time he fairly ran.

The Flower of the Family

"He does need it," said Mrs. Grant; and she thought, even with tears, how long his wife had worn that shawl, that hardly looked as if it would hold together another week.

"It's *dreadful* to be poor!" Lucy burst out, thinking of the same thing. "I don't mind it for myself, but when it comes to not paying Dr. White!"

"He'll get his due from the great Paymaster," said her mother, wiping away her tears; "and He gives full measure, pressed down, and running over."

"Fifty dollars!" said Tom, who had sat all this time in amazement too profound for utterance; "why, we're as rich as kings!"

His mother smiled and sighed too.

"Lucy leave home! To go where?" she thought. "This will take you somewhere, dear," she said.

"No, it won't, mother," said Lucy, kissing the faded cheek, now flushed both with joy and sorrow. "Let it be Arthur's nest-egg. It will help him in college. Do, dear mother!"

"I am not going to college," said Arthur.

"I hope something may happen to make you alter your mind about that, dear boy," said his mother, looking at him anxiously.

"At any rate, Lucy has got to go away," said Arthur. "She's very thin."

"So are you," said Lucy, smiling. "And just think, what a foolish idea to send me off, nobody knows where, and all alone! I shouldn't get well in a hundred years at that rate."

While they talked together, their mother sat silent and thoughtful, and was thoughtful all day. She knew of no spot this side of heaven where her child could find rest. "She'll find it there if anybody does," she said to herself.

"Don't be troubled, mother," whispered Lucy; "there'll be a way provided."

It was provided even then. It was standing at the window of the little post-office, in the shape of a letter, that, ignorant of its own worth and importance, let itself be placed in a row with other letters of "no use to anybody but the owner." It had remained two or three days, quiet, and modest, and unobserved, and many nobodies on its right hand and on its left had been borne off in

The Flower of the Family

triumph, while it, poor soul, (for it *had* a soul,) had stood neglected.

As John Grant was returning home to tea that night, he happened to pass the office, where he saw the letter, and eagerly pounced upon it— letters being rarities in those regions. It was for his father, and although he turned it in every possible direction, he could not even guess who it was from.

"Here's a letter for you, father!" he cried, as he rushed like a tempest into the house.

His father put on his spectacles, and examined the letter with deliberation. He studied the post-mark, pored over the handwriting, and reflected on the seal. People always do so, especially when a host of eager children stand around, saying in their secret minds, "Dear me! will he *never* open it?" At last the seal was broken, and with deliberation still was read and re-read, and folded and tucked into the great family Bible. It was no mere business-letter, that was certain. Mr. Grant would have thought the quaint old volume, that he could trace back almost to the May-Flower, profaned by contact with a worldly document. Nobody dared to ask a question, but everybody felt sure something had happened.

"I shouldn't wonder if somebody had sent father fifty dollars too," said Hatty, in confidence, to Lucy, skipping upstairs that night, two at a time. "And fifty and fifty make a hundred."

"Do they really?" asked Lucy, laughing.

"You needn't laugh," said Hatty; "I'm sure we need it badly."

"We need many things," said Lucy; "things that can't be bought or sold."

"Oh, yes," said Hatty, yawning; "sleep, for instance;" and she hurried off to bed, for fear Lucy should "moralize," as she called it.

As soon as the children had all retired for the night, Mr. Grant placed the letter in their mother's hands. She read it hastily and half aloud:

"My Dear Brother:

"The year is about closing, and I have been very busy settling up accounts. ('He's going to dun us for that money,' sighed Mrs.

The Flower of the Family

Grant.) But I cannot longer delay settling with you that greatest of them all. I owe you, and have owed you many long years— God forgive me for it— a hearty acknowledgment of great and grievous wrong to you and yours. Now that I look at my life in a new light— the light of God's countenance— I seem to myself unworthy the pardon I yet cannot refrain from imploring. My dear brother! my dear sister! can you forgive my hasty words, my unkind deeds?"

"I would have come to ask it in person, but my dear and only daughter lies before me, very ill. I have been prospered in my business— am rich, and increased with goods; and never, till God placed his hand upon this precious child, did I feel my need of aught better than this world had given me. Pray for me, and for this child. She is my only daughter, a most lovely and beloved one. I can write no more, though my heart is full!"

"Affectionately your brother,
"Arthur Whittier."

Mrs. Grant drew a long, relieved sigh, as she closed this letter, as if parting, as was really the case, with the great sorrow and burden of her life.

"I can bear anything now," she said.

"It comes too late," returned her husband. "You have suffered too long. When I think of it, my blood boils!"

"Let us look at our mercies, and forget the rest," said Mrs. Grant. "My poor brother! We should pity rather than reproach him!"

The heart of her husband melted for the moment, as he looked upon the pale, worn face, now lighted with such pure joy.

"I do forgive him!" he cried. "Let us thank God that this feud is swept away!"

Falling upon their knees, they presented their thank-offering unto the Lord; and then, sitting closely together over the fading fire on the hearth, they talked long of past times, and of the days of their youth and love.

"It seems but yesterday that I held brother Arthur in my arms, as I do this child," said Mrs. Grant, as she took the baby from the cradle, and prepared for bed.

The Flower of the Family

"It is not easy for us men to forget wrongs," said Mr. Grant, who felt irritated, he hardly knew why, at the caresses she was lavishing on the child.

"It is not as a *man* you are called on to forgive them," said she, "but as a Christian."

"I don't feel right yet," he answered. "Go to bed, Sarah, and leave me awhile."

She looked troubled, and, standing behind his chair, waited for a parting word of more cheer. But none came, and she left him. He rose as the door closed behind her, and walked to and fro in the long, dark room, with clasped hands and a contracted brow, wrestling with God in such conflict as is never witnessed by mortal eye.

"It was a grievous wrong!" he said. "It has blighted my whole life! Yet I fancied I had forgiven it. O my God, help me to do it now!"

"The wrong was great," whispered a still, small voice; "but did not prejudice and passion aggravate it? Were you blameless and undefiled in this thing?"

"His sin against me is naught in comparison with mine against God!" he cried, at last. And now he ceased from that restless progress up and down the lonely, dark room, and falling upon his knees, he prayed long and tearfully, and without passion or excitement.

The night-watches looked upon the conflict, and the morning dawned upon the victory.

"You have not been to bed at all," said his wife, opening the door of their room, and looking anxiously out.

"I have had a good night," he answered; and as she looked into his face, she, who knew its every light and shade, saw that it had been a good night; such an one as should have come years ago.

"Now my cup runs over," she said.

CHAPTER 7

The Uncle's Visit

THE CHILDREN ALL PERCEIVED, the next day, that they were still to ask no questions about the letter that had excited their curiosity; they were told that it was from their uncle, and nothing more was said. Lucy's health began to improve, however, from that day. Seeing one cloud gone from her father's brow, and catching the sunshine that glowed in her mother's smile, she felt a weight lifted from her heart, that made her appear to herself and her parents really almost well. This proved, however, only a transient improvement, for her cough still continued. Meanwhile, letters from Mr. Whittier became frequent now. The recovery of his daughter was announced as proceeding rapidly, and there was conveyed the hope, at least, that after so many years of separation there would be a speedy meeting. These letters were read to the children who rejoiced in the prospect of seeing, for the first time in their lives, a *real uncle*.

They sat one evening around the great pine table busy with books and work and talk. Tallow candles of home manufacture were dispersed here and there about the table, for the convenience of those who sewed or read, but which failed to light up aught save a circumscribed circle. The great kitchen would have been dark, in spite of them, but for the noble fire on the wide hearth, which illuminated with a comfortable glow every youthful face.

"That's what I call a fire," remarked Arthur, who had just arranged it afresh.

"See how the flames creep around the cold fore-stick, and hug it up!" he cried.

"How do you know they hug it?" asked Rebecca; that matter-of-fact young lady finding the figure incomprehensible. "But you're always saying strange things."

"I know it by my wisdom," he returned, laughing. "And hark, now! Don't you hear the logs singing to the flames, and thanking them for their friendship?"

"No, I don't," said Rebecca, "nor you either."

"I wouldn't thank anybody for friendship that burned me up," said Hatty.

"When Uncle Arthur comes, we'll have a rouser," said Tom, who sat contemplatively viewing the fire. "Mother! was our Arthur named for Uncle?"

"Why, no, indeed," cried Hatty; "he was named for Grandfather."

"It seems very odd that mother should have had a father," said Tom.

"It would be a great deal odder if she hadn't," retorted Hatty. "Oh dear! what a long seam! Lucy, how far have you got on yours! Almost to the end? Well— how you do sew!"

Lucy smiled, and went on; then stopped to cough.

"I can't have this," said her mother. "With that cough, I can't let you sit bending over work."

"I'll sit straighter, then," said Lucy.

"No, dear, that won't do. There, give it to me now. You must get well first."

"We've a great deal to do this winter," said Lucy. "And it's February now. When will the work get done, if I sit still and idle, I wonder?"

"The winter is only half gone," said Rebecca. "Candlemas-day; Half your wood and half your hay.'"

"But not half your work," said Hatty.

"They couldn't get 'work' in," said Rebecca. "But they meant it all the same."

"*You'll* never set the world on fire," said Hatty

"I don't want to," Rebecca answered quietly.

"She's set somebody on fire, though," said Arthur.

"John Wright says she's the prettiest girl he knows." On hearing John Wright's testimony, the children all laughed. Rebecca alone sat silent and embarrassed.

The Flower of the Family

"Who cares for John Wright?" she said at last.

A fresh burst of laughter was the only reply.

Lucy looked up at Arthur, and shook her head a little, though she smiled.

"I wouldn't," she said.

He smilingly shook his head at her, and said, "Well, I won't, then."

After a few moments' silence he looked up again.

"Lucy, can you show me about this sum now?"

She went around to his side of the table; he made room for her on his own chair. She saw that he had written something on his slate for her to read. She looked over his shoulder and read it: "John Wright says he is afraid of you."

She laughed, and wrote back, "Yes. I know I'm a monster."

"But, Lucy, you never say anything to him when he comes here."

"That's because I am afraid of him."

Arthur stopped playing now, and listened to the explanation of the difficulty.

"How quickly you understand," said she.

"How nicely you explain," he answered. "Mother, don't you think Lucy would make a first-rate teacher?" he asked.

"We must make her well first," she answered.

"There's somebody knocking," said Tom, hurrying towards the door.

"It's only John Wright, I dare say," whispered Arthur.

But not all the John Wrights in the world could have made their mother utter such a cry of joy as that with which she now greeted the figure Tom had admitted.

"It must be Uncle Arthur," said Hatty. "Rebecca, look quick: is my hair decent?"

Yes, it was Uncle Arthur; and by his side stood a boy of fourteen, perhaps, whom he soon introduced as his son Charles, and on whom the children looked with reverence. For there was something in the air of this city boy so utterly superior to that of any one in the village that even Hatty hung back a little abashed. He soon made them feel at their ease, however, by feeling so himself; and while Lucy went to see what could be mustered for supper, the whole party became acquainted.

58

The Flower of the Family

"I wish Helen had come," said Charles, looking around with an air of satisfaction, "but she wouldn't."

"Is she older or younger than you?" asked Hatty.

"Older," said Charles. "She's a very pretty girl. Her hair is just like yours."

"It runs in the family," said Hatty.

"I can pop corn," said Tom, finding himself overlooked.

"You must pop some for me, then," said Charles.

"Right away?" asked Tom eagerly.

Charles laughed, and said yes, he couldn't wait; and Tom ran off to get some corn, in a perfect tumult of delight.

Lucy, with Rebecca's aid, soon prepared a supper for the travellers, and summoned them to the table.

"I haven't seen such bread and butter since I was a boy," said their uncle. "You must have an admirable cook."

The girls smiled. "Mother makes all the bread," said Lucy.

"And Rebecca and Lucy make the butter," said their mother.

"You don't mean to say you keep no cook?" said Mr. Whittier.

"I don't mean to say anything about it," she answered.

"Excuse me," he said; "but really this is bad business. Your girls will be fit for nothing." He seemed so troubled that he couldn't help speaking, for his own relief.

"*I* think them good for a great deal," said Mrs. Grant.

"Yes, yes, I dare say; I'm sure they look like nice girls."

"Nice girls!" thought his sister, with a little twinge of annoyance; "I declare, I didn't know I was so proud of them. Well! it does one's pride good to get a fall now and then."

"I am sorry to say," continued Mr. Whittier, "that I have business at H__, which will make my visit to you shorter than I intended. My plan is now to spend to-morrow with you, and then push on to H__, leaving Charles here, if agreeable to you, till my return."

"When I hope you will spend some days with us, at least," said Mr. Grant.

"I cannot do that," answered Mr. Whittier; "but now I've found the way here, I hope to come again. You've no idea what lives we business men lead. We *work*, I assure you."

The Flower of the Family

Mr. Grant thought *he* knew what work meant but he did not say so. He only remarked:

"Yet you merchants are slow to retire from business."

"Well," said Mr. Whittier, "the more a man has, the more he wants, I suppose. As for myself, I hardly care to give up my business till Charles is old enough to take it."

"Then you don't intend to educate him?" said Mrs. Grant.

"No: Charles is no book-worm. I did intend sending him to college, but he was so opposed to it that I had to give up all thought of doing, so."

Lucy and Arthur exchanged astonished glances. In their simplicity, they had never doubted that all young people were like themselves. Their reverence for Charles received a severe shock, and was in danger of running into the opposite extreme. He proved himself, however, a lively, intelligent boy, full of fun and good-humor, and very soon was on the most friendly terms with them all.

"You'll like your uncle better as you see more of him," whispered Mrs. Grant to Lucy, as they went together to arrange a room for him.

"I don't like him a bit now," said Lucy.

"You will like him in time. He has admirable qualities and is my brother, at any rate."

"He doesn't seem like you at all," said Lucy. "And I do not believe I ever shall like him. He ought not to go to finding fault with you the minute he got into the house. I'm sure it is as much his fault as anybody's that we are so poor."

It was long since her mother had seen Lucy so excited. "Lucy, you don't seem like yourself at all. What can make you appear so?" she said anxiously and tenderly.

"I don't know," said Lucy; "but I don't think anything goes just right now. Ever since you said I mustn't stay in my room for fear of getting more cold, I've been very unhappy. And I'm getting fretful again."

"I did not mean to deprive you of time for your devotion, my dear child," she answered.

"I do try to be gentle and kind," said Lucy. "I hope you don't think I've stopped trying?"

The Flower of the Family

"No, dear; I haven't had such a thought. You have appeared as I want you should, this long time, till just now."

She felt greatly disturbed, however. She knew Lucy must be suffering under some kind of nervous difficulty, irritating and harassing, little as it had outwardly displayed itself.

"I've been cross to the children lately," said Lucy. "It makes me very unhappy, but I keep going on so."

"I never call people 'cross' when they're not well," said Mrs. Grant. "And I am sure you are not well."

"I heard somebody coughing badly last night," said Mr. Whittier the next morning. "Who was it?"

"It was Lucy," said her mother. "She has had a bad cough for a number of weeks."

"I don't wonder, in this cold climate," he answered. "Why don't you send her somewhere farther south? You have cold, damp springs here, I believe. She ought to go away before she gets more unwell."

"The doctor said so, long ago," said her father.

"Then why in the world don't you send her?"

There was an awkward silence. Nobody wanted to say, "Because we are poor." It seemed like an appeal to his charities.

"Come," said he, turning to Hatty," suppose you go home with me, and let us see if we can't nurse you up."

"*I* am not Lucy. I'm only Hatty," she replied, as soon as she could recover from the confusion into which her thoughts had been thrown.

"Which is Lucy, then?" he asked.

"She isn't here now," said Arthur; "she's the prettiest one. The one with the brown eyes."

His uncle looked at him and laughed, and looked again, as if he would say, "I've got hold of a curiosity now!"

"So she's the prettiest one, is she? And I suppose she has a parcel of beaux about her, and is very anxious to wear becoming bonnets, and—"

"No, she isn't anything like such a girl as that," said Arthur, indignantly. "She's not at all like other girls. And she doesn't so much as *think* of beaux," he added with infinite disgust. His uncle said no more, and breakfast over, he sat watching them from behind a newspaper, while they busied themselves as usual.

The Flower of the Family

All at once he started up. "Do you keep chickens?" he said, as Tom drew nigh.

"We keep a lot," said Tom.

"Come, show them to me," said Mr. Whittier. "No, go back the rest of you," he said, seeing Charles and Arthur following.

Hatty waited till he was out of sight, when she boiled over. Walking up to John, who sat privately brushing their uncle's boots behind the door, she said in a fierce whisper, "I *hate* him."

"So do I," returned John: "or I mean I should only it's wicked."

"I can't help it if it is wicked," said Hatty.

"He thinks we're all a pack of geese. *I* wouldn't brush his old boots!"

"I've a great mind not to," said John, stopping. "He only did it to plague me, I know."

"Did what?" asked Hatty.

"Why, he came out here before breakfast, sort of spying round, and says he, 'Where's the boy?' 'What boy. Sir?' says I. 'Why, the boot-black,' says he. 'What kind of boy is that, Sir?' says I; 'a boy as black as a boot?' And then he laughed at me and pinched my ear: look, it's red now and I suppose he thought he could make me cry; but I wasn't going to cry for *him*, anyhow. And then says he, 'You're made of hickory; a'n't you?' 'No, Sir,' says I, 'I a'n't made of hickory; I'm made of dust.' 'Who says you're made of dust?' says he, after laughing all to himself ever so long. 'The Bible says so,' says I: and then he went off and left his boots; so I s'pose he meant for me to clean 'em."

Meanwhile the object of this wrath was walking off with Tom by the hand, engaged, apparently, in a diligent pursuit of such knowledge as could be gained from an introduction to the chickens.

"You must eat a great many chickens," said Mr. Whittier.

"Oh, no, Sir; father sends them to market," said Tom.

"Well, you have plenty of eggs, at any rate, I suppose."

"Yes, Sir. But Arthur sells all the eggs *his* hens lay."

"What for?"

"Oh, he buys his books with them."

"What sort of books? Robinson Crusoes and Jack Halyards?"

The Flower of the Family

"He's had Robinson Crusoe, but I don't know about Jack Halyard. But I didn't mean such books. He doesn't buy such books as those. He swaps for *them*."

"Swaps!" said Mr. Whittier.

"Yes. He gives a feller his jack-knife, and a feller gives him a book— most generally old books. But those he buys with his eggs are study-books."

"Why doesn't your father buy them for him?"

"Oh, he can't afford it!" said Tom, opening his eyes as wide as he could, to take in a view of the propounder of this rash question.

"Who washes your clothes?" said his uncle abruptly.

"Mother, and Rebecca, and Lucy. And Arthur, and John, they make their bed. I shall make mine as soon as I'm a little bigger. Arthur said he wasn't going to have mother or the girls make *his* bed. They have too much to do, you see."

"We a'n't so poor as we were," he continued, finding his uncle greatly struck by his remarks, "for a man sent mother fifty dollars at New-Year's."

"And what did she do with it?"

"At first she cried. Then she said it would pay for Lucy to go away, because the doctor said she must go somewhere. And then Lucy begged her to save it for Arthur when he went to college. There was another man wrote father a letter, but he didn't send him any money "

"Perhaps the 'man' did not dare to."

"Why not?" asked Tom, innocently.

"For fear your father would be angry."

"Oh, my father, he don't get angry. And I don't believe that was the reason, either."

"Suppose now I should send him some money; would he like it, think?"

"Oh, yes. Sir," said Tom.

"Well, you needn't tell anybody anything I've asked you. And here's something for you."

Tom put both hands behind him.

"I shall have to tell," he said.

"Why?"

The Flower of the Family

"Because I always tell mother everything. She says it keeps me out of mischief."

"And so you are going to tell her I've been pumping you with all sorts of questions?"

"I didn't know you had, Sir. I didn't know you'd said anything naughty."

"Dear me, I've got myself into a fix," said Mr. Whittier, looking round for solace in his tribulation upon the hens and chickens, to whom his visit had proved so unprofitable. "Well, well, be off with you, child, and be sure you don't forget a word."

Away went Tom, highly indignant, straight to his mother.

"I don't like that man, and he isn't my uncle," he shouted.

"Hush, hush, dear," said his mother.

"I can't hush, and I a'n't a going to, either," cried Tom. "He asked me if you ate chickens; and if we ate eggs; and why you didn't buy books for Arthur; and why you didn't send Lucy away; and he said I mustn't tell a word of it: and when I said I should tell you, he said he'd got into a fix, and gave me a little push, and said, 'Well, well, be off with you, child.' And he is a naughty, ugly man."

"Tom," said his mother, "you are only a little boy, and you make mistakes sometimes, you know. You mustn't call your uncle a naughty man, and get so angry and excited. You spoke very rudely to mother just now. I am sure you did not understand your uncle; and now mind, you are not to repeat a word of this to any one."

"Can't I tell Lucy?"

"No, not Lucy, nor anybody. And sit down here till you are a good boy."

"I'm a good boy now. I've been good ever so long. Lucy says so. And I don't like that man."

"What has got into you all?" said poor Mrs. Grant, half bewildered. "I hardly know which way to turn Tom, I didn't expect this of you. You have been such a dear, good child, lately."

"I'm sorry I've troubled you, mother. I'll try to be good," said Tom, throwing his arms around her neck, but instantly relapsing into his defiant mood, as he saw his uncle approaching.

The Flower of the Family

"I have made an awkward business of it," said Mr. Whittier, "but I had a good end in view, and I hope you understand that I did not pry into your affairs out of idle curiosity. I only wanted to find out in what way I could be of most use to you. And I know you never would tell me yourself, you're so proud," he added, smiling. "But now about that debt; let us talk the matter over, and have it settled; of course you see the impropriety of my letting things go as they are now."

"What do you propose? I don't quite understand," said Mrs. Grant. "Do you want it paid directly?"

"What are you thinking of?" cried he. "I am only asking of you, who know Grant so much better than I do, how it will answer to relinquish my claim. Would it offend him, do you think?"

"I don't know; I shouldn't use the word 'offend,' exactly. But he might feel hurt, just at this time. He might fancy—" she hesitated, not daring to finish her sentence.

"Might fancy I hoped to wipe off old scores with mere money, I suppose you mean. Don't be afraid to say it; I had thought of that myself." He sat silent for a time; then said:

"Sarah, you are my own sister; we are children of one mother; you, at least, ought not to be unwilling that I should help you bear your burdens. I don't want to do anything that would revolutionize your family. I only want to make life easier for you, and for your children, in little ways, neither you nor they will notice much. I am ashamed and bitterly regret that I have not been doing it all these years. How many children did you say there were? Ten? Well, I have something to tell you which will interest you, I am sure. A short time before my father's death, my eldest child was born. A fine little fellow he was! And we called him Arthur. He lived to be four years old, and was the perfect idol of his grandfather, who could never bear him out of his sight. He said one day that he had laid aside a small sum of money for your first-born, expecting it to be a boy and his own namesake; but after waiting several years, and finding your children were all girls, he made it over to my little Arthur. I was poor then— I know what poverty means— and was not sorry to know that means were thus provided for his future education. But God had something better in store for my child, and took him from me almost without warning. It was a heavy blow, but it did not bring me to myself. I was immersed in business, and struggling along from day to day, and had hardly time to think or feel. Poverty spoiled and soured me, and I grew hard and cold under its petty discipline. Well! that money of my little child has been lying ever since in the Savings' Bank where it was first placed. I never could bear to touch, or even think of it. Now let our father's original wish be gratified in its disposal. You can see for yourself that it properly belongs to your son, who bears his name."

Mrs. Grant could with difficulty control herself during this recital. It seemed to her that the hand of God was in the matter, and that He had Arthur's interests even more at heart than she had herself. She went into her room, and thanked Him on her knees; how fervently, only a mother can understand.

CHAPTER 8

New Scenes and New Friends

IT WAS DECIDED, at last, that Lucy should return home with her uncle. He would listen to not one of the many objections urged against it by Lucy herself, who dared not, after all, confide to him her chief ground of hesitation. This was a dread of proving an unwelcome guest to her unknown aunt. She shrank from the bare thought of thus thrusting herself, as she termed it, into a family where all were comparative strangers. But, on the other hand, she was tempted to yield to the solicitations of her parents, whose anxiety in regard to her health made them blind to other considerations,

"Never mind about her wardrobe," said her uncle; "everything she needs can be easily provided in New York."

There was time, however, during his week's absence, to make some necessary additions to this very simple, very scanty stock; and everybody's energies were, for the time, concentrated on this important point. Amid the bustle and labor of this week, Lucy hardly realized that so great an event as separation from all she loved was before her; and when her uncle returned, announcing his speedy departure, her heart failed her.

"Don't make me go, dear mother," she said, taking her mother aside. "Please let me stay!"

"Dear child, I wish you could!" said the poor mother, who at this moment forgot all her secret purposes of self-control and propriety. "I wish I dared keep you!"

"I shan't have a happy moment away from you," pleaded Lucy.

"But, my dear Lucy, you will find God as truly there, as He is here. And He is better than many mothers."

The Flower of the Family

Lucy smiled through her tears; and then she tried to thank her mother for all her dear love and patience, and to tell her how she should think of her all the time, every moment; but she could not. Her uncle was waiting; she ran out, kissed them all over and over again, and was gone. They stood looking out after her, all in tears, for this was the first parting they had ever known; and who could say what should befall between the parting and the meeting? All were in tears; only Arthur stood leaning quietly against the side of the door, looking pale but composed. He thought he was getting too old to cry now; so he stood there, looking down the road, till he found himself alone. Then he went up to his room, bolted his door, and stretching forth his arms, as if to reach and recall her, he cried, "O Lucy! Lucy!"

No other word escaped the brave young heart, that now felt itself so lonely, so deserted; and in a very little time he went down, and about his usual morning tasks. And when Hatty afterwards wrote to Lucy, she said, "We all cried, but just Arthur," and marvelled as she wrote, and then forgot it. But his mother saw that from this day Arthur was, if possible, more gentle, more manly than ever, and that thought for her never left him. And in how many ways a dutiful, affectionate boy can lighten and smooth his mother's lot!

At the close of the third day the travellers reached their journey's end, and Lucy found herself kindly, if not warmly welcomed by her aunt and cousin. She was heartily glad to find herself soon advised to retire for the night, for she felt not only weary, but embarrassed and annoyed. Before leaving home, such very special additions had been made to her wardrobe, that she had only been afraid of being overdressed. But one glance at Helen had shown her the contrast between her own country style and that of the city.

"They will be ashamed of me, I am sure," she said to herself, "and I ought not to have come here, dressed so."

She had read of "country cousins," whose air, and speech, and raiment all conspired to make their city friends blush for very shame; and how did she know that she had not fallen into the same error? She sat down and reflected a little; and after some few troubled, uneasy thoughts, came to a conclusion that quite restored her peace.

The Flower of the Family

"I am dressed as well as father could afford; I ought not to be ashamed then. And it would be wrong and silly to try to do anything else. And if my aunt is annoyed, I shall be very, very sorry; but I must try to bear that patiently." She opened her little Bible, and her eye fell upon the passage beginning, "Consider the lilies of the field," and she read on to the end of the chapter. "Yes," it seemed to say, "God knows that you have need of clothing as well as the lilies of the field; and all you have to do is just to wear, as the flowers do, the dress He gives you." And the meek and quiet spirit with which she took the lesson home, became as an ornament of grace about her neck, which many a well-adorned maiden lacked.

Meanwhile, Mr. Whittier was subjected to a storm— if one may use so harsh an epithet— of questions of every possible form and intent.

"How came you to bring my cousin?" Helen asked half a dozen times, edging in her question at every available point, with a skill worthy of her sex.

"I brought her on account of her health," her father at last answered. "She has a bad cough, and has been advised to try change of air; and I want you to do all you can for her pleasure and comfort."

"What sort of a girl is she?"

"A very good sort of a girl, I believe."

"Then I sha'n't like her at all," said Helen, decidedly. "I don't like 'good sort of people.'"

"Well, then, if you prefer bad sort of people, I dare say you will be suited. There are plenty of such in this world."

"But, papa, can't you tell me *anything* about her? Has she left school?"

"Indeed, my dear, I do not know. I am not sure she has ever attended school. And in the one day I spent in the house, I could not learn the individual character and history of ten children."

"Ten!" cried Helen; "have I ten cousins? O papa, among so many there must be some I should like. Charles, don't you know cousin Lucy?"

"Oh, she's a nice girl enough," said Charles, "Makes first-rate pies and all that, and is quite an oracle among them. Rather good, I fancy."

The Flower of the Family

"I'm afraid I shan't like her. Mamma, do people from the country always have shopping to do? And don't they want to be on the go the whole time, to see what they can see?"

"There isn't the least touch of selfishness about my little daughter, is there?" asked her father, drawing her down upon his knee.

Helen colored.

"Well, papa, you know how I dislike sight-seeing!"

"But you do not dislike doing a kind act, I hope. Now your cousin has spent her whole life in the country. Everything here will be new to her. She is in delicate health, owing, unless I greatly mistake, to constant confinement to those little children; and it is my opinion she needs rest and amusement far more than a doctor. Her mother told me how she had been tied hand and foot to all sorts of disagreeables. The only wonder is, the child isn't spoiled."

"I wonder how old she is," said Helen.

"Let me see; she must be seventeen, I think, more or less."

"But, papa, haven't you talked with her on the journey? Don't you know in the least what she is like?"

Her father laughed, and shook his head at her, and turned his attention to her mother.

"I'm afraid the world has gone pretty hardly with them all," he said. "Yet they seem a cheerful set. Mr. Grant still takes a rather melancholy view of life, yet it is wonderful how much religion has done for him in that respect. He is by no means the gloomy man he was. And the children seem more like their mother. I found it not so easy a matter to arrange about that debt as I fancied it would be. All I can do at present, is just to edge along by degrees, relieving them at this point and that, in a quiet way, and by and by I may venture farther."

"Is Mr. Grant so proud, then?" asked Mrs. Whittier.

"Not that alone: I think, however, as things are, it would not do to press him too hard. My sister hinted he might fancy I hoped to wipe out past offenses with money. I am sure she wished me to use caution. The fact is, Grant is peculiar; one must be wary in dealing with him. But he is a good man; a thoroughly upright, conscientious one."

The Flower of the Family

Mrs. Whittier mused awhile in silence. "I don't know how I should feel," she said, "but it does seem to me I could accept any thing from an own brother— for the sake of the children, at least; particularly if they are obliged to become mere household drudges, as you say this Lucy has been."

"But Grant is not my own brother, you know. And it is not this debt alone that has kept them down. The farm is small and unproductive; and then they have had such a family! I was all the time afraid I should step on some of them; there were always two or three crawling round on the floor."

"Well, why don't you buy a larger farm, then?"

"Who? I? Why don't I buy the sun or the moon!"

"But I am not jesting. If this farm of your brother's is too small, why don't you buy a larger one and settle them on it?"

"Yes, papa," said Helen, "I wish you would."

"Women know a vast deal about business, to be sure," said Mr. Whittier, leaning back in his chair, and laughing. "It's well they have somebody to look out for them."

"But you have not answered me yet," said his wife.

"Well, then, my dear, I will give you one reason out of many equally as good: I can't afford it."

She smiled, and looked incredulous.

"In the next place, then, it would not be the best thing for them. In many little ways, less apparent and therefore less painful to them, I can make their future life more agreeable than it has been. For instance, should this Lucy prove worthy of it, we can give her a year or two of such education as of course she needs; then, as the other children come on, I can do the same for them; or something of the sort; no matter what, so it is for their good."

"But, meanwhile, are you sure of living as long as they?"

"If I do not, perhaps you will; and I could not leave them in better hands. And when we are gone, Charles and Helen will do what we leave undone."

All were silent for a season. At length Mrs. Whittier said,

"I do not mean to press you too far; I only was moved to say what I have done, by the appearance of that poor child. Her dress showed so plainly that life has, as you say, gone hardly with them."

"Why, was she not properly dressed?" cried Mr. Whittier.

The Flower of the Family

"Yes, certainly; very properly. I was relieved to see no vulgar attempt at display in her; yet grieved, too, to think that your sister's child should take this long journey, in the depth of winter, so scantily and poorly clothed. It made me ashamed of the house I live in, and of the garments I wear."

"You women see everything," returned her husband. "I don't know what art you use, but somehow at a single glance you read a whole history in a faded shawl."

"I read more than one in that sweet girl's dress," said Mrs. Whittier. "And more than one in her face, too I am sure, though I have hardly heard her speak a word, that, young as she is, she has passed through trials such as *we* only read about in books."

"Come, come, don't let us get excited about it," said her husband, trying to shake off the feelings of remorse that crept through his whole frame.

"I am not excited more than I always am when I see trouble I ought to have shared and alleviated."

"But why have you let them stay poor so long, papa?" asked Helen eagerly. Her mother shook her head; Helen did not observe it, and pressed closer to her father, looking up into his face with a flushed cheek. He looked down upon it silently a moment.

"I was not always a Christian, Helen," he said.

She asked no more that night. But her heart yearned already to love her yet unknown cousin; and every thought of self vanished before those her mother's words had excited.

"I'll do all I can to amuse her," she said to herself. "I'll go out shopping with her, and I'll get books for her to read, and worsted-work; but perhaps she isn't fond of reading: I dare say she isn't on the whole. Well! then I must think of something else, that's all."

When Lucy rose next morning, a little twinge of pain, as she put on her dress, reminded her of her last evening's reflections upon it. But it was but for a moment, and when she entered the dining-room, Helen's warm greeting made her feel quite at ease again. Her aunt met her affectionately too, and Lucy reproved herself for having fancied them not cordial at the outset. Seated at the table, with a huge paper in its hands, was a little figure she had not seen before.

The Flower of the Family

"Miss Prigott! this is my niece," said her aunt, leading Lucy towards the lady, who, on hearing herself addressed, sprang briskly from her seat, and descended upon them both with ardor and warmth enough for a dozen such meetings. Lucy felt herself more uncomfortable under these embraces than she could understand, for they certainly seemed as sincere as they were vivacious.

"I am charmed to see you, my dear," she said, her little quick eyes running all over Lucy in a twinkling, "and it is an unexpected pleasure to see you looking so robust and rosy. They all tried to persuade me you were in delicate health. But I knew how it was. I have not lived to be fifty years of age to no purpose. Young people get sick of the country, and pine for the city. Yes, yes, *I* know."

"I was not sick of it," said Lucy.

"Oh! of course not, of course not," said Miss Prigott, waving her hand as a final waive to the subject. They seated themselves at the table, and Lucy felt the little eyes running over her again. Now she felt them on her face, now on her dress. Now on the hand in which the silver fork trembled.

"Not accustomed to a silver fork, I presume," said Miss Prigott, sympathizingly.

Lucy answered, this time without embarrassment, that she was not.

"That's right, my dear; always speak the truth, cost what it may."

"If my cheeks burn as I do myself, I don't wonder she calls me rosy," thought Lucy.

After breakfast Helen drew her aside, and whispered, "You mustn't mind Miss Prigott; she's a good little soul enough when one gets used to her, but hard to bear at first. Just let her see you don't care for her, and she'll let you alone, in time."

"But I do care for her," said Lucy.

"I shall just keep you out of her way, then. She does not always live here; at present she is waiting to find a new boarding-house. She was burned out of the last one, and came right here. You mustn't laugh at her; mamma won't like that."

"I sha'n't wish to laugh at her."

The Flower of the Family

"Why, don't you laugh at any thing? Are you so very grave and solemn always as you are now?"

Lucy laughed.

"You can't suppose that what was said at breakfast proved very enlivening to my spirits," she said

"It was too bad, I know."

"Oh! it is all over now: I was only a little taken off my guard. You know I have always lived at home, and have seen nothing of the world. I dare say it is full of strange people."

"I dare say it is," said Helen "but I know as little of it almost as you do. But come; I always take a long walk after breakfast; will you go with me?"

Lucy hesitated a moment.

"Sha'n't you feel a little ashamed to be seen in the streets with a country girl?" she asked, half playfully, yet half in earnest.

"Nonsense!" said Helen pleasantly; and in a few minutes they were in the open air, and Lucy felt herself one of the busy crowd already thronging the streets. The noise confused her; she shrank from the passers-by as they pressed upon her, and of all the attractions with which the shop-windows were filled, she observed nothing. Helen hurried her along, directing her attention to this and that, till at last, stopping short, she asked, "Do you like to walk in such a crowd?"

"No, I do not, indeed. Can't we get out of it?"

"I think we shall agree very well," said Helen. "I hate a crowd." And with this bond of sympathy already established, they walked home, mutually pleased and satisfied.

CHAPTER 9

A Glimpse at "Society"

LUCY WAS FATIGUED by her walk, and looked pale and languid. She sat down in the first chair she saw on her entrance, quite out of breath.

"I am afraid we walked too far," said Helen. "I did not know you had so little strength."

"I am not accustomed to walking much," said Lucy.

"But exercise is good for everybody, isn't it?"

"Oh, I had exercise enough running after the children, and all that; but not much time for walking. But don't wait for me. I shall be as well as ever, in a minute."

Helen went to tell her mother how feeble Lucy was; and as soon as she was out of sight, the little head of Miss Prigott appeared peeping out from the door of an adjoining room.

"What, idling in the morning!" she cried. "Oh my love, that is a sad way of beginning the day. If I had wasted my youth in that style, I do not know what I should be in my age. There is nothing so becoming in young people as industry."

Lucy made a great effort to control herself, but did not succeed so far as to venture on a reply. Miss Prigott therefore stepped forth into the hall and confronted her with a mixture of coolness and excitement in her manner, to which no description could do justice. Lucy's pale cheeks glowed under it.

"A little temper," said Miss Prigott. "I regret it, my dear."

"I was not angry," said Lucy, gathering courage. "I was hurt at being misunderstood."

"Yes, yes; that's the cant phrase of young misses, nobody understands them. They're very intricate indeed."

Lucy looked down and was silent. Her heart only was allowed to speak, and this time to God. It said, "Oh, make me patient! Oh, make me patient!" and felt already grieved that it had not been so from the outset.

"I am your true friend," continued Miss Prigott; "the true friend of the young and inexperienced. And I am sure I can be of great service to you if you will allow it."

At this moment Helen appeared with her mother, and by them Lucy was borne off without ceremony, and made to lie down. Miss Prigott looked after their retreating figures with what she called *regret*; and far be it from us to assign to her emotions a harsher name.

"There they go," she exclaimed, "one to be spoiled and two to be fooled. It is a truly melancholy spectacle." And she returned to her room, and reflected on life, and said it was a dream.

A couch had been placed in Lucy's room during her interview with Miss Prigott, and both her aunt and Helen busied themselves in making her comfortable upon it. She felt ashamed of herself for being unwell, but the shame brought no strength with it. They left her alone, with books within reach, and she lay still upon her pillow and looked about the large pleasant room, at the pretty tasteful furniture, the friendly fire, the pictures on the wall.

"Now, if I had some of them here, I should be perfectly happy," she thought. "If dear mother could see me, how relieved and thankful she would be! And if I only had Arthur here! Dear Arthur! With all these books, and this nice fire, and this quiet room, what would he say?" She smiled at the thought, it was so very pleasant, and then sighed. At the bottom of the sigh lay Miss Prigott, but her little figure floated off upon it, and the image of mother, and Arthur, and the baby, came back again, and hovered around her, and would let no other intrude.

"How soundly you sleep!" said a voice near her.

She started. "Have I been asleep?" she cried.

"Only four hours," said Helen, laughing.

"Oh, why didn't you call me? I am ashamed of myself for sleeping so! But I was very tired, and on the journey I slept very little."

"Are you quite rested now?"

The Flower of the Family

"Oh yes, I feel like a new creature."

"Who is this 'Arthur' you talk about in your sleep?" asked Helen, archly.

"My brother; but did I talk about him?"

"Oh yes, and I was afraid it was some young gentleman."

"Why, I am not yet sixteen; and do you suppose I am so silly as that?"

"Not sixteen, and so tall! Why, Lucy! And as to being silly, all girls are silly. I get tired and sick of their talk about lovers and such things."

"You won't hear such talk from me," said Lucy springing up, and preparing to arrange her hair; "for I neither know nor care anything about the science."

"I'm very glad," said Helen.

And now there was another bond of sympathy between them.

"When shall you be sixteen?" continued Helen.

"Let me see. What day of the month is it? the fifteenth? Well, I shall be sixteen on the nineteenth."

"So soon! We'll celebrate it, then. Did you read before you fell asleep?"

"No, I'm saving that pleasure until I've written home. I must write as soon as I'm dressed."

"You won't have time until after dinner; dinner is all ready now."

"Dear me! why didn't you tell me, and I would have made more haste." She flew about the room looking for this and that, and dressed with a speed and vigor quite opposed to the languor of the morning.

"I advise you not to fly round in that style before Miss Prigott," said Helen. "She'll think you were making-believe sick this morning."

"She thinks so now," said Lucy, stopping short. "I begin to think myself that she was right." On reaching the dining-room, Lucy found them all awaiting her, and apologized for the delay she had caused.

"You look quite refreshed," said her aunt. "I hope you feel so."

Lucy assured her that this was the case. Miss Prigott maintained an ominous silence.

The Flower of the Family

"How have you amused yourself this morning?" asked her uncle.

"To tell the truth, in sleeping," said Lucy: "I was very tired. But I sha'n't do so again."

"I hope they provided you with books?"

"Yes, Sir; but I did not read. I fell asleep as soon as I returned from my walk."

"Not fond of reading," said Miss Prigott, mentally. Her little eyes ran and told the thought forthwith.

"Yes, I am very fond of it," said Lucy; "but to-day I was so tired! And seeing so many books I had been longing to read, and knowing I had time to read them, I just did nothing."

"Young people should be methodical," said Miss Prigott.

"Lucy sha'n't be methodical, or anything else she doesn't like, while she is here," said her uncle.

"Oh yes, this is Liberty Hall," said Miss Prigott.

Mr. Whittier looked at her, and was tempted to say, "I should think *you* thought it so, by the way you visit it." But between a touch of his wife's foot, under the table, and certain prudential forces of his own he forbore.

As soon as dinner was over, Lucy began her letter home; but there were so many things to tell, that she was surprised by a summons to tea before it was half done. While she was thus occupied, her aunt, Helen, and Miss Prigott, sat together at their work. "Lucy seems like a very sweet, intelligent girl," said Mrs. Whittier. "Don't you think so, Miss Prigott?"

"I am a close student of human nature," said Miss Prigott, oracularly.

"I'm sure *I* like her very much," said Helen. "She is different from other girls."

"Yes, very fresh and simple," said Mrs. Whittier.

"Of course, coming from the country," said Miss Prigott.

"Not necessarily. Some young people are as full of pretension as possible, who have never breathed other than country air. Everything depends on education. Or rather, I should say, a *great deal* depends upon it."

"Do you mean to say that simplicity is a matter of knowledge?" asked Miss Prigott.

"Oh! I am no metaphysician. I won't argue the matter with you."

"I always thought simplicity an unconscious virtue. It is a new idea to me that I can educate myself into it."

"But I did not say you could, I believe," said Mrs. Whittier, to whom the idea of old Miss Prigott trying to be simple, proved ludicrous. "I must find what Fenelon says on the subject for you to read."

"I don't read French," said Miss Prigott drily.

"I ask your pardon. I thought you read everything."

"Fifty years ago, young people were taught more useful things than in these days."

"For instance, to embroider on satin," said Helen, mischievously.

Miss Prigott was displeased; but went on: "Pray, if I may ask, how did you discover Miss Lucy's 'sweetness, and intelligence, and simplicity?' For she has hardly honored us an hour with her society."

Mrs. Whittier smiled. "*I* am a close student too," she said. "But, of course, I am not strenuous in an opinion so hastily formed. But I must say that thus far I have been very agreeably impressed by all I have seen."

"What do you think of that?" asked Miss Prigott, abruptly, and presenting for inspection a muslin collar, in process of embroidery.

"I think it very pretty. Did you learn this sort of work at Miss Burton's school?"

"Yes, yes: that was a school where something was taught worth learning. And for an old woman, I think I should not blush at such work as that."

"I hope you'll give it to me when it is done," said Helen.

"No, it is for your cousin."

Helen and her mother looked at each other, and smiled.

"That is really kind," said Mrs. Whittier.

"When girls idle about all day, they need some one to care for them," returned Miss Prigott.

"I do believe you like Lucy, after all," said Helen. "And you said you didn't."

The Flower of the Family

"I said nothing of the sort. Nor have I said I like her, either. But I suppose I can show her an act of Christian kindness?"

"I'm sure Lucy never had such a collar as that," continued Helen. "And you never made one for *me*. I feel really hurt. But I suppose you are waiting for me to arrive at years of discretion, as Lucy has done. Mamma! Lucy will be sixteen in a few days."

"It pains me to see a young woman live so many years in this world in thoughtlessness and irreligion," said Miss Prigott.

"But you do not know that Lucy is irreligious," said Mrs. Whittier.

"I do not *know* that she is; but I hardly doubt it."

"My dear Miss Prigott! She has not spent a whole day under this roof."

"That is true, but my opinions are not formed more hastily than your own. Here you have been making her out sweet, simple, intelligent, and I don't know what not, with no better opportunity of judging than I have had."

"I merely said she impressed me as such. One always receives an impression of some sort in making a new acquaintance. And, until I know the worst, I like to think the best of those I meet."

"It is quite the contrary with me."

"You need not proclaim that," thought Helen. "Everybody knows it."

They were now summoned to tea. Lucy came down looking very happy, for her thoughts were full of pleasant images of home. But her face grew brilliant when her uncle gave her a letter, and she saw that it was from her mother.

"From dear mother!" she exclaimed. "It is from mother! How very kind! She must have written as soon as I left home!"

"The mails travel faster than we did," said her uncle.

"Quite a pretty little piece of acting," thought Miss Prigott, looking with disfavor on the animated, glowing face opposite her.

"It is really quite remarkable for a mother to write to her child," she said.

"But you do not know how much mother has to do, now I am gone," said Lucy. "I am sure she must have sat up late at night to write this:" she gave it a little loving squeeze under the table, as she spoke.

"Then I am sure you ought not to enjoy what has cost her such an effort," said Miss Prigott.

The joyous face clouded over. "I *am* selfish." thought Lucy. "All I care for is my own pleasure. But it did seem so good to have a letter from mother! The very first I ever had from her in my life!"

Her aunt looked embarrassed and displeased, and mentally revolved a plan for Miss Prigott's ejectment from the premises.

Lucy ventured, after tea, to run to her room long enough to read her precious letter. Very precious indeed it was, and she felt tempted to read it once more, before rejoining the family, when a knock at her door arrested her. On opening it, she found Miss Prigott standing before her.

"My love," said she, "you will thank me, I am sure, if I use the privilege of a friend, and give you some little hints that may be of service to you."

"Yes, ma'am," said Lucy: "will you come in?"

Miss Prigott entered and seated herself.

"My dear, you are ignorant of the world, and having never been accustomed to good society, cannot be expected to conform to all its usages."

"What is good society?" asked Lucy.

Miss Prigott, thus arrested in the full tide of her remarks, fixed her little astonished eyes upon Lucy, and was for a time speechless. Was the question malicious? or was the girl, after all, really a simpleton?

"Because in my dictionary it may not mean what it does in yours," said Lucy.

"It can have but one meaning, of course."

"I think it has more than one. I mean, I have been taught to think so."

"Perhaps, too, you think you have been accustomed to it?"

Lucy smiled.

"The society of farmers, and farmers' wives and children," said Miss Prigott, contemptuously.

"Is that bad society?"

"You will find my patience without limit. You can go on. I shall bear your rudeness with equanimity."

"I hope I am not rude; I did not intend it."

The Flower of the Family

"Then you really mean to say you have been in good society?"

"Yes, I do say so!" cried Lucy with spirit. "I know I have seen little of the world, and that I am very ignorant of its manners and customs. But I never can know them so well as to doubt that, in the best sense of the word, the society of my parents is good, very good."

"I thought your father was a farmer."

"Yes, he is a farmer; but he is a man of education and refinement. And my mother was well educated too."

"What insufferable pride!" cried Miss Prigott, clasping her hands. "I suppose you even think you find nothing better here than you did at home!"

"No, I do not think so. I do not say so. But I only say I was used at home always to see real goodness, real refinement, and real worth; and I never knew before that it would be questioned anywhere."

"Of course, then, my wish to be of service to you is a vain one. You are already so entrenched in wisdom."

"Oh no. I know nothing about the usages of society in your sense, and I shall thank you if you will be so very good as to teach me anything you perceive I ought to know. And if I am so proud as you say, I am very sorry. I don't wish to be proud. I do want to be and do right, in all things."

Miss Prigott was mollified by the eager, earnest tone.

"I came to say to you that it is not proper to spend so much time by yourself. But I dare say your mother, who is so well educated, mentioned that in her letter!"

"I was just going down; I only wanted to read my letter. I know I ought to be careful not to keep too much aloof from my aunt and Helen."

"Oh, of course they do not *need* your society; they are sufficient to each other."

Lucy shrank back. All her past fear of intrusion rushed upon her with new force.

"What *shall* I do?" she cried. "If I stay by myself, it is neglecting them; if I join them, it is an intrusion. Oh, Miss Prigott! I never spent one hour from home before, and I always asked mother what I should do, and she always seemed to know!"

"And have not I tried to be a mother to you, ever since you came? And you pay no heed to what I say."

"Yes, I do, indeed I do. I will go or stay, just as you advise."

"Go, then, of course."

Lucy went; and if her spirits were not brilliant, and if the long evening seemed very long, who can wonder, who has ever felt the little eyes of a Miss Prigott?

CHAPTER 10

The Sixteenth Birthday

LUCY WAS SURPRISED and delighted on the morning of her birthday, to find her table adorned with many little tasteful gifts. There was among them a small neatly-folded package, and on opening it she found a religious tract, addressed to the "unconverted," from between whose leaves there fell the collar on which she had seen Miss Prigott expend so much labor.

She took it up with astonishment. That Miss Prigott, after all that had passed, should attempt to gratify her, seemed incredible.

"What unjust thoughts I have had of her!" she cried. "I'll go this minute and thank her. But let me look at this tract first. 'To the unconverted!' Did she mean that for me? Is it possible I have appeared so little like a Christian that she could feel *sure* I was not? But of course she was sure, or she would not have sent me this."

A bitter pang seized her, and her tears fell fast. She thought how good God had been to her all her life, and that she had dishonored Him; and then she began to question herself as to how she ever had dared imagine she knew anything about real love to Him. The longer she looked at herself, the more discouraged and wretched she became, and for a time she paced her room in anguish. At last she threw herself on her knees, and laid her fears and her despair at the feet of her Saviour, to whom the first alarm should have driven her. And as she prayed and ventured herself upon Him, peace returned to her heart; she *felt* that she was His, and that there was needed no righteousness of hers to make her acceptance with Him sure and steadfast. As she rose from her knees, her eyes fell upon a little book that had lain unnoticed among her other birthday gifts. It was from her aunt;

The Flower of the Family

and on opening it, its very title cheered her: "Daily Food for Christians."

"My aunt then guessed what I needed," she thought, and hastily turning to the verses for the day, she was struck by their sympathy with her present mood. "Who is among you that feareth the Lord, that obeyeth the voice of His servant, that walketh in darkness, and hath no light? Let him trust in the name of the Lord, and stay upon his God." And "Though He slay me, yet will I trust in Him."

"Yes, I may distrust and doubt myself, but I will *stay upon my God* and trust Him!" she thought. She stood with the precious little book in her hand many minutes; it comforted her inexpressibly.

They were all awaiting her in the dining-room, anticipating pleasure from her enjoyment of the surprise they had prepared for her. But though there was a tranquil expression on her face as she joined them, all remarked that she was paler than usual, and that she had been weeping.

"Are you more unwell this morning, dear?" asked her aunt.

"Oh no, aunt; and I have been delighted with my beautiful birthday presents. I thank you so much, dear uncle! and you too, aunt! And for my pretty collar, I suppose I must thank Miss Prigott."

"*Miss Prigott* wishes no thanks," remarked that lady, drily.

"You gave me an unexpected pleasure, at all events," said Lucy, determined not to be annoyed.

"I wish I could give profit as easily."

Lucy understood this remark to refer to the tracts and she said in a low voice,

"I thank you for the wish."

After breakfast, as she was passing through the hall, Miss Prigott's head once more made its appearance from the side-door.

"If you can spare time, I should like to see you," she said.

Lucy entered the room with a beating heart hardly knowing what she feared, yet certainly afraid.

"You were displeased at my sending you a tract!" Miss Prigott began.

"Not *displeased*," replied Lucy. "Only I was sorry."

"For what?"

The Flower of the Family

"That I had given you occasion to do it," she said, in a voice so gentle, so humble, that Miss Prigott for a moment was touched. But only for a moment. Instantly gathering up all the dignity she could concentrate in her little person, she fastened her eyes upon the shrinking figure before her.

"What do you mean, child?" she asked.

Lucy was silent.

"Do you mean to pretend that you are capable of judging for yourself what sort of tracts you need? Or what?"

"At my age, I ought to have some opinion on such a subject. But I feel just as grateful to you for your wish to be of service to me, as if— " she hesitated.

"Go on."

"As if you had chosen the best way. If you had called me in here, and told me you feared I was not a Christian, and had pointed out wherein I had given you occasion to think so; then, I think, I should not have felt so very, very wretched as I did." Tears started to her eyes as she recalled the misery of the morning, and she rose to go.

"Sit down, child," said Miss Prigott; "sit down. I'm sure I had no wish to make you wretched! But girls do use such strong language! I am sorry my tract was not to your taste. And I can't account for it that I should have made a mistake in my choice of it. Are you *sure* you are not yourself mistaken?"

"No, not sure. But I hope not! I trust not!"

"Well! I must say I never dreamed you were religious. I have not heard you speak a word that would indicate it, since you came here."

"It is not my way to talk much on such subjects."

" '*Your way*!' Do you mean to say that Christians have different ways peculiar to themselves, and in which they all are right?"

"I did not say that; but I always was taught to think so."

"Then there is no standard? Every one is to judge for himself?"

"Christ is the standard. Every one is to try to be like Him."

"And I suppose it was not *His way* to talk much about religion?"

"No, I don't think it was," said Lucy, rousing herself, and speaking with animation. "Not to talk *about* it. I never could see that that was expected of us, either."

"Poor child! you have been sadly taught, I fear. Now, listen: Christians are the disciples of Christ. They are either like Him, or they do not deserve the name. And if they are all like Him, they are, of course, all like each other, just as coins are all similar to each other when the casts of one die."

"My father has often told me that natural characteristics modify the Christian life," said Lucy. "For instance, that Paul could not be John, nor Moses, David."

Miss Prigott was astonished and puzzled.

"I never saw such a girl in my life!" she exclaimed. "I thought I was going to have such comfort in you! First, I gave you that tract; and then, I was to give you others, as I found you prepared for them. But now, all my plans are disarranged. Nothing in this world gives me such pure pleasure as doing good. But you have thwarted me from the outset."

"I do believe she wishes I was a perfect heathen, whom she might convert at her leisure," thought Lucy. But in an instant she reproached herself for the thought, and said:

"There are some tracts I want very much. There is one of Newton's, called 'The Progress of Grace,' that I have long wanted. If you would be so kind as to give me that, I should be very glad."

She hoped thus to appease Miss Prigott's troubled soul, but hoped in vain. Miss Prigott looked negligently over the great bundle of tracts upon her table, and said at last it was not among them. In fact, it formed no part of her scheme to *build up* the objects of her compassion in faith and good works. She was one of a large class of good people who, in their zeal for the utterly irreligious, lose sight of those babes in Christ who stand in almost as pressing need of *culture* as they once did of warning.

"You may return that unfortunate tract you despise so much," she said, as Lucy once more rose to go.

"I do not despise it," said Lucy, "nor your good will, either. I thank you for both. And I am very sorry I can't make you understand me, and see how much, how very much obliged I am

The Flower of the Family

to anybody who wishes to help me become that which I long for!"

The sincere, earnest tone went to Miss Prigott's heart

"I believe you do mean right," she said; "but you need training, much training. If you are really a Christian, why not show the simplicity of one? Why all this parade of curls about your face, that every body notices wherever you go?"

"My hair was not made by myself," replied Lucy, who could hardly speak for surprise.

"At least you could cut off those long curls. Why should Christians conform thus to the world?"

"I was always taught to make myself look as well as I could, without too much time and thought. Mother always said people owed so much to each other. And she always would have us neat and clean, whatever else we lacked. She said that was our only ornament."

Ah, I see how it is! you love that pretty hair more than the will of God?"

"I hope not," said Lucy. "I don't know that I ever gave it so many thoughts at a time in my life, as I have just now. But I supposed, as it *would* curl—"

"Just as if it would curl if you did not spend an hour every morning upon it!"

"It would be in sad confusion, certainly, if I did not take care of it. But I do not spend that time on it, nor anything like it."

"But you are vain of it; come, you can't deny that."

Lucy was silent.

"If not, of course you won't object to my relieving you of it." As she spoke, Miss Prigott approached her with scissors in hand. Lucy instinctively put up both hands in self-defense.

"I am not vain of my hair," said she; "but I do not wish to lose it. You might as well cut off my skin because it is not black. Or, if you must cut, suppose you begin at this collar," she added, laughing. "I'm sure it's not simple at all."

Miss Prigott laid aside her scissors, and smiled too. She liked opposition as much as she liked simplicity. Her eye rested complacently upon the collar Lucy wore. "Well, we shall none of us stagnate while *you* are here," said she. "And, on the whole, you look so very ugly with your hair off your face, that I think

The Flower of the Family

Providence meant you should wear it as you do. There's a philosophy in hair, as there is in everything."

Lucy now made her escape. Helen met her as she was hurrying through the hall.

"Where have you been? And what's the matter with your hair?"

"I've been in Miss Prigott's room, and she wanted to cut off my curls to bring down my vanity."

"Your vanity! Well! I should like to cut down hers. But it would take too long. She's been lecturing you, I dare say. What about? Do let us Hear!"

"Oh, about various things! But she means it for the best."

"These old maids are always busy-bodies," said Helen. "And Miss Prigott was an old maid when she was born."

"How do you know? Were you there at the time?" Helen smiled and shrugged her shoulders a little; a trick she had caught, unconsciously, from her French master. Lucy went on, and shut herself into her room. She felt uneasy and restless; and only in solitude could she look into her own heart, and learn the reason. At first she felt disposed to charge it to Miss Prigott; but she soon perceived that her perplexity lay far down in regions to which that lady had not penetrated.

"What is it I want now? What would I have if at this moment I could be endowed with that which I need most?" was her anxious question. And the answer soon came. "I want an *anchor*. I want to feel myself fixed somewhere."

Yes, it was just this. The fitful temper wanted something whereon to fasten itself. The changeful humor yearned for something that knew not change. The distrustful heart must have a rock on which to plant itself. Hitherto there had been much of doubt, and darkness, and conflict in her soul. Every wind that blew, affected the aspect of life to her view. Even a Miss Prigott could shake her faith in God, make her doubt His love and mercy, and cut her loose from the Rock on which she was moored. Should this be so? Amid the multitude of her thoughts within her, the idea of God alone offered repose. To Him then she turned. To Him she confessed her capricious, changeful temper; her doubts, fears, mistakes; and besought Him now and *once for all* to fasten her to Himself. The Spirit of God chooses to work by simple means. The experience of that morning

The Flower of the Family

assured her of this. For amid days otherwise dark, in the fitful moods of a sensitive, impressible nature; in the weariness of ill health and languor, there was, ever after, one point where was no darkness at all, one centre where all was peace. Friends disappointed the eager heart that asked too much; change and uncertainty brooded over the path as yet untried; but far above chance and change, rose the sense of Him to whom she was "safely moored." "He is my *rock*, and there is no unrighteousness in Him!" was now her joyful, and now her tearful, but ever her thankful assurance. Does any young heart regard this picture of Lucy's birthday as somber; and shrink from it with disgust? It is surely not meet that they who have had sad experience of the vicissitudes of life should throw back upon a younger and more joyous and more fearless temper, the shadows they have worn as a garment. But there is sorrow and disappointment and change for all. And there is no soul strong enough to face life alone. In its plunge into the billows it must have the assurance that one who has buffeted those waves in human infirmity and suffering, stands upon the bank with outstretched, unwearied hand, to rescue, and to support.

When Lucy left her room, she found Helen equipped for a drive.

"You must go too," she said: "mamma thinks you should not try to walk at present."

"I have a visit to pay just out of the city, and as it is a fine morning, I think you must accompany me," said her aunt. Lucy felt not at all disposed to meet strangers in her present mood, yet she dared not object; and they were soon on their way, Miss Prigott forming one of the party. Whatever terror and shyness went with her was put to flight at once by the benignant, friendly face with which Lucy was charmed on her introduction to Mrs. Lee.

"It wouldn't be very hard work to love her!" thought she; a thought whose echo at that moment was making itself sensible in the heart of her new friend. After Mrs. Lee had held some moments conversation with her aunt and Miss Prigott, Lucy was not sorry to find herself addressed.

The Flower of the Family

"You remind me of an old and very dear friend of my youth," she said. "How singular these resemblances are! Miss Prigott! Do you remember our schoolfellow, Sarah Whittier?"

"Of course I do," returned Miss Prigott.

"And does not this young lady resemble her! Excuse me, my dear," she added, observing the color that had rushed to Lucy's face; "I forgot for the moment that it is not pleasant to be thus scrutinized. But this was a dear, very dear friend!"

"The likeness is not miraculous," remarked Miss Prigott. "This is her daughter."

"The daughter of Sarah Whittier!" cried Mrs. Lee, drawing Lucy to her and kissing her tenderly. "My dear child!"

Pleasure and pain struggled together in Lucy's heart, and her eyes filled with tears, while her face shone with smiles.

"How unkind in Miss Prigott never to tell me she had known my mother!" said the tears.

"How delightful to meet one of her old friends!" said the smiles.

There was an opening to her heart in the embraces Mrs. Lee so cordially gave her. She needed few questions to lead her into such a glowing, tender description of her mother, and brothers, and sisters as only love and her simple unspoiled nature could give; and Mrs. Lee sat holding the hand she had clasped at the outset, almost as simple, as loving, and as child-like herself. Mrs. Whittier and Helen looked on and enjoyed the scene which Miss Prigott at last interrupted by a dry, "Are we to spend the day here?" and then there was a hasty leave-taking, and a whirl into the noise, and uproar and hurry of the city, and so home.

CHAPTER 11

Good Intentions, If Not Good Works

THE NEXT DAY Lucy was more unwell. Miss Prigott said it was just what she expected; though on what grounds this expectation was founded, she declined to state. Her aunt would no longer delay consulting a physician, and Lucy pleaded against it, this time, in vain. She cast a longing glance back to dear, good, homely Dr. White, and wished herself in his hands; but the wishes could not bring him, and her dread of Dr. Thornton could not keep him away. He came, looking, as the saying is, as if he had just "come out of a bandbox;" with few words, a grave, almost solemn face, and an already careworn expression on his still youthful brow. His visit was brief; Lucy fancied he had hardly looked at her. But his eye had been as busy as it seemed quiet. He had felt the changing pulse that indicated so faithfully every sudden emotion; had observed the color that came and went in the young face, and the compressed lips that shut back complaint, and had said as plainly as speech could do, that a strong will dwelt in the fragile form. Yes, he had even taken note of that sunny flood of luxuriant hair that shone around the sweet face, and the large, brown eye, rare in color as it was in size. But though doctors in stories always shake their heads, he had not shaken his; and when Mrs. Whittier followed him as he left the room, his few words reassured her. He thought Lucy's illness not serious. Yet for many days he continued his visits, and Lucy soon learned, in spite of her fear of him, to enjoy these brief interviews. One day, in the course of conversation, Helen, exclaiming at some playful remark Lucy had made, cried, "Why, Lucy Grant!" Instantly the face of Dr. Thornton flushed with a new interest.

"Are you from the country?" he asked.

Lucy answered that she was, with a momentary surprise at the question. He looked at her now with real interest; she felt the difference between his present manner and that polite, unconcerned air he had hitherto worn, and smiled with a half satisfied, half inquisitive air.

"My brother has made your acquaintance, I think," he said.

"I don't remember," said Lucy, trying to think whether she really knew any person of that name.

"Oh no, Lucy does not know him," said her aunt. "He went abroad before she came to us."

He made no reply, but still looked with a new, not unkind, interest upon Lucy. "I have a sister to whom I must introduce you," he said at last.

"Oh, I have had the pleasure of doing that!" said her aunt. "Lucy dear, Mrs. Lee is a sister of Dr. Thornton."

Lucy's frank smile said she was glad of that, and she was going on to tell him how Mrs. Lee and her mother had been old friends, when a look from Miss Prigott restrained her. How she knew Miss Prigott's eyes were upon her, nobody knows, but they acted instantaneously upon and froze her up.

"Your mother must have had an immense family," said that lady, addressing the doctor.

He smiled. "Pray, by what rules do you judge?" he asked.

"Why, there must have been at least twenty years between Mrs. Lee and yourself."

"There were fifteen. But what then?"

"Why, if there was a child every year or two—"

"But, unfortunately for your theory, my good lady, there was not. There was an awful chasm between Mrs. Lee and myself."

" 'My good lady!' What irreverence!" Miss Prigott felt it to her fingers' ends, and her little soul rose against Dr. Thornton, and said it wouldn't stand such treatment.

No sooner had he taken leave, then, to the surprise of everybody, she broke out with:

"Well! when *I* was young, we didn't employ *boys* for our physicians! If we had, I wonder where I should be now!"

"Quite an interesting question!" whispered Helen to Lucy.

"And I am surprised, Lucy, that you expect to get well under such treatment," continued Miss Prigott.

"I thought you said she wasn't sick!" said Helen.

"Sick! she's seriously sick, I've no doubt. And this little snipper-snapper of a fellow, this Dr. Thornton, pretends that she is improving!"

"He is six feet high," said Helen, smiling.

"Lucy certainly does look better," said her aunt. "Sometimes she has quite a good color."

"A hectic flush," said Miss Prigott.

Lucy laughed; and so did her aunt.

"You've quite a 'hectic flush' yourself," said Helen, playfully.

Miss Prigott was silent, but from that hour Lucy became the victim of a thousand petty, wearisome annoyances, that it required patience piled on patience to endure with equanimity.

She must have mustard on her chest, and camphor on her throat; a cloud as big as a man's hand must forbid her going out, lest she should take cold; a ray of sunshine not wider than a knitting-needle must not creep into her room, lest it should make her feverish. If she sat up she was conjured to lie down; if she read, books were pronounced exciting. If she ate her food with a gusto, it was proof that there was an unnatural appetite to check; if otherwise, she was destroying herself by starvation.

"Is there anything you feel you could fancy, my love!" she inquired so many times one day, that Lucy said at last, in despair, she should like a bit of chicken. When it was brought, and in process of consumption, Miss Prigott hovered around the plate, not to say *over* it, with so many cautions, provisos and suspicions, that the poor child could not take a morsel. Then the little sagacious head was shaken, and Miss Prigott pronounced it as a feature of consumptive cases, that the appetite was always capricious. In her weariness and languor, these little trials wore upon Lucy sadly. She would have found the mouth of a cannon a pleasant exchange for any one of them. Meanwhile Miss Prigott took care to restrain herself when Mrs. Whittier and Helen were present, and not a tithe of the annoyances to which she subjected their dear Lucy ever was known to them. At last she armed herself with an immense medical book, and in the intervals when alone with her victim, proceeded to study her case.

"Does it hurt you to draw a long breath? Have you raised anything rust-colored?" she inquired; to both which questions Lucy said nay.

"Have you a pain in your chest, inclining to the left side, sometimes affecting the left arm?"

"I had once a dreadful attack," said Lucy.

"Then your heart is diseased. It is ossified; or in process of ossifying."

"But I don't have such pains now," said Lucy.

"Oh, well, you'll be having them, depend upon it. You must be careful when you go up a hill; and how you run upstairs. I've often seen you run upstairs two at a time."

She read on, leaving Lucy to her own cheering reflections. Suddenly she started up. "Let me look at the corners of your eyes," said she. "Yes, they're as yellow as beeswax. Do you ever have a pain in your right side? Do you ever feel depressed and melancholy? Have you a bitter taste in your mouth? Oh, yes, I know you have; your liver is inflamed; it is in an alarming state. That causes your cough. Your liver is swollen, and crowds on your lungs and tickles them; then you cough; and that good-for nothing Dr. Thornton says you're in consumption."

"Did he say that?" cried Lucy, starting up.

"Why, if he didn't, he thinks so, I know. And I've said all along it was your liver."

"By the time you've read that book through, I shall be pretty thoroughly diseased," said Lucy.

"You need not laugh. Your case is really serious. And if it had not been for me, you would have died of liver-complaint long ago."

At this moment Charles put his head in at the half-open door.

"There's a little, dried-up, fussy old woman down-stairs, who wants to see you, Miss Prigott," said he.

She bustled away, and he looked after her, laughing.

"She'll be delighted when she sees who it is," he said.

"Who is it?" asked Lucy.

"Mrs. Nobody," he answered.

"Oh, Charles! how very unkind! And you said what is not true."

The Flower of the Family

"It is April-fool's day," he answered; "besides, what business has she to be scaring you to death with her old doctors' books? Mamma would be so angry if she knew it! And if she looks in the glass on the hat-stand, she'll see just the little old woman I sent her to see."

"I've done a great many things I ought not," said Lucy, "but I don't think I ever tried to tease a respectable old woman in my life."

"Perhaps you never wanted to. Now, I *did* want to; so there's the difference."

"Yes; but still, I'm very sorry you did that."

"She's Prig by name, and prig by nature," said Charles.

He felt nettled at Lucy's reproof, and revenged himself thus. Lucy was silent. He got up, and went whistling through the room. His conscience smote him, and the longer he reflected, the more ashamed he felt.

"I didn't mean to hurt her feelings," said he. "I only wanted to have a little fun."

"Mayn't I tell her so? Do let me!" She caught his hand as he passed her couch, and her pleading look prevailed. "I'll tell her myself," he said.

He went out, and met Miss Prigott on the stairs, but instead of the exasperated look he expected to encounter, he was surprised by one of the most kindly and forgiving nature.

"It's the first of April," she said, smiling. "I should have remembered that."

"I never saw anybody like her in my life!" thought Charles. "The least she could have done was to fly in a passion."

He felt disgusted with her that she had shown so little spirit, though he would have been indignant if she had shown more. So consistent are we all! Lucy's face expressed some surprise, and Miss Prigott observed it.

"Is it so strange to see an old woman control herself?" she asked.

"It is strange to see anybody do that, old or young," said Lucy; "and as pleasant as it is strange."

She felt already a kindly glow of interest in and sympathy with Miss Prigott, hitherto quite unknown; for she saw that the provocation to anger had been great. The little yellow face

The Flower of the Family

seemed lighted with a charm that attracted her; and as she looked upon it, she saw that two tears twinkled on the short eyelashes, although the thin lips wore a serene smile. The next time she spoke, though it was only to say "thank you," when Miss Prigott offered her a fan, the tones of her voice said what a score of set speeches could not have done. They said, "I have begun to love you!" And Miss Prigott's lonely heart had won for itself a treasure that cheered and blessed it as no earthly object had ever done before.

Charles walked hither and thither, in an unenviable mood, wishing Miss Prigott to all manner of places— to "Joppa," and to "Jericho," and to the "bottom of the Red Sea;" but she sat still in her chair, as unaffected by his maledictions as she was unconscious of them. At last she rose and went to her room, where her Bible and her hymn book waited for her with words of comfort and sympathy. As soon as she was out of hearing, Charles drew near again to Lucy.

"What makes you look so grave?" he asked.

"Who, I?" said Lucy. "I was only thinking."

"A penny for your thoughts, then."

"They are not worth that. I was only thinking of poor Miss Prigott."

"Poor! rich Miss Prigott, you mean. She's as rich as can be."

"She may be poor, for all that. Though, if she has plenty of money, she's better off than I supposed. But I meant that she is poor in friends. Nobody seems to like her; at least, no one *loves* her."

"*Loves* her!" said Charles, making a face at the bare thought.

"Well, I do think I shall get to loving her in time. At first, I didn't at all. I only saw her disagreeable qualities. But I see that underneath them she has something good."

"Do look at me through those rose–colored spectacles."

"Well, but, Charles, was it not really good in her to take no offense at your calling her such dreadful names? Think how pleasantly she trotted down to the parlor and back again."

"Pooh! she did not understand that I meant her by those titles. You'd have seen her angry enough, if she had."

Lucy was silent again. In his present mood, she thought it not wise to argue with him.

The Flower of the Family

"You think me a perfect scamp!" said he.

"Oh, no! I only wanted you to be just; as boys are apt to be."

"Well, what do you want me to do? Go and fall on her neck, and cry, and tell her I am sorry?"

Lucy smiled, and he could not help smiling too.

"I like fun as well as you do," she said, "only, as this is your father's house, and Miss Prigott is a visitor in it, and an old woman too, I felt a little sorry; but never mind now. I dare say I've made too much ado about it."

He looked as if he thought so; but when he met Miss Prigott at the tea-table, shortly after, his kind, attentive manner said just what he was ashamed to say in words, "I am sorry if I have hurt your feelings." When he entered his room that night, he found on his table a set of books he had long desired. They stood in elegant bindings, a little army of pleasant surprises.

"Papa knew I wanted them!" was his delighted thought. He opened one; a paper fell from it, on which was written in an old-fashioned, but familial hand, "Please accept, from a little, dried-up, fussy old woman."

"I'm the April fool now," he said, throwing the volume angrily down. And if Miss Prigott had been within reach, he would gladly have harmed her. He rushed from his room in pursuit of sympathy. But to whom should he go? What would his mother say when told that he had applied such epithets to a worthy old woman, her guest? As to his father, nothing would tempt him to face his ridicule. And Helen? She would not know what to say. But there was Lucy; *she* knew all about it: he flew to her.

"I've gone to bed," she cried out, as he assailed her door.

"Get up, then, and dress yourself."

"Oh, Charles!"

"I sha'n't sleep a wink to-night, if you don't."

Thus adjured, Lucy rose, threw on her dressing-gown, and opened the door. He rushed in, candle in hand, and held up the paper before her eyes. On reading it, Lucy could hardly help laughing, but on the other hand she felt for Charles in his mortification.

"Between Miss Prigott and me, you fare pretty badly," she said.

"You! You are an angel compared with her! Was there ever anything so mean? But I won't keep her old books! I'll lay them on the floor outside her door. If she falls over them in the morning and breaks her neck, it won't be my fault."

Lucy deliberated a little before she replied. From what she knew of Miss Prigott, she felt pretty sure that she had sent the books as a peace-offering. It was mistaken kindness, certainly; but then, if kindness, it should be received as such.

"I am sorry for you," said she: "I know just how you feel. A box on the ear wouldn't be half so irritating. But I do believe Miss Prigott *meant* kindly. And if I were you, I would let it go at that."

"Do you call it kind to make a fellow feel like a fool?"

"But if she did not intend to make you feel so? And I do not think she did."

"How should *you* feel to be served so?"

"I should feel badly; but I would try to make the best of it. To-night I would sleep over it, at any rate." Her friendly, kind tones soothed him somewhat. He took the paper and went back to his room in silence; and when he met Miss Prigott next morning, her unconscious face confirmed Lucy's suggestion, that she had meant it all in good part. In fact, on reading in her Bible that passage, "If thine enemy hunger, feed him," etc. ; she had resolved to obey it literally; and while Charles was tossing impatiently on his sleepless pillow, she reposed peacefully on hers, in the blissful conviction that she had accomplished a deed as Christian as it was ingenious and witty.

CHAPTER 12

The Consequences of a Prescription

LUCY FOUND HER POSITION more agreeable now that something like an understanding was established between Miss Prigott and herself. Her uncle, too, became better known to her; and she had occasion to regret the hasty judgment she had formed against him at the outset. In his great anxiety to spare the feelings of his friends, he was continually exciting their prejudice; one needed to know him well in order to like him. While he was studying the best mode of doing you a favor without seeming to do it, Miss Prigott would hop on to the field with her little brisk figure, and force that same favor down your unwilling throat. Perhaps you are strangled in the effort to swallow it. But she'll never know it; so there's no great harm done.

"You must take a teaspoonful of this mixture every hour," Dr. Thornton said to Lucy on the next visit; and all that day she was asking somebody what o'clock it was.

"She needs a watch of her own," thought her uncle.

"She ought to have a watch," likewise decided Miss Prigott. And while Mr. Whittier edged towards the subject by asking Lucy how she expected to manage in the night without one, and deliberately went from place to place in search of a particular, not expensive kind. Miss Prigott was hurrying through Broadway as fast as horses could carry her, and had selected, triumphed over, and put into Lucy's hands an article, expensive, ornamental, and every way unsuitable.

Poor Lucy's grateful heart ached with more than one emotion, and she needed nothing now to keep her awake that night. That such a sum should be expended for her by an almost stranger, was of itself a pain; but to own such a watch when her father

The Flower of the Family

even had none; when her mother stood in such pressing need of almost everything money could purchase; when Rebecca and Hatty were going so poorly clad! She lay and thought what books could have been provided Arthur with a tithe of this expense; what a shawl she could have given the doctor's wife; what hosts of neat, comfortable garments for the children! And let no one deem this ingratitude. Her heart was more than full of thankfulness; it only shrank from so much selfish pleasure. Of herself she did not once think. "This for mother, that for Arthur," was the sum of the matter. She passed the night in great perplexity, but towards morning, coming to the resolution to speak freely to her uncle on the subject, she grew easier and fell asleep. When he came to pay his usual visit before going out, she drew the watch from her pillow and placed it in his hand.

"Why, where did this come from?" he cried.

She told him, watching his face as she did so. It expressed anything but approbation or pleasure. Lucy even fancied she heard him say something about "these officious old maids;" but she was not sure.

"What shall I do about it, uncle?" she asked.

"Oh, enjoy it," he returned.

"But how *can* I enjoy it, when"— she hesitated. In the middle of the night it had seemed the easiest thing in the world to open her heart to her uncle, but now it was quite another affair.

"Come, tell me the rest," said he.

"Dear uncle, I was thinking of the time when my father sold his watch, and how mother cried, because it had been *her* father's once, and then to think of my having one, worth, I don't know how many such as that!"

"Your father sold that watch!" cried her uncle. "My father's watch *sold*!"

"It was to get things for Rebecca, when she was sick," said Lucy, humbly. "She was out of health for three years. Father made a crib for her, with rockers, and we used to take turns rocking her when she was in pain. And her appetite was so poor all that time, that mother could hardly persuade her to eat enough to keep her alive. So one day— I shall never forget it— father went to H__ , about five miles from us; and when he came home he had oranges and other nice things for Rebecca. She began to gain strength after that. The orange-juice seemed to refresh her so much. Father sat watching her as she took it, and looked so happy, and yet so pale. We did not know then that he had sold his watch, and we wondered what made mother cry."

Her uncle covered his face with his hands; but Lucy knew that he was in tears.

"Oh, uncle! must I keep it?" said she.

"We'll think it over," he answered. "I hardly see what else you can do. Miss Prigott intended to do you a favor; you must try to feel grateful to her."

"Oh, I do feel grateful! So grateful that I *ache*," cried Lucy, putting both hands to her heart.

He kissed her, and left the room.

There had been nothing gained by the interview, she thought. She reproached herself for having betrayed that point in their family history; wondered how she came to do so; accused herself of always telling things she ought not; wished— oh, how fervently!— that she could fly to her mother's sympathy and counsel, and so find rest. But now Miss Prigott came to flutter about her room, and to make herself, in spite of her good qualities, as undesirable a companion as ever.

"You look feverish, my dear," she said; "let me feel your pulse. It is as irregular as possible. Have you had any more of those pains in your chest?"

"Only pangs of gratitude," said Lucy, trying desperately to smile.

"My love, let us drop that subject;" and the thin bony hand waved it off" into the air. "I have never told you anything about my school-days, I think."

"No, and I have so wished you would!"

"Why didn't you ask me then?"

"I thought you had some reason for not doing it, after you said my mother was a school-mate of yours. I kept hoping you would speak of her."

"There's nothing special to tell about *her*," said Miss Prigott, her old dry manner coming back.

"Indeed, I scarcely remember her at all. She was a great beauty, forsooth, and an independent piece. Somewhat of a romp, too."

"Mrs. Lee said she was remarkable for her fine spirits."

"Yes, yes, a regular hoyden, I remember, she was."

"Mrs. Lee did not say so," said Lucy, uneasily.

"My dear, Mrs. Lee minces matters. That's her way. Now I recollect distinctly that although your mother and Mrs. Lee were both members of the Church, they used to amuse themselves by throwing beans and peas at the other girls."

Lucy laughed, privately, down among the pillows, but the little sharp eyes detected her in the act.

"What are you laughing at?" she inquired.

"Oh, I don't know. It seems so funny that my mother should ever have thrown peas at people;" and this time she laughed heartily.

"Funny! It was a very rude, improper thing. And they *members of the Church*!"

"I don't see what that had to do with it," said Lucy, turning restlessly on her pillow.

Miss Prigott looked things unutterable, as she always did when pushed into a corner.

"Of course, there's no use in arguing with *you,*" she said.

"But, Miss Prigott," said Helen, who had been greatly amused by this conversation, "do you mean to say it is a sin to throw beans and peas at people?"

"No, I don't."

"Then why shouldn't members of the Church do it, as well as other people?"

"Because it is not becoming."

"It is not becoming to anybody, I suppose. But if being a member of a church is going to make it wicked for me to laugh, and all that, I'm glad I am not one; that's all."

Lucy's eyes rested on Helen long after this remark was made. There was a levity in its tone that pained her. Helen felt the look, fidgeted under it, pretended not to observe it, but at last cried, "What are you looking at me so for?"

"I'll tell you, some time," said Lucy.

"Well, to return to your mother," said Miss Prigott. "I remember she used to be after the young men a great deal."

"Mrs. Lee said they used to be after her," said Lucy.

"Well, that's the same thing."

"I don't think so."

"And let me tell you how she got me into disgrace once. I was studying grammar; I came to a word I could not parse, and as she sat near me, I asked her about it. She told me. Just then our teacher observed us speaking, and marked us both. That mark ruined me. I never had had one before."

"But I don't see how my mother was to blame," said Lucy.

"Oh, of course not. She's your mother."

"Yes; my mother," repeated Lucy softly; yet concentrating in her tone so much reverent affection, that Miss Prigott was struck dumb.

"Well, well! she was the flower of the school, everybody agreed!" said she at last. "Beautiful, and talented, and I don't know what not. And she might have married the President, for aught I know. But she chose to go and throw herself away on a man nobody knew; a divinity student he was."

"On my father!" cried Lucy. "Oh, Miss Prigott! Please don't say any more! I can't lie here and hear you say such things!"

"Dear me!" said Miss Prigott, looking round astonished; "did I say anything?"

"I know you don't mean to be unkind; but you are. You do say such strange things! And Mrs. Lee says my father would have made a distinguished man if he had not lost his health, teaching to obtain means for his education, and all that."

"Oh, of course. Everybody knew that. But what did he go and lose his health for? That was the most foolish thing he could have done.

"Lucy looks very tired," said Helen, "and mamma charged me to keep her quiet. She was obliged to go out on business. There was a great fire last night, and some of her poor folks were turned adrift."

Miss Prigott caught at this intelligence with alacrity.

"Why didn't she take me?" she cried. "I'll go this minute. Lucy, my dear, do you think you could spare me a little while?"

Lucy smiled her assent, and had the satisfaction of hearing the door speedily close upon the active little figure, that sped so zealously on deeds of mercy.

"How tired you look!" said Helen, kindly. "She'll kill you, I'm sure."

The Flower of the Family

Lucy lay still and made no answer. She felt two-thirds "killed" already.

"Is there anything I can do for you?" asked Helen, kneeling by the side of her couch.

Lucy looked up and smiled.

"Dear Helen, there is one thing. If you would just read to me a little. One or two hymns."

Helen took Lucy's little hymn book, and began to read. The book was full of marks; she read wherever she found one.

"These very hymns were my favorites once," said she.

"And are not now?"

"No, not so very," said Helen, shrugging her shoulders a little, according to her wont.

"I thought— I hoped you were a Christian," said Lucy sadly.

"I thought so once, myself. As little while ago as when I was sick. But it all passed away as soon as I got well. And now, I'm as bad as ever."

"Oh, Helen! And yet you seem in such good spirits!"

Mrs. Whittier now returned from her morning labors, and came at once to see Lucy.

"They have not been good nurses, I fear," she said. "You look worn and tired."

"Miss Prigott fretted her," said Helen.

"I charged her to avoid exciting subjects. She said she would enliven Lucy by talking of her mother."

"Lucy has been enlivened to the last degree," said Helen. "Miss Prigott was determined to torment her to death; but I drove her off."

"You shall have some rest now, then," said Mrs. Whittier. "Come, Helen."

Helen waited a moment; stooped down to kiss Lucy, and whispered, hastily: "But I am not in good spirits;" then followed her mother.

Left alone, after her long, sleepless night, Lucy lay quietly, and tried to rest. Anxious thoughts about home assailed her; the watch, ticking beneath her pillow, wearied her; above all, Helen's last remark disturbed her serenity. She opened her precious little "Daily Food," and read here and there a verse till her heart found repose, though her head throbbed with fatigue and pain.

The Flower of the Family

"Lying here, doing nothing, is the hardest work I ever did in my life," she said to her aunt, when two hours later she crept softly in.

"Have you slept at all, to-day?" her aunt inquired.

"No, aunt, I think not. But I don't mind it. Pray, don't look so anxious."

"Shall you be glad or sorry to learn that Miss Prigott is to leave us to-day?"

"To-day!" cried Lucy. " I don't know. I hoped to get well, and to be of some comfort to her. I do not know how, exactly; but she has been very kind to me."

"Mrs. Lee has just been here, and has insisted on taking Miss Prigott home with her. She says you never will get well with her hanging about you. And I am not sure she isn't right."

"Oh, pray, pray don't let her go on my account! I never shall get well if she does."

"Don't be uneasy, my dear. She is fond of visiting her friends; and Mrs. Lee is always hospitable and full of company. It will be a good thing for all parties."

Lucy said no more, but she felt sadly disturbed, and even guilty.

"Why can't I love poor Miss Prigott better?" she asked herself. "She's so kind, and has been so friendly!"

Yet, in spite of the question and the shame, the certainty that Miss Prigott was going, proved soothing. Under its influence her weary eyelids closed, and she slept quietly. Miss Prigott stole in on tiptoe to take a farewell look, and kneeling down by her side, lifted the thin hand tenderly, and kissed it more than once. They all flattered themselves that everything had been so skillfully arranged, that the unsuspicious little woman was going in blissful ignorance of the facts of the case. But she had overheard an incautious whisper of Helen's; had learned that they believed her absence essential to Lucy's recovery, and her kind, busy heart was full. She said not a word, but speedily made her arrangements for leaving, and when Lucy awoke, she was already on her way. Lying back in the carriage, with firmly-closed eyes, she was lost in a painful reverie.

"From the very first hour I loved that young girl!" she said within herself; "and my foolish old heart hoped for love in

The Flower of the Family

return. So it is after fifty years' experience of life; I am still childish, still hopeful, yet still disappointed."

Two or three tears wet the faded, wrinkled cheek and humble, gentle emotions came with them. Mrs. Lee was struck with the subdued, mild air, so unusual and so unexpected, and went as far as possible in kindly attentions to her guest.

"I shall not trouble you long," said Miss Prigott. "My room will soon be ready for me, in the country, and I shall go there in a few days."

"It is too cold for the country as yet," said Mrs. Lee. "I hope you will spend some weeks with me."

Miss Prigott was silent, and a dejected air hung unnaturally about her. Mrs. Lee sent for her little children, with whom she knew no one could long remain melancholy. They came smiling in; and Miss Prigott soon had one, a plump, happy little creature, upon a table before her, and was feeding it with sugar-plums, with which she always went armed.

"You don't know where I've been!" said the little one, archly.

"Where was it?" asked Miss Prigott.

"To a wedding! To my cousin Mary's wedding!"

"Well, when I am married, will you come to mine?"

"Oh, *you'll* never be married!" said the child, opening its astonished eyes very wide, and surveying the old, yellow, wrinkled face.

The expectation of such an event formed no part of Miss Prigott's thoughts; yet the words of the child jarred painfully on her ear. To her excited fancy they seemed to say, "Nobody can love *you*!" and so, cheerless and solitary, she went to her bed.

CHAPTER 13

The Storm Before the Calm

WHETHER OWING TO MISS PRIGOTT'S DEPARTURE, or to a favorable change in the weather, Lucy began rapidly to improve. Dr. Thornton's visits became few and short, and at length ceased; some reading was now allowed; letters home could once more be written, and her life was busy and agreeable. It was decided between Dr. Thornton and her aunt, that she must not return home for some months; and Helen was revelling in the thought that during their summer journeys she would be with them.

The letters from home all assured Lucy that she was not needed there; every one rejoiced that she could be spared from among them, for this necessary season of refreshment and repose.

One evening Helen came to sit with Lucy, and they talked over their summer plans together.

"We must take books with us," said Helen. "I am sure I don't know what; but books we must have."

Lucy named several she wished to take; one of them was "The Imitation of Christ."

"That's as dry as chips," said Helen. "How can you want to read such books?"

"It doesn't seem dry to me," said Lucy; "if it did, perhaps I should not care to read it."

"But it puzzles me when I see how interested you are in religious books. I don't understand it. For even when I was thinking myself a Christian, I must own they did seem dry."

"What, *all* religious books?"

Helen deliberated a little.

"Yes, all; unless I except some few hymns."

The Flower of the Family

"Perhaps your youth is to blame for that. I don't know. I am pretty sure there was a time when I did not relish Thomas a' Kempis, because I did not understand him."

"But I did not like those I did understand, very well. If I had taken my *choice*, I should have read nothing but stories and poems, and so on. Novels I am not allowed to read yet."

Lucy made no reply. She felt puzzled in her turn, now.

"Do tell me," said Helen abruptly, "do tell me one thing; that is, if you are willing: Do you really *like* to read religious books?"

"Yes, I really do."

Helen sighed. "And do you like the pious talk these good sort of people forever keep up?"

"I do when it comes right out of their hearts. I don't like anything that isn't genuine."

"And you enjoy Miss Prigott's cant, and all that?"

"No, I did not say I like 'cant.'"

"But do tell me; am I such a heathen? Am I so much worse than you? For such talk as Miss Prigott's enrages me. I can't bear it. She might talk to me forever, and do me no good. When I am with her, I feel that I never want to be a Christian."

"Oh, dear! what shall I say? I am not much older than you, Helen; I am not fit to talk with you. But surely it is not Miss Prigott's religion that makes her disagreeable. You don't know how much worse she might be without it."

"So mamma says. But, Lucy, do let me ask one question more. You needn't answer it if you don't wish to; but I do so long to know." She crept close to Lucy's ear and whispered, "If you knew you could get to heaven with just what goodness you have now, should you still keep on praying and trying to grow better?"

"I should not wish to live another moment if I could not pray," said Lucy, earnestly.

"Then there *is* something in religion, after all. And something I know nothing about. Oh, Lucy! seeing you from day to day has made me so dissatisfied with myself; has put such new thoughts in my mind!"

She retired to her room, and there threw herself across her bed, in tears. Her life seemed to her full of mistakes, full of contradictions, full of sins. She thought she would give all she possessed in the world for that peace with God that Lucy

The Flower of the Family

understood, while to her it was such a mystery. Underneath her misery, however, lay a latent satisfaction with the tears she was shedding. She had a vague hope that they were tokens of penitence, and seals of her acceptance with God. For the moment, she forgot that her room had witnessed many scenes like this.

Lucy, meanwhile, had closed her door, and was thanking God that He had used her in the accomplishment of one of His designs. She felt humbled by His goodness; and it seemed to her, that if He would only take her and use her just as He pleased, and let her do something for Him who had done so much for her, she could ask no higher happiness. When they met again, Helen appeared very much as usual; but there was a new expression of holy peace and gratitude on Lucy's face. Helen observed it with a pang.

"Why cannot I feel as she does?" she asked herself. Ever since Lucy's arrival, she had watched and unconsciously studied her. She had loved her from almost the first hour, and admired her too; and the next step after love and admiration, is imitation. She wished herself like Lucy. But in many things Helen was a mere child. Life had always smiled on her, and had given her all she asked for; she had never known a real sorrow or a real privation; nor had she been obliged to put forth an effort to win a desired object. But the "kingdom of heaven suffereth violence, and the violent take it by force."

"I shall not rest till all is right with me," she said one day to Lucy, in answer to an anxious look. She was dancing and singing about the house at the moment, and in no mood to be restrained even by a look. But though it half-displeased, it drove her to her room and to her knees, and for a brief season to reflection.

Not an hour after, she came to Lucy with tickets for a concert in her hand.

"See!" she cried joyously, "tickets for the concert this evening! Papa took the trouble to go to Dr. Thornton, to ask if you might venture out, and he says you may go— in the carriage, of course. Isn't it delightful!"

Lucy laid aside the book she was reading, and looked at the tickets in silence.

"Why, I thought you would be so pleased!" said Helen in a disappointed tone. "I took it for granted you had never heard fine music, and that, after being cooped up so long, it would be delicious to get out once more!"

"Dear Helen, and so it would, if I were sure— if I only knew certainly one thing. If all is right with you!"

Helen colored. She felt irritated and embarrassed.

"I don't want to be driven in this way. You are getting as bad as Miss Prigott. Stiff and prim! I'm sure I did not dream of committing a sin in just going to a concert!"

Amid her anger she saw Lucy's face, so grieved, yet so loving, so lovely! It troubled her as she flew back to her room, and for a season it made her indignant tears flow faster. Meanwhile Lucy sat as one benumbed. All had passed so rapidly that she could hardly realize that a great breach separated her from Helen; that her dearest friend in all this great busy city was alienated from her, perhaps forever.

"Have I done wrong?" asked her bewildered conscience; and she knew not what to say. She thought it all over; tried to recall her words, and tones, and looks.

"I am always making mistakes!" she said to herself; "always. And now I've offended Helen, and have done so much harm!"

Great sorrows drive every Christian to God; but we are only too prone to try to bear our little trials alone. We fancy such petty affairs beneath His notice. Yet, may it not one day appear that the mountain was after all only a hillock; the great burden but a grain of sand? We *must* throw ourselves as children upon Him. We must be willing to consult His pleasure in the meanest affair of life; to seek His compassion and sympathy in "*every* pain we bear." Let Him be the judge of their worth and consequence, and perhaps He who seeth not as man seeth, will detect the mountain in what is called the hillock, and mark that as our intolerable burden, that men regard as the small dust of the balance.

Lucy struggled to recover herself, in vain. In vain she assured herself that such a little affair was not worth praying about. Perhaps there was a vague notion in her mind, that she would not have dared shape into words— that God should not be required to note our petty cares and wants. These are not humble views of

The Flower of the Family

ourselves and our interests; they are low, inadequate views of Him.

But at last she laid aside her book, in which she had tried to forget herself, rose hesitatingly, closed her door, and stood leaning against it, as if still in doubt.

Why should she linger? Had she not borne to the ear of her Father more than one trial, not greater than this?

"I *must* find comfort somewhere!" she cried at last; and now she was on her knees; and now she confessed her ignorance, and sought direction, and did find comfort. Then seating herself at her table she wrote a little pencilled note to Helen, so kind, so loving, so Christian! surely this must prevail! She went to Helen's door, and knocked. There was no answer. She tried to open it; it was locked. She waited a moment; then pushing her little note under the door, into the room, she retired.

Helen had shed floods of passionate tears, and was sitting forlorn and wretched at her window, whence she could look down into the street. She watched the passers-by with a moody, unsympathizing air; even with a sort of disgust at their life and activity when her own soul felt so dead. Perhaps every one of these objects of her contempt would have gladly exchanged the home to which his feet were bearing him for that of Helen. Very few, if any among them were hastening to such an apartment as that she now occupied; not one towards a larger, a more airy, or more luxurious. There goes a little figure, almost bent double with age and infirmity. A basket is in its hand, from which, off a stone step, apples and candies have been patiently sold all day. There is a home for that all day houseless head; it lies down, down that long, dirty street, and up, up, up those narrow, noisome stairs; and in that close and crowded room. Wicked children quarrel and shriek all through that street; every door sends out half a dozen of them, with white heads, and grimy faces, and bare legs and feet. Children of larger growth, too, congregate at all the corners; heads not so white, faces not so grimy, legs and feet not bare; yet the defilement from within staring from the red eyes; and the voices harsher, the words more profane, the whole air more revolting. Floods of liquid filth flow down this street, unfit for the abode of savages or wild beasts, and sin and sorrow and clamor and crime brood over it, and claim it as their own. Yet here the sweet word "home" ventures. Here the little bent figure pauses, and has found hers. How cheerily would she exchange it for Helen's abode; how speedily lay those weary limbs on that soft, clean bed; how sure of happiness in that stately abode! Yet if peace with God has found its way into that old heart, it may see in Helen no object of envy; and that poor wretched child may gladly exchange all the luxuries of her outer life for one glimpse of the joy that adorns and illumines the meanest Christian soul!

"What harm is there in going to a concert," said Helen, "that she need have looked so solemn about it! And I mean to go, whatever she says. She may stay at home and mope: I don't care; I *will* go."

Something within feebly remonstrated against this injustice. It said, "You know perfectly well why she wished you to relinquish, for once, even an innocent pleasure. You paved the way for her to say what she did, by your own remark."

She rose hastily, and left her room. It was growing dark, and she did not observe the note Lucy had placed beneath her door.

"Are you ready for the concert, dear?" her mother asked pleasantly, as she entered her room.

"I don't care about going; Lucy doesn't seem to wish to go."

"That's very singular. But one dreads going out after confinement to a sick-room. I'll speak to her myself."

""I think, dear," she said, on entering Lucy's room, "that it would really do you good to go out this evening. Are you not fond of music?"

"Oh, yes, very fond. And I never attended a concert in my life."

"Helen must have misunderstood you, then; she fancied you did not wish to go. It is time to dress we must hurry away, directly after tea."

"Is Helen going, aunt?"

"Certainly; but she is not dressed, either. I must tell her there is no time to lose."

"Is she really going, after all?" thought Lucy sadly. *"Can* she go, and enjoy it?"

She dressed, hardly knowing what she put on, and went down to tea.

"Miss Prigott ought to be here to put you to rights," said Charles, as she entered the room.

"Why; is anything the matter?"

"No, only you look as if you had lost off your collar."

"I look as if I hadn't put it on," she answered, laughing, and running back to supply the omission.

Helen met her on the stairs, and felt displeased that she could run joyously about the house, when she *knew* how miserable she was. She pushed by, without a smile of greeting, and went loftily to the table, at which her mother was now seated. Lucy, meanwhile, in passing Helen's room, saw her little note lying on the floor, and, hastily picking it up, observed that it remained unopened. Her eyes filled with tears; she felt herself aggrieved. On seating herself at the table, she saw that Helen wore a resigned, martyr-like expression, and that she carefully avoided every little attention she strove to pay her. If she spoke, Helen did not hear; if she offered to help her to any article, she did not see. And when they were all at last seated in the carriage, Helen was missing. Her father was not fond of waiting for his family; he was always punctual, and required them to be so. He ran impatiently into the hall, where she stood with her bonnet in her hand.

"Why do you keep us all waiting so?" he asked, a little sharply.

"I'm not going; I prefer to stay at home," she answered.

"Why, you foolish child, come along. You have been teasing to go, all this week."

"I sha'n't go; so there!" She was frightened at herself for speaking thus to her father. He looked highly displeased, and went out, closing the door violently behind him.

"Why; isn't she coming?" asked her mother, as the carriage drove off.

"No; she's getting amazingly ill-humored of late."

"Don't let us go without her; I do not think she's well. She said not a word to me about staying at home. At least, not after she found Lucy was going."

"She's well enough; she's only out of humor about something. I dare say she repents by this time staying behind. It will be a good lesson for her."

"I should prefer to return," said Mrs. Whittier.

The Flower of the Family

He replied in a low voice; Lucy fancied he said something about "not disappointing" her.

"Oh, don't go on my account!" she cried.

But her uncle made no reply and they drove on, all thoroughly uncomfortable, but Lucy most so of all. The brilliantly-lighted, well-filled hall, dazzled and excited her. The youthful performers, all clad in pure white, and making such melody as she never had dreamed of, seemed like angels in heaven; she almost fancied herself there. How much she would have enjoyed it, had Helen only given her a parting smile as she came away; or if she sat now by her side, loving and joyous as was her wont! Her aunt watched her, and was pleased with her rapt attention. She had a slight suspicion that all was not harmony between her and Helen; and if her heart unconsciously said, Lucy must be in fault, let no one smile. Who shall judge charitably the child, if not the mother? As they drove home, Mr. Whittier asked:

"Well, Lucy! have you enjoyed the evening?"

"Yes, sir, very much," she answered.

"I'm afraid Helen could not have said as much if you were left out of an expected enjoyment," said her aunt, in a tone half playful, half serious.

Lucy colored. Her spirit rose against this unjust suspicion. She was on the point of saying, "I did not deserve that!" She had been excited into high spirits by all she had seen and heard this evening now came the reaction. "This is *such* a world!" was her mournful sigh, as she leaned back in the carriage, restraining her tears.

"Miss Helen has gone to her room, and desires not to be disturbed," said one of the servants, on opening the door for their admission.

Without laying aside her bonnet, the anxious mother proceeded to Helen's room. She found her lying on the bed, apparently asleep; her face looked flushed and swollen: she had been weeping— that was plain.

"Are you asleep, darling?" she whispered.

"No, mamma, not asleep; but if you would just let me alone this once!" she answered, peevishly.

"There is something wrong here," said her mother, "and I must know what it is." She placed her candle on the table, and deliberately took off bonnet, shawl, and gloves. Helen watched her.

She understood the air of decision with which all was quietly done, and a defiant spirit rose within her.

"I won't speak another word," thought she.

"Now, my dear," said Mrs. Whittier, drawing a comfortable chair to the side of the bed.

Helen had risen from her recumbent position. She sat now upright on the bed. Her eyes were heavy, and her hair hung about her face, damp and disordered. She looked steadily at her mother, but was silent.

"What is the trouble?" repeated Mrs. Whittier. "Is anything going wrong between yourself and Lucy?"

Still no answer.

"Shall I find the explanation in this note?" asked her mother, taking from the table Lucy's note.

Helen leaned over to look at it. Surprise conquered her resolution not to speak. "I don't know what that is!" she cried. "Give it to me, please." She seized it eagerly; opened it, glanced over its contents, and burst again into tears.

"May I read it?" asked her mother, who was now seriously concerned. Helen wept on violently, and made no reply; but as she heard the paper rattle in her mother's hands, she made no effort to oppose her, and it was read. A loving, touching appeal it was: Mrs. Whittier's heart was moved; it yearned towards Lucy, to whom she felt that she had been unjust.

"Oh, my daughter! what can you have done to grieve this sweet girl?" she cried.

Helen was melted now: she tried to explain, but her tears choked her. She got up from the bed and threw herself into her mother's arms.

"Oh, mamma! I have been so rude, so unkind to her! And only because she wanted me not to go to the concert."

"But I don't understand: why did she wish you not to go?"

"That's the worst part of it, mamma. It was because she was afraid it would divert my mind from something better. Ask her, mamma; she will tell you."

Mrs. Whittier went at once to Lucy. She found her still up; reading, apparently.

"My dear Lucy, Helen has sent me to you. She says she has treated you unkindly, and seems greatly distressed about it. She says you will tell me the whole affair."

"It was nothing, dear aunt; I dare say I was wrong myself. Helen told me, a few days ago, that she had once thought herself a Christian, but that she did not think so now; and she seemed thoughtful at times, and as if she wished to be one in earnest. And when she said she was going to the concert, I was afraid it would distract her mind, and before I knew it, I had said something— I do not remember exactly what— about her staying at home, and she was hurt; then I was so sorry!"

Her aunt kissed her. "May God bless you!" she said fervently: "I thank Him for sending you to us. Shall I tell Helen you forgive her; I fear she will hardly sleep, otherwise."

"Dear aunt! I had nothing to forgive! May I go to her, just for one moment?" Her aunt assented, and lingered outside Helen's door, that they might speak together without restraint; and when Lucy came out, her step was elastic as a glad child's.

"And now, my dear Helen," said Mrs. Whittier, "I wish you to go to bed. There must be no more of this excitement to-night."

"Oh, mamma! how can I sleep, after being so wicked, so angry?"

"Think of the Friend of sinners, my child."

"Mamma, could you pray with me? Dear mamma, don't you think you could?"

Mrs. Whittier hesitated. Only a very few months of Christian life had she as yet known; she had never prayed with Helen; God's ear alone had heard her petitions in her behalf. Yet surely this was no time for the dominion of earthly fear; she knelt with the two hot hands in hers, and forgot that she was not alone.

"Put yourself right at the foot of the cross," she whispered, as they rose from their knees; "and lie there this night."

"It is the only place I'm fit for," said Helen and thus penitent and humble, she retired to rest.

And in the valley of humiliation there are green pastures, how strange that one who has reposed there should ever pine for the mountain-tops!

When Helen awoke next morning, she felt like walking softly all day. She went early to Lucy's door to tell her how sorry she should be, all her life long, for those angry words: then to her father, with whom she was so thankful to make peace. Very sorrowful indeed she seemed for many days, and Lucy laid aside all other pursuits to devote herself to her. Together they read the Bible; and when Helen in a kind of gloomy despair sought out and dwelt upon those passages that described the exceeding sinfulness of sin, Lucy always had a host of precious promises ready to meet them. When Helen spoke of herself, and was sickened with all she saw of her own heart, Lucy spoke of Christ, till the glow and fervor of her words awakened a kindred glow in her eager listener. Thus step by step Helen was led on; giving herself in earnest to the influence of God's Spirit, and thankful to sit like a little child at the feet of any true Christian who would teach her the way heavenward. There was no fear of her taste being offended now: she was too anxious to know and to feel the truth, to be fastidious as to the modes of its reception. Lucy saw with delight, almost with enthusiasm, that even Miss Prigott was welcomed and treated with respect; and that her words were received with as much gratitude now, as heretofore with disgust. And so it will ever be with the earnest seeker after life eternal. What matters it to the drowning man in his extremity, by whom or by what method, he is saved from death? And when Helen found herself breathing a new atmosphere, and felt within herself the first struggles of Christian life, the affections of that whole household encircled Lucy as the instrument in God's hand of so great a blessing. It was the happiest hour she had ever known; for the highest honor God can lay upon His children, is to permit them to do something for Himself.

CHAPTER 14

Cases of Conscience

AS LUCY'S HEALTH CONTINUED TO IMPROVE, she began a regular course of reading and of study. Both Helen and Charles owned books to which she had never before had access; and her old thirst for knowledge, though it had lain silent during her illness, seemed to have gained strength by its weeks of repose. Her love of method, thwarted all her life, yet not slain, started up now afresh; she divided her time into regular hours, and no one pursuit encroached on others. Helen, meanwhile, devoted herself exclusively to religious reading. She had not attended school since her own serious illness; and now she began to dread returning to its temptations. She lost her interest in all her old pursuits; and even began to regard everything not directly religious in its tendency, as dangerous and sinful. She withdrew herself not only from her former associates, but, by degrees, from her own family, and spent her whole time in reading, meditation, and prayer. And while some Christian graces were thus exercised, and bade fair to thrive in what appeared a favorable atmosphere, others of equal worth were left to dwindle and die. Her Christian character failed to attain the symmetry it obviously lacked. We are to live in the world, yet above it; safety is not found in solitude, nor out of it, but in the happy mixture of the two.

"How long are we to stay at the sea-side?" Lucy one day inquired.

"About four months," Helen answered.

"In that time, don't you think I could learn to draw? That is, if you are willing to teach me."

"Oh, do you wish to learn to draw? What good will it do?"

"I don't know. But as I never can learn music, I should like one accomplishment so very much!"

"But what is the *use* of drawing?"

"I was not thinking of its uses; I was only thinking of its pleasure. It would be an amusement to me all my life; and useful too, I dare say."

Helen returned to her work in silence. She was making a mat for Miss Prigott, in a fanciful style then in vogue.

"Don't look so sober," said Lucy at last, playfully. "It makes me think you are not exactly pleased with me."

"I am puzzled," replied Helen. "I don't see where the line is to be drawn between right and wrong. Now I had made up my mind not to draw any more myself, and I was surprised to hear you say you wish to begin."

"I've been all over that ground. If it hadn't been for father, I should have turned into a regular fanatic. I got so at one time, that I thought it wicked, or something near that, to eat anything nice. I fancied I must not indulge myself in amusements of any sort."

"Well?"

"But father said that was slavery of the worst kind. That it grew out of low conceptions of God. Just as if He were a Task-master who wanted us to work all the time without any rest."

"But we shall have time to rest when we get to heaven."

"I don't know how to argue about it; I know father made it very plain to me. He said God had Himself given us tastes that could only be gratified by indulgence and culture; for instance: for music, painting, and all that. These pursuits cease to be innocent only when we put them in God's place and love them better than we love Him."

"And haven't you the slightest scruple about learning to draw?"

"No; not more than you have in wasting your precious time over that mat."

Helen smiled, and yet looked a little suspiciously upon the mat.

"Oh, I was only jesting," said Lucy.

"You were playing chess with Charles all last evening. I watched you, and you seemed perfectly enchanted at winning."

"Yes, I always want to win!"

"Isn't that selfish?"

The Flower of the Family

"Yes, I suppose so. But I don't pretend to be perfect."

"But, Lucy, is it right to play chess all the evening?"

"Anything is right, in the way of innocent amusement, that makes a boy's evenings pleasant. Father made a little set of chessmen, and used to play with us all. He wanted us to enjoy home above any other place."

"I thought your father was a very grave, silent man. I had no idea he would let you play anything."

"That's because you've never seen him. And I have quoted grave things of his saying, and none of the funny ones. I think he *is* a very grave man; but he liked to see us cheerful and happy—and besides, he has plenty of fun in his nature."

"Well! I'll teach you all I know about drawing, and I hope things will look plainer to me in time."

"They will, I don't doubt. At first one sees 'men as trees, walking;' but after awhile this isn't so."

They were interrupted by Mr. Whittier, who came to bring letters to Lucy, from home: one from her mother, on a large sheet, on which Rebecca and Hatty had also written; and one from Arthur. Helen watched Lucy's face as she hurried through the former, and a pang of jealousy, obscure, but sharp still, shot through her heart, as she saw how animated and joyous it was.

"It is so good to hear from home!" said Lucy as she folded the great sheet. "But it makes me want to be there. I am sure they need me. But they won't own it. It seems almost wicked for me to go off to the sea-side for so many months, while they are all so busy at home!" She turned now to Arthur's letter; and as she read that, her smiles grew less frequent, and she sighed as if with the awakened remembrance of an old sorrow. It was a boyish, simple letter enough.

"Dear Lucy:

"I've got something to tell you that I am sure you won't like; but I *must* speak to somebody; and father and mother are full enough of care already. It is about John. He has taken it into his head to go to sea. About a month ago, father let him go to H__ on business: he fell in there with some wild fellows who are going to sea, and they talked to him till he felt as big as a man. He came home with his cap stuck on one side of his head,

The Flower of the Family

singing sailor songs; and when father blamed him for being gone so long, he owned he had been off in a boat with some other boys; and father was displeased, and said he shouldn't go to H__ again. It's a wicked place. Well, the very next day, Mr. Robbins called to see us, and he told mother he thought John a very smart boy, and that he ought to be fitting for college; and offered to have him come to his study every day, and recite in Latin. But John wouldn't listen to it; he told me, then, how he had set his heart on going to sea. Now, you know he isn't big enough yet; besides, he would get to be such a wicked boy, that I don't like to think of it. So I coaxed him to put off all thoughts of it till you come home, because two couldn't be spared at once. But he's just as fidgety as he can be; and those boys prowl round here sometimes; and they have money; and seeing it makes him wild. Do, dear Lucy, write to him, and try to make him contented.

"A few days ago, mother told me that she had money in a bank in New York, that would send me to college; but perhaps you know it already. But if John insists on going to sea, I mean to go with him and I wish father would take that money and pay off his debts. I am reciting to Mr. Robbins; he is a very good man, and knows everything. But, somehow, if I thought I shouldn't be more of a man, I think I'd stick to farming. John is growing like a house on fire, mother says. He seems to grow up fast. Some things he knows better than I do. Not things in books, but about men, and all that. Do write to him. Oh, how I miss you!"

Then followed a few lines, badly written and badly spelled, from John himself. Lucy was struck with their confident, bold tone; it seemed that of a boy of eighteen, rather than that of one of his age: how could he have grown old so fast? She sat down and wrote him at once; and, in her ardor and trepidation, she told him that if he would promise not to say a word about going to sea until her return, which would be in a few months, she would give him money to take a long journey, as soon as he could be trusted from home. A desperate resort to her watch could be then made, she thought anything was better than for such a boy to be left to go to ruin. This hour of anxiety decided her not to make use of her watch; and, no questions being asked, she fancied that no one observed that it was not worn.

The Flower of the Family

Gladly now would she have flown home; but she dared not even say that. She saw that both her aunt and Helen wished her to accompany them, and that they would be hurt should she propose to relinquish a pleasure so long looked forward to. Besides, when her friend Mrs. Lee came with Miss Prigott to make her parting call, before going into the country for the summer, she assured Lucy that Dr. Thornton had spoken very decidedly in reference to her not returning home at present; and she made her promise not to think of it. The matter was, therefore, once more settled, and they began to make preparations for their summer flight. Miss Prigott always went after mountain-air, somewhere. This was her hobby; and when one set of mountains failed to rejuvenate her, she sought new ones. She was determined that Lucy should reap the benefit of her experience. Mrs. Whittier's hobby was the sea-air; and into no other would she allow Lucy to be carried. Miss Prigott grew warm on the subject, and urged her loneliness as an argument in favor of a project she had formed. This proved to be neither more nor less than a design to make Lucy her companion for the summer.

"Well!" she said at last, when she found her hopes blasted in the most summary manner by Mrs. Whittier, "how could an old woman of my age expect a young girl like Lucy to consent to accompany her? Without father or mother, brother, sister or child, how can I dream of anything better than solitude? And I ought to have learned better years ago!"

Lucy was touched by these words; she had never heard that the lot of Miss Prigott was so very lonely. She longed to throw her arms around the little, wrinkled figure, and tell her she would go with her anywhere, and love her too. Perhaps nothing restrained her but an awful sense of the wealth of which the object of her sympathy was the not happy possessor.

In a few moments Mrs. Lee rose to go. Miss Prigott lingered behind, and whispered to Lucy:

"I hope you will be candid, my dear, and speak the exact truth. If I give up my mountain journey, and follow you to the sea-side, shall you be sorry? Shall you wish me away?"

Lucy answered, and with truth, that far from being sorry, she should be very glad. This answer proceeded, in part, from a benevolent impulse; yet it was sincere.

"Thank you, my love. I shall not do so; I only put the question. And now, good-bye: may we soon meet again!"

Lucy was conscious of a sense of relief when these last words were spoken; she felt sorry for and was displeased at it.

"Ah! I may well say I am not perfect!" she thought. "I wish I was! I wish I were more like Christ! He is no respecter of persons!"

Then she thought, that in poor Miss Prigott His eye detected real grace and goodness, or, at least, desires after goodness; and that the life blessed by His approval and presence was not, after all, solitary.

CHAPTER 15

The Sea-Side

THE CLOSE, OPPRESSIVE DAYS in June hastened Mrs. Whittier's preparations for their departure, and by the middle of the month they were all established for the summer, near the sea-side. Everything here was as new to Lucy as the great city they had left. Now for the first time she saw and heard the ocean; and she saw it with no careless eye; listened to its music with no ordinary ear. She felt like throwing herself into its embrace, like the child that once asked, "Can anything so beautiful be dangerous?" Books seemed tame, and lay neglected; but many voices spoke to her, even the voices of many waters, that were full of life and truth. Day after day slipped by, and her enthusiasm rather waxed than waned; and her aunt and Helen indulged her still in her ecstasies, without entirely sharing them. They had seen the sea all their lives; and, if the truth must be owned, had caught the spirit of those about them, who saw in the ocean nothing but a great bathing-tub, in which men, women, and children, dressed, not to say screaming, like Indians, might dip, and dive, and spatter and splash, without wetting anybody's carpet, or crowding anybody's neighbor. There is "but a step between the sublime and the ridiculous"; and he who sentimentalizes on the shore at one hour, spouting, "Roll on, thou deep and dark blue ocean, roll!" goes shrinking into it the next, gasping for breath, a sorry picture of "majesty stripped of its externals." Thus fared Lucy, and her frolics and her laughter in the water were as genuine as her moralizings and poetizings when out of it.

It soon became apparent to everybody that everybody had brought too many books, too many plans of all sorts, too many collars to embroider, too many slippers to beautify. There was positively no time for anything. What with bathing, and dressing, and being civil, and driving out, each day slipped away in the most unexpected manner. People sat with books in their hands, making believe read; and brought out needlework, pretending to sew; and made desperate efforts to appear industrious and literary; but it wouldn't do. Everybody saw through it; knew it was a great humbug; felt like a martyr and said, originally, forty times a day, "Where *does* the time go?" But "time" never came back to tell where it went. There would have been a melancholy pleasure in knowing. One might at least have written its epitaph.

To Lucy's observing eye, these months among people were full of amusement and instruction; and although she could not have told you what each man and woman wore on their backs, she could have given you a pretty just idea of what they carried in their heads. Here was Mrs. Somebody dressed as simply as a child; and there was Mrs. Nobody with a whole trunk full of magnificence flying from various points on her person. Here was Mrs. Smith, who wondered how "everybody" dared come here, even if they could afford to, which she doubted; and there was Mrs. Jones, who would enjoy herself amazingly if those Smiths had stayed at home. Mr. Tompkins pined for "society," and threatened every day to go somewhere else. Mr. Williams thought solitude charming, and was often seen wandering in by-places, which everybody said was pride. Mrs. Perkins let her children eat everything; Mrs. Parkins wouldn't let hers taste of aught agreeable, that they might learn self-denial. Mr. Simpson thought his wife a pattern to all in the house. Mrs. Sampson was sure nobody had a husband like hers; which no one denied or cried about. Miss Irkton wished she had the training of all those dreadful children. Mrs. Lewis said, that old maids should not come to watering-places, and felt that none but mothers could appreciate babies.

Lucy's age forbade her having much to say; she therefore saw and learned the more. She saw that everybody had faults, whims, hobbies; also that everybody had good qualities, real and reliable. If Mr. Tompkins was lofty, he was also generous. If Mr. Williams was unsocial, he at least spoke ill of nobody. And although Mrs. Perkins did indulge her children, she indulged you too, and would spend a whole day nursing you, if you were sick

The Flower of the Family

and solitary. And what if Mrs. Parkins did teach her children self-denial? were they not the happiest family in the establishment, in her intense devotion and affection? All the books in the world could not have taught lessons so beneficial as Lucy was now learning. Lessons of charity and "psalms of life," that to the last hour of her existence made her more genial, more forbearing, more tender-hearted. She saw that she was not the only being in the world, in whom human infirmity and foible was to be found, and that all wisdom and goodness were not locked up in her own head and heart. If her brothers and sisters had faults, they were not the worst in the world; and if they were dear and precious and affectionate, so were hosts of others, likewise. It is no small attainment to learn what to expect of the world in which we dwell; and it is not from books, however wise, but from living men and women, and children too, that we shall make it

The season so profitable to Lucy, proved unfavorable to Helen. She looked less into the heart of things, and more upon the surface. She saw many professedly religious people doing things her conscience had forbidden, and so began to think she had been too strict. Then her very social disposition attracted her more and more to the society of the young people about her; and when with the Romans, she did as the Romans did.

She very soon found it difficult to keep up regular habits of devotion; and by degrees grew somewhat careless in regard to them. While Lucy resolutely hedged herself about with a *habit* of prayer, Helen wavered and was fitful in this respect.

"Mrs. Smith is a good woman, and yet she does so and so," said Helen. "Therefore why should not I? Besides, no one wishes to appear better than the rest." Sometimes, when conscience said, "You have not prayed to-day; go now," she was talking with that delightful Miss Woodman, or kindly listening to tedious Mrs. Young; then she would reply, "In a minute;" or, "How it would look if I should go and leave her!" or, "I'm sure I should be thankful to do so, if it were not for seeming to neglect Mrs. Young." Yet the example of Lucy was of service to her. She saw that *the business of her life* was to serve God; and that nothing was allowed to interfere with any one of the duties she owed

The Flower of the Family

Him; and which she performed evidently with pleasure, and out of pure love of His will.

"I shall be glad when it comes time to go home," Helen one day said to Lucy. "I am getting so tired of these people here. It is a clear waste of time to spend one's summers away from home."

"How soon shall we go?" asked Lucy.

"In a few weeks, I think. Papa is obliged to go then; and we may as well do the same. Don't you think so?"

"Yes, indeed!" cried Lucy with so much energy that Helen could not help laughing.

"We must make up our lost time this winter," said she. "I long to see how you'll like Mr. Jackson. He's considered an admirable teacher."

"What do you mean, my dear Helen? I am to go home as soon as we return to the city."

"Oh! that then is the reason you are so eager to cut short our stay here? But, Lucy, papa says you sha'n't go home at present. He has written to your father about it."

"I *must* go. I've written to father that I shall certainly be there by the first of October."

Helen smiled and shook her head. "You know you are to stay till you are quite well; and besides, I've set my heart on having you at school with me. And papa and mamma have been planning it all along. You know they think you must be the flower of your family."

"There are nine more just such flowers," said Lucy, smiling.

"I don't believe it. And if there are, I don't care. I never shall like any of them so well as I do you."

Lucy dismissed the subject at once from her mind. She looked upon it as impossible for her mother to spare her longer; her health was now perfectly good; she felt anxious about John, and could have cried like a baby to see them all.

"Papa has written to your father to come on, and talk the matter over. He was to meet us as soon as possible, after our return."

"He can't leave home at this season."

"Here he is, at any rate!" cried Helen, almost beside herself with delight at the pleasure she had the satisfaction of announcing. "I was told to break it to you gently, and I'm sure I have; but you're as pale as a sheet."

Lucy was in her father's arms; she did not hear the concluding sentence. Surprise and joy made her lose her color for a moment; but it returned speedily; and as he held her off, and looked tenderly in her face, he thought he had never seen her so beautiful, so well in her life.

"How *could* you get away, dear father?" she asked, as soon as she had satisfied herself by a long embrace that he really was there.

"*I came!*" he answered, smiling.

"And how long can you stay? And did you come to take me home? And are they all well?"

He sat down, and took her on his knee, and looked so satisfied, so happy, that she forgot he had not answered her questions.

"There are not many such children!" he thought.

Mr. and Mrs. Whittier and Helen now joined them, and there was a deal of talking, and laughing, and rejoicing; yet Lucy's oft-repeated question, "Have you come to take me home?" was not answered.

"Give your father a little peace," said her uncle at last; "you do nothing but cross-question him. Don't you know it is rude to ask people what they have come for, and how long they're going to stay?"

Lucy smiled and held her peace, satisfied that all was right that her father did; and so content to wait his pleasure.

As he was about to retire for the night, he asked her, jestingly, if she should be ready to return with him in a day or two; and her animated reply made him smile, while it brought a cloud over Helen's brow.

The next day they were all busy lionizing Mr. Grant. He had not enjoyed such a season of refreshment since the days of his youth; and Lucy enjoyed seeing him fish, and bathe, and drive, so keenly, that this seemed the happiest day she had ever spent. It proved an eventful one to her, too, for she now learned that arrangements had been made for her remaining among her friends, as Helen had assured her. Her aunt, taking her aside, made known all the plans of which the past few months had been full, and expressed her strong pleasure in the prospect of keeping her yet longer.

The Flower of the Family

"But I feel that mother needs me at home," said Lucy. Mrs. Whittier put into her hands the kind, cordial consent her mother had given to her remaining to attend school with Helen; and when she looked up, with a face radiant with gratitude, to thank her aunt, she found herself alone.

"How can I ever thank them?" cried her full heart; "and how can I ever thank God for His goodness?"

At this moment her father came in, very cheerful and happy, to congratulate her.

"Now your great wish is gratified," he said.

"Father," replied Lucy, "it ought to be Hatty."

"What ought to be Hatty?"

"Why, you know how bright, and pretty, and lovable she is; and how she has always disliked the country; and I have been here now a long time, and it is her turn now."

"As to the prettiness, I am no judge. You all look pretty to me. But as to the brightness and lovableness, why, I hardly think they need complain. Why should Hatty be brighter or more lovable than you, pray?"

"Oh, because I am older than she."

"Older than she! Dear child, how much older now?"

"A year and a half," said Lucy, smiling at the apparent failure of her argument. "But I feel a good many years older than she. And now Arthur is provided for, I do wish it could be Hatty! Oh, how can I let you go home and tell her I am well and strong, but am to stay here and enjoy a life of ease and pleasure, while she is to toil and wear out at home?"

"I see how it is; you are old in experience of the cares of domestic life; and I am thankful you are to be released from that incessant drudgery, and grow young again."

"It was not drudgery, dear father; and, besides, if it was so, my absence must throw the more upon mother. It will be hard for her!"

"To see you grow young again? Come, cheer up, darling! You know you can be of the greatest service to Hatty and all of them, by these advantages. Two years, or even three, are not a lifetime."

"Two years! oh, father! am I to stay so long without seeing mother!"

The Flower of the Family

"That's the hard part of it; hard for you; and for her, and for us all. But you know, my dear child, how gladly I would take you home with me, if I could."

"I can't stay; I must see mother, and tell her how it grieves me to leave her, and hear her say she spares me willingly." She yearned to feel herself folded in her mother's arms; once there, she thought no temptation could draw them apart.

"My dear Lucy, I know you better than you know yourself," said her father, after a pause, "If, in this moment of excitement, you decide to relinquish the opportunity for an education so freely offered you, I am sure you will regret it your whole life. You know that you have thirsted for knowledge ever since you can remember, above everything else."

"Except goodness!" she said, gently.

"Except goodness!" he responded, laying his hand lovingly on her head. "Come, let me decide for you, as your mother has already done. You will stay."

She clung to him, dreading to ask how soon he would leave her.

"Don't let us be seen crying," he said, hearing approaching footsteps.

"I did not know I was crying," said Lucy, smiling away her tears. "I hope I am not ungrateful to uncle and aunt— only, when I get thinking about home, I so long to be there!"

Her uncle now entered. He was in fine spirits, and drew Lucy affectionately to his side, where she stood lost in thought, while he talked with her father

"Poor mother!" she repeated to herself again and again. "Ought I to stay from her so long? How hard it is for her to lose us just when we are becoming useful! The baby will be a great boy before I see him again. And Arthur! ah, nobody will watch him as I have done! Nobody will have time; for my absence will throw more labor upon them all."

Helen now came to express her pleasure. She caught Lucy in her arms, and wheeled her about the room, crying, "She's mine! she's mine!" till they were both out of breath, and glad to sit down upon the sofa. The ecstasy of Helen did Lucy good; she felt pleased to find herself the object of so much affection.

"I must return home to-morrow, Lucy," said her father; "that is, I must be on my way thither early in the morning. So, if you wish to write, you must make haste."

Lucy lost no time in doing so; and her heart relieved itself, as she wrote a long, glowing letter to her mother, full of love, and tenderness, and hope. And then a note to Arthur; dear boy! How her pen flew over her paper as she thought of him! And after that, such a deprecating message to Hatty was appended to her mother's letter, as if it were wrong to be here, if she must be there! As she wrote, and all their dear faces came up before her, she felt tempted to give utterance to the cry that lay smothered in her heart, and to exclaim, "I will not, I cannot stay!" and perhaps she would have done so, and our story would end here, if she had been used to obey the voice of feeling rather than that of conscience. But this opportunity might never return— she dared not neglect it. And there was not much time now for deliberation; her father was preparing to depart; there were scores of last things to be done, and amid the confusion, she could not realize what was befalling her.

"Oh, my God! only let me do just *right*!" was her reiterated prayer; and she rejoiced that she could add, "I *delight* to do Thy will, whatever it may be!"

CHAPTER 16

Life at School

IMMEDIATELY ON THEIR RETURN TO THE CITY, both Lucy and Helen began to attend school. Lucy met with some difficulties at first; for her education had been quite fragmentary, and it required time to put her on the same level with her new companions. It soon appeared, however, that in some respects she was superior to them all. Her general knowledge was, for her age, and the circumstances in which it had been gained, quite remarkable; her tastes were refined and mature, and her lively imagination made her often brilliant. Those who at first smiled at her country breeding, taking for granted that nothing but ignorance and dullness were the occasion of her modest, retiring air, shortly became her admirers and friends. Every week her teacher returned her "composition," adorned with marks of approbation. His object with his pupils was to excite their ambition; he did not scruple to appeal to their pride and vanity, in the prosecution of this design; and Lucy's talents won his genuine admiration. He pressed her with studies she was only too willing to take up; selected for her a course of reading; boasted of her success everywhere, and even wrote a glowing letter to her parents, congratulating them on the possession of such a child. Her uncle could not sufficiently rejoice that he had rescued her from the home in which he imagined her not appreciated. In his satisfaction, he went so far as to persuade himself that he had detected her remarkable talents during his visit at her father's, and that thus she had been brought hither.

"What a providential thing it was that I should have been so struck with her!" he said more than once to Mrs. Whittier, who smiled a little, but would not dispute it. Less prosperous days

The Flower of the Family

have turned older heads than Lucy's, and so have been exchanged for long nights of weeping. But God had abundantly blessed to her heart the discipline by which, through many years. He had been preparing her for these very temptations. And she now so loved and longed for His favor and approval, as to feel the worthlessness of that of the world. "None of these things move me!" is the triumphant exclamation of many a saint, when tempted by all the honors life can offer, to look away from those imperishable rewards awaiting him on high.

Mr. Jackson, who was always trying experiments in the management of his pupils, opened this new term with the offer of prizes in all the departments. save that to which Lucy belonged. He privately whispered to her, and to her class-mates, that they needed no such stimulus to exertion. Helen had at first a little hesitation about becoming a competitor in the race, but finally entered the lists; and, having done so, soon manifested great zeal and energy. One evening when she had been hard at work for several hours, reviewing old lessons, Charles came sauntering in, and threw himself listlessly upon the sofa.

"How busy you girls are!" he said. "Come, Helen, do put away those old books, and read me that French story. You know you promised to read it some day this week."

"I'll certainly keep my promise; but I can't now. I am reviewing Day's Algebra, and you needn't be surprised if you see me very industrious nowadays."

"I thought industrious people could find time for everything."

"Oh dear! no, indeed! there you are quite mistaken. But don't talk to me now, please, for I am going to undertake a sum a mile long. Yes, every bit of a mile long."

"Do let a fellow see it!" cried Charles, with pretended curiosity. "A mile long! What remarkable girls you must have at your school! We boys never dream of sums more than two feet long, at the utmost."

Helen laughed. "What a good-for-nothing fellow you are!" said she. "You know very well what I meant. Or, perhaps you do not perceive the difference between literal and figurative language!"

"Dear me! how wise we are getting!" said Charles, provokingly. But Helen would not be provoked; she let him laugh till he was tired, while she went on half-aloud: "Let me

The Flower of the Family

see: x represents the sugar; y, the tea; z, the— what's z to represent? Oh, I see— the coffee; no— not the coffee, either. Why, I'm as stupid as an owl, to-night."

"Is that so very unusual?"

"Oh, Charles! please don't look over my shoulder so. Nothing puts me in such a fidget as having people looking over my shoulder."

"*People?*" said Charles; "what people? Am I people? Yes, she must mean me, for there's no one else in the room. Well, I declare! I never knew I was in the plural number before! But this must be *figurative* language!"

"Oh, Charles! you are a real torment!" said Helen.

"That's *literal*, isn't it?" he asked.

"Charles," said Helen, now laying down her slate, "do go away, there's a good boy. Come, now, I'll tell you why I am so anxious about this particular lesson. Mr. Jackson has offered a prize, which I want very much to win. I meant to keep it a secret, but there's no use."

Charles could not resist the tone in which these words were spoken; neither could he refrain from saying, "I don't think much of prizes, anyhow."

"Don't you? but why not? I am very sorry."

What boy ever gave a reason for the belief that was in him? "I don't know why," said he. "I don't like them, because I don't!" and away he ran, leaving Helen to return to x, y, and z; which she did, till her head ached, and she was tired in every limb.

The hope that the prize would be hers, and with it her father's satisfied smile, her mother's gentle caress, made her lose sight of and forget other objects of interest. The lamp-mat that had been commenced in honor of Miss Prigott's approaching birthday, was thrust hastily into a bag already fain to burst from its plenitude of like fragments; and a lovely handkerchief, in process of hemming for the cook, shared a similar fate. Every night when she retired to her room, her mind was so filled with the thought of school, and so wearied with the labor she had imposed on it, that she approached with reluctance this season of devotion. She would then force herself through her usual duties, and go to bed in a most cheerless state. "It ought not to be thus," she would say to herself; "and tomorrow I will not allow the thought of that foolish prize to distract me so! But there is one comfort! When all is settled, I shall be free again. Now I must get along as well as I can."

One must live many more years than Helen had done, to be quite free from such mistakes as this. What a blessed day that is, when we learn to expect nothing better from life than distractions; nothing better from our own hearts than a heedless absorption in every petty, passing interest! Then first we throw ourselves on the simple grace of God, forsaking forever the fancied stronghold of our own good purposes.

When Helen awoke on the morning after her conversation with Charles, all the interests of her school-life rushed, like armed men, to meet her. In the very midst of earnest words of prayer, her plans for the day came to claim attention.

Her thoughts wandered to her books and studies and then, urged back to their solemn task, came reluctantly, and flew away from her grasp.

But that struggle with temptation was not lost. How full of love and tender compassion was the invisible, yet present Saviour before whom she knelt! How willingly He accepted that poor, feeble, half-uttered prayer, and how that sigh for deliverance found its way to the ear of Him who hath been touched with the feeling of our infirmity! And when Helen walked sadly on her way to school, filled with self-upbraiding, yet too weak in faith to tear herself at once away from temptation, shall we doubt that Jesus Himself went with His little disciple, pitying and resolving to rescue her?

"How glad I shall be when Helen is herself again!" sighed her mother more than once. She thought it not best, however, to interfere with her in her present mood. Experience is a good teacher; without her instructions and discipline, no character is complete. All the mother's wisdom fails to supply to her child the place of that each must acquire for herself.

"Hurrah! here she comes, prize and all!" shouted Charles, as one day, on his return from school, he encountered Helen, smiling, and blushing, and bearing a large package in her arms.

"Do tell me if you brought that home yourself?" he cried.

"No, Mr. Jackson sent it for me. I met it at the door."

She looked around for her mother's smile and kiss, and for a moment they made her completely happy.

"I'm glad you've got this pretty desk," said Charles, removing its covering. "There's that hateful Mary Anna Milman expected it; didn't she?"

"She is not hateful at all, but my dearest friend!"

"*I* think her hateful," retorted Charles. "For her hair is as red as fire; and when she walks, she goes mincing along, just so. Look! on her tiptoes; just so. I can imitate her perfectly."

Helen was tired and excited. She had been through a long public examination, and her head ached.

"You are very unkind, Charles," said she, indignantly; and as usual, when angry, she ran to her own room, crying with all her heart.

"Mamma," said Charles, replying to his mother's glance of regret, "I really did not mean to vex her. The least thing makes her cry."

"She has over-exerted herself, and we should make some allowance for that," she answered. "You know I begged you to try to enter into her pleasure, should she win the prize; for, after all, it is valueless to her without our sympathy."

"Well, mamma, I tried to sympathize with her. I'm sure I did not know Mary Anna Milman was her dearest friend. And her hair is red, and everybody knows it; and she minces when she walks. I don't see how Helen can endure her."

"But the truth is not to be spoken at all seasons, my dear boy, unless in case of need. Suppose I should take this opportunity, when you are vexed, to point out the faults of Carlo; would you not find it an ill-chosen time? And, as you could not cry like a girl, would you not rush from the room in a passion, like a boy?"

Charles smiled. "Oh, I dare say you are right, mamma. I do wish I could help teasing Helen. But it is such fun!"

Mr. Whittier now came in to dinner, and as they seated themselves at the table, he missed Helen.

"Where is she?" he asked.

"She'll be here presently," said her mother, who did not care to annoy him with the information that she was crying in her room.

But Charles volunteered the intelligence without delay.

The Flower of the Family

"What is she crying for?" asked her father. "Has she lost the prize? Well, I am glad of it. I never liked this system of emulation. And now it is all over, I hope she'll honor us all with a little attention."

Her mother explained that the prize was safely in Helen's possession.

"Then why is she crying?" persisted her father.

"She got angry with me," said Charles, "because I teased her about her 'dearest friend,' as she calls her."

"She was very tired, uncle," said Lucy, "and her head ached when she went to school."

Mr. Whittier said no more, and dinner was anything but a social meal that day. Lucy slipped away as soon as possible, to find Helen, and tried to persuade her to take refreshment of some kind; but she lay rather obstinately on her bed, and looked quite unlike a heroine. Her mother soon followed Lucy; she had a little tray in her hands, on which was a cup of tea and a bit of toast.

"Come, darling," she said, "you must take this."

Helen rose, and obeyed in silence; and Lucy left them alone, knowing that thus sympathy could best be offered and received.

"Mamma!" said Helen, "I hope you do not think I've been crying all this time at what Charles said. I was vexed at first; but I soon got over that. But I was so disappointed! I thought it would give me such pleasure to win the prize; and I worked so hard for it! And it seems now such a trifle to sacrifice all those months to!"

"I understand it all, my dear child. But I must have you rest now. Lie down again and sleep; I am sure you need it."

Caressed and soothed by her mother's soft hands, Helen's tears soon ceased flowing; she became quiet and composed, and at last fell into a refreshing sleep. Mrs. Whittier sat and watched the young sleeper, as an angel sits, and watches, and loves. Gladly would she bear in her own person all the disappointments, trials, and sorrows life can offer, if thereby her child could be spared them. But this may not be. The utmost a loving mother can do, is to pity and to pray for the objects of her affection; each one for himself must suffer, and suffer alone.

Helen awoke refreshed, and thanked her mother with many grateful caresses, for her gentle watch over and sympathy with her. When left alone, she sat some minutes in thoughtful silence. She felt, now that all excitement was over, that she had been selfish, and careless, and peevish during many months; and all to gain a momentary pleasure. And this pleasure was not so real, so substantial as she had expected it to be. It was, moreover, dampened by the fact that some of her school-mates envied her, while others disputed her right to the prize. These little school experiences are of service, however, to a heart once turned heavenward. They proved so to Helen. She felt now, and feeling led in time to conviction, that she never could be satisfied with mere worldly honor, and that she must give herself with more earnestness to the love and service of God. She knelt and prayed as these thoughts urged her to do; and as she prayed, the petty interests and disappointments of life grew more and more insignificant. Nothing seemed worthy her pursuit but the fear of God and the love of Christ.

Thus humble and happy, she went now to join her mother and Lucy. Her father was in the hall; she ran to meet and to kiss him, and to help him take off his coat, as she had not found time to do of late. Nothing but a certain feeling of timidity, a consciousness of the source of her present peaceful and loving mood, restrained her from kissing every one in the house. Charles was alone in the dining-room, reading or trying to read— for he was a very poor scholar— the French story he had often vainly asked Helen to read to him. She sat down by him and whispered, "I am sorry I was vexed with you about Mary Anna." He looked up, astonished. Never before had her pride allowed her to make any concession of this sort. He made no answer, for he felt embarrassed, and knew not what to say.

"After tea I'll read that story, if you'll let me, after making you wait so long," she continued.

"The reason I wanted you to read it was because Barrows and I had a dispute about one part. I wanted to ask you what you thought."

"Lucy's thoughts are worth more than mine; why didn't you ask her?" asked Helen.

"Does Lucy read French?" he asked, in surprise.

"Of course she does. Mr. Lennox says he never has had a pupil of whom he was so proud."

The Flower of the Family

After tea, Helen read the story, and her father laid aside his paper to listen. She then hemmed the cook's handkerchief, so long buried in the depths of her great bag.

"You look tired, Helen," said her mother. "Do amuse yourself in some way till bed-time."

"She has worked too hard of late," said her father, "and must unbend her mind a little."

Helen laughed, and let her father pinch her cheeks at his leisure.

"Come, I'll tell you all a story," said he.

Charles, who was busy in a private attempt to adorn Carlo with Dinah's new handkerchief, instantly snatched this unwelcome appendage from the poor dog's head, and drew near to his father. Lucy and Helen also prepared to listen; and Mr. Whittier began on this wise:

"There was once a man who said to himself, 'I mean to walk across the world, and see what there is on the other side.'"

"Oh, what a fool!" cried Charles.

"Perhaps he was insane," suggested Helen.

"The man set forth on his journey, and proceeded to follow his own nose, whithersoever it led him, provided it led in a direct line, diverging neither to the right hand nor the left. Pretty soon he ran bolt up against another man, who was walking in an opposite direction. The collision threw the other down."

'What a monster of cruelty to run over a blind man!' cried the bystanders.

"The man did not stop to explain his conduct. He felt too eager and anxious; and so he hurried along in a straight line, till he came to a little child that had fallen upon the pavement.

" 'Mamma, mamma! I want my mamma!' shrieked the child."

'Run home to her, then, and move out of my way,' said the man.

"But the child lay upon its face, and cried louder than ever. The heart of the man smote him. He knew he ought to lead the little one to its home, but to do this would take him out of his way. So he stepped over its head, and proceeded on his journey.

"Presently he came close up to a house. He opened the window and stepped in.

The Flower of the Family

" 'A thief! a thief!' cried the children, as the stranger appeared in the room. In rushed, armed with pokers and brooms, the father, the mother, the maids."

" 'Hear me!' shouted the man, trying to raise his voice above the tumult. 'I have taken a vow to walk straight through the world. Allow me to pass through your house, and I never will trouble you again.'"

" 'Don't talk to me of your vows!' cried the enraged father, punching him with the poker.

" 'He is a thief! he will be robbing us all!' cried the mother."

" 'Let us throw him out of the window,' said the maids.

So out of the window they threw him.

" 'I shall have to begin all over again,' said the man, as soon as he picked himself up. 'Or, stay; could not I climb over this house?'

"With incredible exertion, aided by lightning-rods, shutters, chimneys, and the like, the man at last succeeded in accomplishing this object, while the owner of the house ran to summon the police and the children cried within."

"He now went rapidly on his way in the open country, where neither men, children, nor houses arrested his progress. He went through ditches, he trampled down sweet flowers, he ascended and descended high hills. On he went, tired, dusty, lame, caring for nobody and nobody caring for him. He met with many hardships and resisted many opportunities of doing good; at first through violence to his own feelings, but after a time coming to be cold, selfish, and hard of heart."

"At last he came to the shores of a great sea. Here he stood still, in despair. What should he do? At last, stripping himself of everything, even to the gold that he had hitherto borne about his person, he plunged into the waters and swam for his life. Cold, exhausted, hungry, bare, and penniless, he at length reached the opposite shore and continued his journey. Every step was now one of pain and strong effort, and when a little hillock obstructed his path, he wept like a child. Through summer and winter, seed-time and harvest, still he toiled on. At last he reached the end of his journey."

The Flower of the Family

"And what did he find there, papa?" cried Charles, whose interest had been waxing stronger and stronger as his father proceeded.

"What do you think he found?"

Charles's opinion wavered between all manner of possible and impossible things. He thought of a race of giants; of men with but one eye or of men with six eyes, and the like; while Helen, who had been lost in thought, started up, crying,

"Why, he found his own house!"

"What! his own house? How could his house be on the other side of the world?" asked Charles.

"Why, don't you see," cried Helen, snatching up an apple, "if I set out from this dent and walk in a straight line, I come right back to the dent again?"

"Any fool might see that," said Charles. "But what has this to do with the story? The man was not walking *round* the world, but *across* it."

"But, my boy, is the world a flat plane, or a sphere?"

"Why, it is a sphere. Ah! I see now! Of course the man would come to the point he started from."

He looked discomfited, however.

"Well," said he, "what did they say to him when they saw him coming home?"

"His mother looked at him from the window, and when she saw the miserable state to which he had reduced himself, she said, 'We will get him to bed as soon as possible, poor fellow, for he seems to need rest sadly. And we won't upbraid him for his folly. He has had his punishment.' But his wife said to him, 'A pretty state you are in, to be sure! I wonder you have not been carried to Bedlam, where you belong. Who do you suppose fed and clothed your children while you ran such a wild-goose chase over the world? Did I not tell you how it would end?'"

"And that's the last I ever heard of him," said Mr. Whittier, bringing his story to so sudden a close, that both children cried out,

"Is that all? What became of the man? How did he feel?"

"I have told you all I know," said their father.

"Well," said Charles, "he was a fool, anyhow. He might have known he was a fool, if he had stopped to think a moment. His

The Flower of the Family

wife gave it to him well, though, didn't she? It was just good enough for him!"

"Oh, that was the part I liked least," said Helen. "His wife might have known he would feel ashamed and sorry enough to need no scolding."

"That is one of the morals of my story, but not the only one," said her father.

"I hate morals, and am going to feed Carlo," said Charles, laughing and hurrying off.

Helen suspected the story had some reference to her own heedless course during the few past months, but she had not time to say so, for her father, pointing to the clock, admonished her that it was time to go to bed. He kissed and blessed her with great tenderness, as she bade him good-night, and, half amused and half reproved, she retired to her own room,

"Nonsense is wholesome sometimes," said Mr. Whittier to his wife, half apologetically.

"Yes, indeed it is," she answered.

CHAPTER 17

The Holidays

"Mamma," said Helen the next morning, "after hearing papa's story, I concluded not to try to finish that mat within a given time."

"Then you did not understand its object, my dear."

"Why, mamma, I get so absorbed in whatever I undertake, that I care for nothing but to reach the end. And I don't know how I can help myself."

"You surely do not intend to sit with folded hands and an idle mind, all your days, I suppose?"

"Why, no, mamma. But I thought I would not allow myself to set about anything very interesting, for fear of becoming too much in love with it."

"On the contrary, I advise you to finish the mat. Miss Prigott likes to be remembered on her birthdays. And it will be good discipline for you to oblige yourself to be interested in, but never overcome by such work."

Helen hesitated. "Oh, mamma! you don't know how weak I am!" said she.

"Almost any one can run away from temptation," returned her mother. "It is far nobler, and requires a higher degree of strength, to meet and conquer it."

Helen ran for the mat, and sat down to her work, which proved a sore temptation to her.

"I must just put in these crimsons, to see what the effect will be; or I will only finish this rosebud to see how it is going to look;" says the inveterate embroiderer, when the still small voice of duty whispers of another and less agreeable task. Many an innocent lamp-mat or fire-screen has borne witness to frowns,

The Flower of the Family

shrugs, and sighs, when it should have seen bending over it only a fair and unclouded face. Old Mr. This, and tiresome Mrs. That, if they intrude on this fascinating pastime, may be thankful if they are not consigned, in wish at least, to the bottom of the Red Sea, by lips that ought only to know how to shape words of friendly greeting and cordial welcome!

Helen was going on bravely with her work, and interruptions proved excessively annoying, so that when her friend Mary Anna was announced, she felt a slight emotion of vexation, and failed to rush to meet her with the ecstasy of delight that young lady deemed requisite. In fact, Miss Mary Anna had not found herself in the best possible humor that morning, and had had her feelings already wounded by a suggestion from a little sister, that she had "got out of bed on the wrong side." She therefore assumed an air of injured innocence, and seating herself at a distance from Helen, proceeded to make herself as disagreeable as possible.

"I am glad," said she, "you find time for worsted-work and such amusements. You must enjoy life vastly more than young ladies who have to descend to such vulgar employments as darning stockings!"

"Indeed," returned Helen, "I hope my happiness does not depend on my employments. I think I could darn stockings if it were necessary."

"But it is not necessary, as you can afford to have everything of that sort done for you. I only wish other people were so fortunate."

As Mary Anna's father was very well able to have her stockings mended for her, Helen knew not what reply to make to this speech.

Mary Anna, thus arrested in the progress of her remarks, turned to another point.

"I suppose you were much delighted to find you had won the prize. To be sure you deserved it, for how you *did* work! For my part, I did not think it worth so much trouble. It was only a paltry desk, after all!"

"Oh, it was not the value of the prize!" said Helen.

"But the glory, I suppose?"

Helen colored a little.

"Well, I suppose it *was* the glory, as you call it."

The Flower of the Family

She felt annoyed, however, and looked in surprise at Mary Anna, who sat smiling with an air of sweetness with which it seemed impossible to quarrel.

"I should have been very happy to have you win it, glory and all," said Helen, kindly.

"Oh, I assure you I care nothing about it. I value my friendships far more highly. Indeed, I made no effort to obtain the prize."

Helen was surprised at this announcement, which however, she would not contradict.

"The girls all say they did not try for it," pursued Mary Anna, "because they saw how determined you were to win it, cost what it might."

"Mary Anna!" said Helen, "I am afraid you do not love me so well as you did once. I never heard you talk so before. Why, I really thought you would be pleased to have me win the prize!"

"Well, and am not I pleased?" cried Mary Anna "I am sure I came this morning on purpose to congratulate you. But I cannot go into raptures. It is not my way. My feelings are deep and strong."

So saying, Mary Anna rose to take leave, and departed, with the same agreeable countenance which she had preserved through the interview.

The moment she had gone, Helen caught up her work and tried to go on with it. But she could not see to take one stitch. Her eyes kept filling with tears, and were determined to keep full. She felt pained and grieved beyond measure. What had she done to deserve such treatment from her dear friend? But, after all, what treatment? Had anything unkind really been said?

Her mother entering the room, detected the tears, and came towards her full of that sympathy a mother always has ready.

"Mamma," said Helen, returning her mother's silent caress, "please don't ask me any questions, for I hardly know myself what I am crying for."

"To tell the truth, I was in the next room, and unavoidably heard all that passed."

"Oh, mamma! I am so sorry! Pray don't judge Mary Anna by her appearance this morning! I never heard her talk so before! I dare say she is sorry for it by this time."

The Flower of the Family

"I advise you my dear, not to commit your happiness too entirely to those who will trifle with it when occasion suits. Understand me, however, I do not counsel you to love Mary Anna less, but Christ the more. Then every little trial will drive you to Him who never tampers with the love yielded Him."

"Lucy thinks Mary Anna has some excellent qualities mamma."

"I do not doubt it, dear. And by the by, do you know that Mrs. Lee has sent for Lucy to spend the holidays with her?"

"Oh, mamma! But Lucy is not going, I hope?"

"I don't know. On some accounts, I think it would not be amiss. Lucy has left the decision with me."

"She admires Mrs. Lee, I know, and Mrs. Lee seems really to love her. But I don't think it fair to take her from us; why couldn't she go and spend one day and come home at night? We had planned to do such a number of things together!"

"I will see what your father says. But don't look so dismal, my dear. What will you do when Lucy leaves us altogether?"

"I don't even dare think of that."

Mrs. Whittier stood reflecting a few moments, and then went in search of her husband whose key she heard now in the door.

"You're just the little woman I want to see," he cried, as he encountered her. "Come here, and let me exhibit some of the things I've been getting for those girls. And by the by, I have determined that on New-Year's day Lucy shall begin to have an allowance, equal to Helen's. I wonder I never thought of it before. How has the child got along without money?"

"I've taken care of that," said Mrs. Whittier smiling a little triumphantly as he shook his head at her. "I dreaded proposing it; but on the whole, she bore it pretty well. Of course I provide her dress, as I do Helen's, and I gave her to understand that her quarterly allowance was to be used just as she pleased."

"You manage these things admirably," he answered.

"Why, to tell the truth, I fancy that Lucy receives favors with less pain and more pleasure from me than from you."

"What possible difference can it make, from which of us a favor comes?"

"I have tried to put myself in her place, and to feel as I should suppose she feels. And it has occurred to me that she might regard all you do for her as done because you feel obliged to relieve your sister; whereas what *I* do must clearly proceed from pure love, and for my own gratification."

"I don't know that you are not right. But now look at these things. Which shall be Lucy's and which Helen's?"

"You must come and look at mine first. And have you got nothing for Charles?"

"Oh, yes; a trifle or two. But I did not know what would best please him. Now, with girls it is different."

Mrs. Whittier prudently restrained the smile with which she was tempted to honor her husband's purchases. They were silks, of a quality and color quite *mal a` propos* for school girls, who went into no company.

"You haven't said which shall be for which," said Mr. Whittier. "Now I thought Lucy would look best in the green, and Helen in the— what color do you call it? Red?"

"I call it a dashing pink; and as for the 'green,' as you call it; why, my dear, it's sky-blue! Just to think of our sober little Lucy in sky-blue!"

"It is green, I assure you. I asked for green; and the shade of this struck my fancy. And as to the other: why, I am sorry you don't like it; but what can I do? I'll exchange them in the morning—"

"Which is Sunday, you know."

"Dear me! And Monday is Christmas! Well! I did my best; I must run down after tea and see what else I can find. As to those 'sky-blues' and 'flashy pinks,' I'm sure I don't see what you will do with them, unless you'll wear them yourself. I wish you would."

"I'll save them for wedding dresses for Lucy's sisters," said Mrs. Whittier, laughing. "As for Lucy herself, her taste is too Quaker-like for such colors. And now let me tell you; Mrs. Lee has invited her for the holidays."

"Indeed! she must go then, of course."

"So I said, at first; but Miss Prigott has sent me such an odd little note on the subject, full of dark hints and mysteries; I hardly know whether to heed her warnings or not."

"How can you pay the least attention to anything Miss Prigott says on a subject in which she has no concern?"

"Why, she seems to know or suspect something that may be worth our heeding. She reminds me that Dr. Thornton once spoke to Lucy of his brother Edgar Thornton, you know, as if he were an acquaintance of hers. Lucy denied, at the time, ever having seen him; but Miss Prigott says Dr. Thornton evidently did not believe her, and that she heard Mrs. Lee afterwards allude to it."

"Oh, these old maids!" cried Mr. Whittier.

"How much they do contrive to see and hear! Now, my own opinion is this: Let Lucy go. It will make a pleasant change for her; and the society of Mrs. Lee would be an advantage to any young lady."

"But Helen will be so disappointed!"

"Helen must learn that selfishness is an unbecoming, unchristian trait."

"Oh, my dear! Do you think Helen selfish?"

"There is danger in that line for an only daughter whose every wish is gratified."

"We will consider it settled, then, that Lucy is to go," said Mrs. Whittier, reluctantly; and ashamed to own that she too felt a little selfish about it.

Lucy therefore went to Mrs. Lee's, where she found herself in a most congenial atmosphere. Mrs. Lee herself, though not young in years, was at heart a perfect child; as fresh and as simple as Lucy. She felt real interest in hearing everything she could learn of her old friend and school-mate; and was never weary of the little sketches Lucy gave of her sisters and brothers. She suggested books which it would be well for her to read, as she found leisure, and subjects on which to write, But the cultivated mind, the refined taste, the simple air, were not the highest attraction to Lucy, charming as they were. The genial piety by which the life was adorned, won her heart, when talent and acquirement only won admiration. The influence of a genuine Christian is noiseless and silent as the continual droppings of a summer shower, which refreshes and enriches oftentimes more than the heavy fall of rain. Who has not felt his heart glow with quickened warmth at a mere glimpse into a holy soul? Or stimulated to like grace in witnessing an act of patience or forbearance? If, amid the pressure of labor at school and at

The Flower of the Family

home, Lucy had lost aught of that devout temper habitual with her, she was now in circumstances to recover it ten-fold; for every word, and look, and tone of Mrs. Lee, free, and cheerful, and untrammelled as true liberty in Christ could make it, yet said, "I am not of this world." There were throngs of visitors, and the claims of many children, and the pressure of many cares; yet there hung ever about her, like a halo, that serene air, unbroken, unagitated. There are two ways in which genuine piety develops itself. One busies itself chiefly in lopping off useless, diseased, and unsightly branches, and this work occupies it so incessantly that it has not time to perceive that fruit of good quality is not thus produced. The other rather lets the branches take care of themselves, and goes to the root of the matter, assured that if all is right there, all will become right outside. To this latter class Mrs. Lee belonged; and there was, so to speak, a naturalness about her, that mere religious surface-work would have destroyed. She could afford to be enthusiastic, and joyous, and, in a good sense, careless and impulsive. The *branches took care of themselves*. Some vague notions of this sort had long floated in Lucy's mind; but conversation with Mrs. Lee, and close study of her ingenuous, open character, shaped these notions into convictions that were of service to her to an unlimited degree.

But this happy week came to an end, as even wretched weeks will, and Lucy returned to her uncle and to school, greatly refreshed, and with her head and heart as full as they could hold. So full of better things, that the united flatteries of Mr. Jackson, Mr. Lenoux, and all the other teachers, only reached the outside, whence they fell harmless.

On the evening after her departure, Dr. Thornton, who formed one of his sister's family, was sitting by her side reading a foreign letter, one sentence of which, if it is not impolite, we can read over his shoulder, without troubling ourselves to hear the whole sheet.

"Your mysterious hints relative to a certain little maiden who shall be nameless, were duly pondered. Anything farther in that line will receive attention."

"There, you see, he is still weak in that point," said Dr. Thornton. "I told you how it would be. Edgar is not a man to

The Flower of the Family

move his affections from post to post, like men on a chess-board."

"But did you not tell me he had seen her but once?" asked Mrs. Lee.

"Once, more or less," said Dr. Thornton, smiling. "But you don't consider how you have kept the fire alive by your letters."

"Fire! If he has got so far already, I yield the field. I supposed it the merest fancy, that the first pretty face he saw would dispel."

"Well, if I take the field, what am I to do? Skirmish about, and attack the enemy by degrees?"

"My dear brother, do remember what a child she still is, and how improper it would be to put such notions into her head."

"Meanwhile, she grows every day older; and the first thing you'll know, some country lover will bear down upon the field and carry her off. I declare, I am half tempted to do it myself."

"You shan't have her; you're not half good enough. Besides, you're too old. No, Edgar found her, and I hope will win her, but there's time enough; they're both young."

"Well! I think I'll run over Miss Herbert's little brother, and half-kill him, and then make love to her while she's nursing him. Edgar shouldn't be allowed to do all the courting in the family."

Mrs. Lee looked at him. He yawned and half-smiled, as he observed it.

"I don't think that case so hopeless," she said, "Miss Herbert's father may yet relent. Do not be discouraged." Dr. Thornton made no answer, but got up, and walked with an uneasy whistle through the room.

At length he said, "How old did you say Miss Lucy is?"

"Nearly seventeen now."

"And Edgar is nearly twenty-two. Supposing he stays abroad four years; she'll then be twenty-one. Old enough, in all conscience."

"But are you so sure that he will remain constant to a mere shadow? For such, one look at even a girl like Lucy, seems to me."

Dr. Thornton stopped walking, and came and stood before her.

"Mark my words," said he. "Edgar will marry either Miss Lucy or nobody. I say it, who will have either Grace Herbert to wife, or none."

"What wills you boys have!" said Mrs. Lee. "I hope this time, however, they'll not be put to the test."

CHAPTER 18

Lucy in Trouble

HELEN WAS NOW VERY HAPPY. Walking in the steady light of Lucy's example, she made fewer mistakes in judgment, and was less easily led astray by her own ardor and precipitation. Charles, too, allowed himself to be guided by Lucy when he would listen to no other voice. And this was no small point gained; for he was at that age when boys think it particularly manly to pick up all sorts of odd and questionable habits, to ornament their conversation with slang expressions, and to defy authority and laugh at reproof. His mother quietly rejoiced in the gentle, refining influence now exerted over him, while she admired Lucy's tact, her forbearance, her wonderful sagacity in her interaction with him.

One person, however, regarded Lucy with an unfriendly eye; and this was Helen's friend, Mary Anna. Things had never been just right between the two since the interview heretofore described. Not that Helen cherished unkind feelings towards her friend; but that Mary Anna herself ever retained an embarrassed, painful remembrance of her envious and selfish temper on that occasion. Naturally, however, Helen had been drawn more and more closely to her cousin; and that not solely on account of Lucy's attractions. It was the result of their entire sympathy in that Christian race which they pursued together. Mary Anna was full of worldly tastes, though she regarded herself as a Christian. She had not so learned Christ as to delight in forsaking even *innocent* pleasures for His sake, and she knew little of the serenity and the peace to be found in a life of faith. There are many uncomfortable Christians in this world. Mary Anna was one. She performed many religious duties because others did so,

The Flower of the Family

and because she thought she must. Lucy and Helen, on the contrary, performed these same acts because it was their privilege so to do. With what cheerfulness and alacrity we sometimes see a child run to offer a flower to its mother! But how sluggishly, with what apparent difficulty, the same act is performed, when, instead of the lively emotion of love to its parent, there is only the principle of obedience to her commands in exercise!

Poor Mary Anna was always doing something to appease her conscience; and this was made necessary by her so frequently doing something to torture it. Sometimes for weeks together she would lead a perfectly worldly and thoughtless life; then she would have spasms of goodness, and nothing could be more ardent than her devotion. One day she was sure she did not deserve to be called a Christian, and on the next her mountain would stand strong, and she would say, "I shall never be moved!" Now there was doubtless a little true grace in her heart; but it was but a spark, and a slight breath of temptation threatened its existence. But feeble as it was, Mary Anna tried to warm and animate herself thereby, and she kept wondering why she was always so cheerless and benumbed. And all this time the great Fountain of light and life was open to her; she only needed to turn forever away from the contemplation of herself, to be henceforth vivified, strengthened, and filled with all the fullness of Christ. How strangely it would look to see a plant constantly employed in watching its own growth, and bemoaning itself on account of its tardy progress, when all it had to do was just to give itself up to the nurture of sun and rain, and the kindly influences of the soil to which it had been transplanted!

"I wish I had your happy disposition!" she one morning said to Lucy, as the two cousins entered the school-room. "But everything depends on temperament. I was born with a desponding temper, and I suppose there is no escaping it."

Lucy wanted very much to infuse into this cloudy mind some of her own sunshine, but she hesitated because she felt herself young and inexperienced.

"I was not born with a particularly happy disposition," she said. "Indeed, I think I used to suffer a great deal of either real or fancied misery."

The Flower of the Family

"And are you always happy now?"

"*Always!*" replied Lucy, emphatically.

"Oh, well, you have everything to make you so. Your uncle's family just bow down and worship you, and you have all sorts of elegances and comforts. Perhaps you would miss them a little if you should lose them."

Lucy was a little pained by these remarks. She felt that she could leave all these "elegances and comforts" cheerfully, should it be necessary. Her happiness was built on less perishable objects.

"Oh, Mary Anna!" said Helen, "I wish you could only catch a little of Lucy's faith! I wish you knew how very happy you might be if you would!"

Mary Anna sighed. This was one of her desponding days. She retired with a heavy heart to her desk, where amid her books she forgot for a season her depression. Indeed, she soon appeared cheerful and even merry. But Helen, who knew her well, perceived that her friend's mirth was only assumed, and that the comfortless expression was not long absent from her face.

"Ah! what can I do for her?" thought she. "I wish I might tell her how many real troubles Lucy has; then her cheerfulness would puzzle her, I'm sure: and she would see how well it is worth seeking."

Everything seemed to be going on prosperously with Lucy; but one evening, as they all sat variously occupied together, she suddenly fainted and fell from her chair. In a few moments she recovered herself, and would have resumed her lessons had her uncle allowed it. But he looked at her with anxiety, and ordered her to proceed at once to bed. Accordingly, Lucy was preparing to take leave for the night, when Helen, who had been not a little agitated and alarmed, cried out reproachfully: "Oh, Lucy! it all comes of those everlasting shirts!"

"What everlasting shirts?" inquired Mrs. Whittier.

"Oh, Helen! how could you?" cried Lucy. She ran from the room, and Helen was hurrying after her, but was detained by her father.

"Let your mother accompany Lucy," said he. "For my part, I wish to know the meaning of all these 'Oh, Lucy's!' and 'Oh, Helen's!' Come! What is it all about?"

"Indeed, papa, you must not ask me. It is a secret of Lucy's. I never meant to tell it. What I said just slipped out before I knew it."

"Upon my word," returned he, "it must be a mighty secret which you are not allowed to repeat. But your mother assuredly is a party to it?"

"No, papa; Lucy would not allow me to tell mamma."

"I hate mysteries," said her father, "and, above all things, the secrets of school-girls. I am sure there is something wrong in this affair. It is strange, indeed, in Lucy to confide to you matters you deem it your duty to conceal from us!"

Quite thrown off her guard, by hearing Lucy thus attacked, Helen proceeded to tell, in the most incoherent and eager manner, that Lucy had learned that her eldest brother, John, *would* go to sea, and that her mother was killing herself by working at night on his outfit; how, after writing in vain, to beseech him not to go, Lucy had undertaken, by way of relieving her mother, to make up his shirts; how she had bought, cut out, and made up eleven, and was now at work on the twelfth. That she had risen early and sat up late to do this, and finally, how she had conjured herself never to lisp a word on the subject.

During this story, her mother had returned to the parlor, looking grave and anxious, and Helen thought both her parents were hurt or displeased

"Lucy has shown great want of confidence in us," said they.

Helen looked on in dismay. She felt that Lucy had done wrong; but then it was an error of judgment; such an one as she might herself have fallen into. In fact, she was sure she should have done as Lucy had, in a like case.

"Mamma!" said she, encouraged by her own reflections, "I am sure you cannot blame Lucy for wanting to relieve her mother!"

"Certainly not. I admire her devotion as much as you can do. But she knew I would cheerfully have had this work done for her; and her keeping it such a secret, proves that she knew she was doing wrong."

"Oh, mamma! I told her you would have it done for her, but that always made her entreat me to say nothing to you about it. She said she should be ashamed to have you do anything more for her family, after all you had done."

The Flower of the Family

"*Nonsense!*" cried Mr. Whittier.

"*I* should feel just so in her circumstances, at any rate," cried Helen. "And I know both you and mamma would have thought it presuming in Lucy to come here and ask you to have John's shirts made up for him."

Her father laughed. "Well, keep cool! Keep cool! I am not inclined to send Lucy to the stocks, my dear."

But now Lucy, the very picture of sweetness and ingenuousness, came back to plead her own cause.

"I know I have done wrong, uncle," said she; "but at the time I did not see that I was wrong."

She had shed many tears, and looked pale and ill. Her uncle and aunt were touched, as they regarded her, and her aunt drew her into a comfortable seat at her side, while Helen threw herself at her feet, and kissed her hands again and again.

"Foolish child!" said her uncle, patting her on the head. "Did you think your aunt would refuse you the comfort of having this sewing done?"

"No, uncle, but—"

"But you thought she could not afford it?"

Lucy thought no such thing. She looked embarrassed and anxious.

"My dear Lucy," he continued, "too much gratitude annoys me far more than too little could. You need not feel so terribly burdened under the weight of what your aunt and myself are doing for you. What is it, after all? A matter of a few dollars and cents!"

Lucy allowed herself to be cheered by her uncle's attempt to cheer her, and by her aunt's and Helen's caresses; but there remained a sore spot about her heart still. It amounted almost to physical pain. Full of refined and sensitive feeling, and the daughter of a man who lacked, and would ever lack, abundance; how many mortifications had she met with! How many still lay before her! And yet a queen, with a worldly and proud spirit, might have envied this young girl, as she passed through life, and have given the very crown from her head and the sceptre from her hand, for the Christian fortitude and cheerful endurance with which, by its very discipline, Heaven was arming her.

"Which of the boys is this John?" asked her uncle.

The Flower of the Family

"He comes next to Hatty; he is about fourteen now. He got restless some time ago, and wanted to go to sea, but gave up going on finding how we all felt about it. But Arthur, who really seems older than John, has written me about it since; and not many weeks ago, mother wrote herself. She said she and father had never been so tried and perplexed, but that they had at last decided to let him go. It was after this that Arthur let me know how hard mother was working to get him ready, and how the labor and the anxiety had worn upon her. I made him promise to tell me exactly how things went on at home, for I know father and mother would try to keep all their trials and cares from me."

"But this John; why, was not he the little fellow who undertook to black my boots? He surely is not fit to go to sea."

"He has grown astonishingly fast since then they say; and feels as big as a man."

"But excuse me; if he isn't a fool, he's a rogue, I am sure. For he pretended to me, he thought himself made of dust, and I don't know what other nonsense."

Lucy laughed. "He *is* a real rogue," she said, "and until you know him well, you wouldn't know what to make of him."

"Has he any really bad habits?"

"Oh no, sir! he is only a little wild and restless. He is a bright boy about some things; but he never liked going to school, nor confinement of any kind. Arthur says he told father he felt *crowded* on the farm. He wanted more room."

"I fancy he would find himself more 'crowded' in a hammock at sea. I'll tell you what you may do— but stay, I'll do it myself; it is not safe for you to be sitting here, looking so pale. Go to bed, dear child, and I will write to your father about John. I do not doubt we shall devise something better for him than going to sea, at present at least."

Lucy thanked her uncle warmly, and went to bed with one care the less. For, however she had tried to leave John in the hands of God, she knew too well the temptations and dangers of the life of a boy at sea, to be free from great concern on his account.

Helen saw plainly that her parents loved Lucy better than ever, since this little occurrence. As for herself, her head was as full of plans as it could hold.

The Flower of the Family

"What if she should have a fortune left her? Would it not be delightful to send it all to Lucy's hard-working father?"

"Suppose some rich old man should meet Lucy in the street, admire her lovely face, take the trouble to inquire into her history, and then suddenly die, leaving her heiress to all his property? Stranger things had happened."

"What, if she should herself make up and send to Lucy's mother a great box of garments for those children?"

This last idea, it must be owned, had a matter-of-fact air about it, hardly worthy so brilliant an imagination as Helen's. Her mother, while she smiled at the first, thought favorably of the latter suggestion.

"But not at present," she added, as she saw Helen's eager countenance. "For it would perhaps annoy Lucy, now that she has been so disturbed about those shirts. By and by we will manage it so as to give her unmixed pleasure."

"Shall you let me make up the things, mamma?"

"I think not. There is that poor girl of whom we heard yesterday; she supports both herself and a blind mother by her needle. I will give her this work."

"Shall you do nothing yourself, then?"

"No, I think not."

Helen looked disappointed.

"I don't think there is much merit in giving things that it costs us no trouble to give," said she.

"There is no want of merit in it; is there?"

"Why, no, not exactly. But I was thinking, mamma, that if you and I should make up the things all ourselves, it would cost us some self-denial to do it, and—"

Her mother smiled.

"I see how it is," said she. "You wish to earn a right to think highly of yourself."

"Oh no, mamma! I do not, indeed!"

"I will not dispute this point with you, my dear. But tell me, what is your object in preparing this box for your aunt?"

"Why, to relieve her from sewing so much, and to please both her and Lucy."

"Well, and is not this object gained by the plan I propose? You see it is not a question of merit at all. The question is, how can

The Flower of the Family

we do most good? not, how can we secure most honor to ourselves?"

"Then there never can be any merit in your giving, mamma. You have only to put your hand in your pocket and take out the money."

"Well," returned her mother, smiling, "I ought to be thankful that the money is there when I want it, and that I have the heart to give it away when it is needed. But let me tell you, for your comfort, that I have to deny myself every hour the pleasure of relieving others, as I should like to do."

"But, mamma, does not the Bible urge us to do other things for the poor than just give them money?"

"Undoubtedly, my dear Helen. We were speaking now of only one case. You are confined by your studies at school and at home a very large portion of each day, and absolutely need refreshment and exercise during every spare moment. Otherwise I would allow you to make up as many garments as you chose. But you must wait, in patience, till the proper time comes. There will be some merit in that, my dear."

"Well, then, when I leave school I mean to spend all my time in sewing for poor people and fitting up boxes of clothing for them. And I will send cartloads of nice, comfortable things, to old women, and poor sickly girls, and neglected little children!"

Her mother would not check her youthful enthusiasm by even a look of dissent or of doubt.

Her father now threw down his paper and called Helen to come to him. "When I was a young man," said he, "I heard some friends of mine speaking of a young lady in the neighborhood; and one of them said to me, 'Whittier, you are a good-looking fellow; why don't you deliver this damsel from the hands of the cross old lady who has charge of her? She is an heiress, it is said.'

"Now, I had a notion in my young head, that heiresses were, of necessity, proud, heartless, and worldly, so I took no notice of the conversation, although I unavoidably listened to it."

" 'They say this aunt is a stingy old soul, who won't let the poor girl spend a penny. But at night, when the old lady is in bed, she sits up and makes garments for the poor in the neighborhood with her own hands.' "

The Flower of the Family

"Several of the young men laughed and shrugged their shoulders. For my part, I thought such a maiden, without a penny in her pocket, would be a richer treasure to me than many another, with her weight in gold at my disposal. And, as it happened, I met, admired, and loved her, and even asked her to become my wife."

"And what did she say, papa?"

"You can ask her yourself," he answered, pointing to the corner where her mother sat, smiling and shaking her head at him.

"Oh, mamma!" cried Helen, throwing herself upon her knees at her mother's feet, and kissing the hands which had so many years ago done these works of mercy, "how I love you! How glad I am that papa married you!"

She could find no words with which to express her surprise and pleasure.

"My dear Helen, you must not think of my beloved aunt as a 'stingy old soul!' That was just the folly of those young men, you know!"

Her father looked affectionately upon them both, and even got up to kiss one of those hands Helen was caressing.

The influence of this hour followed Helen through life. Again and again, when denying herself a passing pleasure for the sake of administering to the wants of others, the image of her mother, an unworldly, loving young girl, came and stood as it were by her side, smiled upon her at her task, and made it sunshine in the very depths of her heart!

"I must tell you one thing, however," added her mother, "of some importance. Before your father 'met, admired, and loved me,' every cent I possessed, with the exception of a small sum in the hands of Miss Prigott, was lost at sea. All my property, with that exception, was invested in a clumsy manner, so that even the insurance had not been renewed when it should have been. The very day after the insurance ran out, my worldly wealth sank like lead in the mighty waters."

"That's the best part of the story!" cried Helen. "I'm so glad papa married you for *yourself*, and not your money!"

"You're a romantic little thing," said her father. "What do you suppose people live on who haven't money?"

Helen did not know; nor did she much care.

"How came Miss Prigott with money of yours, mamma?"

"Oh, it happened so. At the time of my downfall, she was very kind; she came and stood by me when other friends grew cool: I shall never forget it. She even offered to divide her own property with me. But of course I could not allow her to do that."

"I hope I shall learn to like her after this, mamma."

"I hope so too, my dear; for, with all her oddities, she is a generous, kind-hearted woman and her life has been full of trouble."

CHAPTER 19

A Visit from Miss Prigott, and What it Led To

"What are these little odd-shaped things?" said Charles one day, approaching the table where Lucy sat writing.

She looked up and smiled.

"Little letters for the children," said she.

"Two, four, six, eight, nine! But some of them must be too young to read."

"They're just as pleased as if they could," said Lucy; and opening one of them, she showed him that it contained nothing but a host of paper babies, neatly painted; and paper furniture to match. "The baby can understand such a letter as that," said she.

"He'll tear them all up, and put the rest in his mouth and choke himself. You had better send him a hammer and some nails."

"I would, if they'd go in a letter."

"Well, what's in the next biggest letter?"

She opened it, and showed him a number of pictures that she had drawn for Horace.

"He'll throw them down the well."

"Perhaps you'll like this better, then!" and she opened a third little sheet, on which, with great care and patience, she had printed with her pen a miniature epistle in verse. Charles shouted with laughter as he read it, and was about seizing the five remaining letters, but Lucy put her hand over them. "You can't read those," said she.

"Oh, yes, I must," said he, seizing them and running off.

Lucy smiled, and went on with the letter she was writing, simply saying, "I know you won't read them, when you know I don't wish it."

The Flower of the Family

"There is no fun in trying to tease you," said he, throwing the letters down before her. "Now, if it had been Helen, she'd have screamed, and run after me, and we should have had a regular time of it."

"It puts me out of breath to run, and Miss Prigott says I mustn't."

"And I suppose you never do! Oh, no! Never hurry upstairs? I hope Miss Prigott will remember you in her will."

"What's that about 'Miss Prigott?'" cried a little fine voice; and that lady came smiling in, in the most unexpected manner. Charles lost no time in retreating, under pretense of calling his mother and Lucy rose to meet the little woman, very cordially.

"It is a long time since I've seen you," said she. "My aunt said yesterday, you had quite forsaken us."

"I've come to spend the day now, knowing you would be at home from school on Saturday. And so you must just put away all this writing, and sit down with me, unless you think the old woman's company will be tedious."

Every school-girl knows the value of Saturday; few would consent to sacrifice one to a Miss Prigott. Lucy looked dismayed for a moment at the prospect, but would not let herself look so longer.

"Can't I give up one day?" thought she, as she prepared to lay aside books and papers on which her heart was intent. She had planned to do so much this day, and it was not easy for her at once to change these plans; her mind felt stiff, and would not turn readily to a new class of interests. But she ran— yes, she *ran* up to her room, found her stocking-basket, and came smiling back, saying to herself, "It's well to find out how selfish one is, now and then."

"There, give those to me," said Miss Prigott. "I brought my thimble on purpose."

"Oh, I shouldn't like to have you mend my stockings."

"I shall do it, nevertheless; and you, meanwhile, are to sit down here by my side and tell me all about your school. For I hear they are spoiling you there, and making you think yourself a genius."

"I haven't begun to think so yet; but I am afraid I shall, if I get beyond mending my own clothes."

"Nonsense, my dear. Now, what are your studies?"

"French, for one."

"What's the use of that? Who do you ever meet that can't talk English?"

"I meet no one now, but I may. And in these days, no one thinks of not reading French, at least."

"Well, what next?"

"Latin."

"And who talks Latin, pray?"

"No one; it is a dead language. But I study it in the hope of being of use to my brothers in time."

"Well; one tongue is as much as I can master. If yours is as troublesome as mine, I wonder you want to give it a helping hand. I suppose you study Greek and Hebrew, too."

"I don't yet; but perhaps I shall one of these days. Intellectual Philosophy comes next."

"But don't you study grammar?"

"Not English grammar. Mr. Jackson says that is the last study to be taken up, rather than the first— as at most schools."

"I suppose, then, his pupils learn their A B C's after they've learned to read."

"We have none so young; perhaps they would, if we had," said Lucy, smiling.

"How do you expect to speak correctly, if you do not study grammar?"

"By listening to those who speak good English, I suppose. And then our compositions are corrected every week, and mistakes there are pointed out to us."

"Everything goes backward nowadays!" sighed Miss Prigott. "I expect to see babies taught to fly before they can run. Though I hope I shan't live so long."

"I think aunt does not know you are here," said Lucy. "I'll go up to her room and see."

"Have you told me all your studies?"

"No; I'll tell the rest when I come back."

"I dare say you don't touch a needle at your school."

"Oh, no! we have only gentlemen as teachers!"

Lucy returned in a few moments with other work, and sat down again near Miss Prigott, who was getting a little deaf.

"Aunt will be down presently," said she.

The Flower of the Family

"What have you got there? Let me look at it. How beautifully you sew!"

"I am quite proud of my sewing," she answered.

"Proud! that's very wrong, my dear."

"Well, I am. And of my bread, too. Because I had no taste for such things, and disliked doing them excessively; and when I sew well, or make good bread, or anything of the sort, I know it is clear gain on myself. So much wild land cultivated and made useful."

Miss Prigott meditated on this speech, and turned it over and over in her little mind; but did not understand it at all. Lucy was glad to see her aunt come in; and took refuge behind the large piece of work on which she was occupied.

"Do you still like your boarding-place?" asked Mrs. Whittier, after welcoming her guest.

"Yes; but my life is very solitary. I think of taking a house on that account. To tell the truth, I came to consult you about it. I suppose you wonder how I have been so busy as to have no time to come to see you. But my time has been fully occupied, I assure you. Now guess, if you can, what I've been doing. But I may as well tell you, first as last. I've been building a house."

Her hearers were as much surprised as she wished them to be; and she was herself so overcome by the shock she felt she had given them, that she was obliged to fan herself into breath again.

"Yes, I have built a house. All last summer, while you were idling in the country, my house was going up; by the first of May it will be habitable. Every brick I selected with my own hands; I found fault with every board; and examined every nail. I lost seven pounds of flesh, by coming into town so often to remind the workmen that I was in a hurry, and to watch them, lest they should squander away their time. They treated me very ill, indeed, and once began to joke in my hearing, and say to each other, they hoped I had picked out my husband as carefully as I did my bricks and nails. I assure you I never went nigh them again."

"I wonder we have not heard of your exploits," said Mrs. Whittier, trying not to laugh.

"Ah, I know how to keep a secret! I've not lived fifty years for nothing. I contracted for the house under a feigned name."

The Flower of the Family

"And what was that?" asked Helen, who had entered in the midst of the conversation, and had been pinching Lucy to make her laugh, ever since.

"Mrs. Trogip, my dear."

"That's the very house papa was describing to us a few weeks ago!" cried Helen.

"What did he think of it, my dear?"

"Oh, he said it was a fine house— to look at," she added in a low voice, for she did not wish to inform poor Miss Prigott that he had pronounced it badly built.

"But, my dear Miss Prigott," said Mrs. Whittier, "you surely don't intend to occupy that great house by yourself."

"We shall see," said Miss Prigott, mysteriously.

"I do believe she's going to offer herself to somebody," whispered Helen to Lucy.

"I've been half-distracted with the way people have served me," continued Miss Prigott. "One man sent me a card on which he stated that he could furnish wedding-cake cheaper and better than any in the world; another sent word at what rate he could provide white gloves by the dozen. All those saucy clerks at Horton's asked, whenever I ordered anything, 'Shall I send the bill to Mr.__?' as if any Mr. in the world had the settling of *my* affairs!"

"But this looks really suspicious," said Mrs. Whittier. "I certainly think it must be inquired into. Who can be the happy man?"

Miss Prigott was in ecstasies; but not one word further would she declare, and Helen, hearing her father in the hall, rushed out, laughing, to tell him the news.

"Papa, don't you think Miss Prigott is going to be married?" she said, as well as she could between her paroxysms of laughter.

"Nonsense!" was the brief response, as Mr. Whittier took off his coat and gloves.

"She is, papa, she really is. And she's built a house for him to live in. That very house you were telling us about!"

"I shall not believe it till I see the man, and hear him own it," he replied.

When Helen returned to the parlor, she found Miss Prigott's ecstasies subsiding sufficiently to enable her to go on with a description of her house, quite coherently. In addition to the usual rooms, there was to be a library well filled with books; all the works of Baxter, Owen, Bunyan and other good men were to be there, and a host of others, besides.

"The happy man must be a minister," said Mrs. Whittier, willing to indulge Miss Prigott in riding her hobby as long as she chose.

"You are as wide of the mark as ever," was the answer. "My dear Lucy, you will ruin your eyes over that fine stitching. If I had used my eyes in that way in my youth, where would they be in my age? Besides, I want you to keep your eyes in good order; for I have some furniture yet to purchase, on which I want your judgment."

"But I know nothing whatever about furniture," said Lucy, in astonishment.

"Then it is time you should learn, my love," said Miss Prigott sharply.

"She has made a whole set of chairs and tables," said Charles.

"Has made what, did you say? Chairs and tables? Why, my dear Lucy, is there anything you don't do? Did you not find it very hard work?"

Lucy explained that the articles in question were made of paper, and required little skill; and she was glad to hear dinner announced, and to escape the expressions of amazement she saw shaping themselves on Miss Prigott's lips, by a precipitate retreat to the dining-room. She found it so irksome to have every little thing she said or did, commented on and praised; it made her feel foolish and ashamed. Yet she might have been proud, according to her own theory, for the pleasures she had prepared for the little boys at home. It had cost her both time and labor; and was indeed a work of love, worthy to be classed with the "cup of cold water."

As they sat at the dinner-table, Mr. Whittier said to Miss Prigott, "I hope you have lost nothing by the failure of that foolish Savings' Bank?"

"Not a penny!" she answered. "But many a poor old woman has."

The Flower of the Family

"I had a trifle there myself," said Mr. Whittier. "Fortunately, not much. It was my boy's; and I would gladly have lost a greater sum elsewhere.

"Ah! that was a fine boy!" said Miss Prigott. "Haven't I heard you say his grandfather wished to educate him?"

"Very likely; for that was the case. I intended the sum he left him should pass to your little brother, Lucy; it just occurs to me that I had not transferred it to him."

The presence of a little foot upon his own, under the table, recalled Mr. Whittier's thoughts; he looked embarrassed, and began to say, in a confused way, that of course it made no difference; there was more money in the world than that promised Arthur; but it was too late. Lucy's quick comprehension took in the whole matter at a glance. Some things in Arthur's letters had puzzled her; he had hinted at some difficulties in the way of his education, which she could not understand: everything was plain now; her uncle had forgotten to send her grandfather's legacy to Arthur, and now it was all gone! While she had been perfectly showered with luxuries, and was so happy at school, and so at ease about Arthur, he had been unable to pay his school-bills, or buy necessary books: what a year of mortifications and disappointments it must have been to him and to her mother! Her mind was able to seize only one point of relief, there was the watch Miss Prigott had given her; with that she could supply Arthur's present wants, and have something left for the future. She went to her room the moment dinner was over, and speedily dressed herself for going out; then, taking the watch in her hand, she quietly left the house, and was driving down Broadway before she had collected her scattered thoughts.

"I am almost afraid!" she said to herself. "I may be going on a foolish, or even wicked errand. Oh, may God direct me, and keep me from doing wrong!"

But when she entered the brilliant establishment where the watch had been purchased, her courage failed. She lingered near the door: it was not too late to return; but no— the image of Arthur, tall and slender, and not strong, came and stood by her side and gave her courage; she advanced, and offered the watch for sale. Hardly had she done so, when Dr. Thornton approached her, with an air of surprise, under which she shrank.

The Flower of the Family

"May I ask the meaning of this?" he asked kindly, and in a low voice.

She hesitated. "Excuse me, I should not have asked," he said, and was moving away, but she detained him.

"It is nothing wrong, I hope; nothing I should be ashamed to have you know; but I could not explain it here. Only, pray don't think my uncle does not provide me with all I need. I do not want anything for myself; it is for some one else."

He stood by her side in silence, but with kindness still, and in a few minutes the precious money was in her hands. Yes, precious; for it should fly as on the wings of the wind to Arthur.

"If my uncle hears of this, it should be from me," she said to Dr. Thornton, as they passed into the street; "and no other person has a right to know it."

He smiled. "I think you may trust me," he said; and so they parted. Lucy soon reached home. It was getting late, and as she entered the house, the bell was ringing for tea. She hastily laid aside her shawl and bonnet, and joined the family. To her relief, she found they had not missed her, or, at least, had fancied her in her room. But after Miss Prigott had taken her departure, and she had leisure for reflection, she began to feel disturbed by a new question. Ought she not to go frankly to her uncle, and tell him what she had done? But should she do that, would he not feel that she recklessly had chosen to give him pain? "There is a right and a wrong to this matter," she thought. "Oh, if I only knew what I ought to do, I think I would do it, cost what it might!" She could hardly sleep in this doubtful state; and all the next day she felt perplexed. But by degrees it began to be very plain that she owed it to her uncle to confess the whole transaction.

Her mind once made up, she lost no time in taking him aside, and laying before him the facts of the case:

"Uncle, I have done something that I am not sure you will approve. I have sold my watch."

"To whom?"

"To Mr. Kent, of whom it was bought; and for a trifle less than the original price."

"It is just what I expected of you, Lucy," said he. "And, let me tell you, you have lost nothing by confessing to me that you have sold it. I saw you hurry off, after dinner; and as it needed no enlightenment to tell where you had gone, I followed you."

"Are you displeased with me, uncle? Have I done wrong?"

"I am displeased with myself for giving you occasion to sacrifice your watch, my dear. I will not say it was quite right for you to run off, without consulting any of us, and sell Miss Prigott's gift. But I knew how you felt about it, and ought to have given you my advice unasked."

"Dear uncle, when I first showed it to you, I wanted to ask if I might exchange it for a less expensive one; but I said all I dared. And I was writing home yesterday morning; and that made me think, as it always does, how I should delight to take them all by surprise, by sending them something not any heavier than pictures and paper-babies, but worth a good deal more."

Her uncle smiled, and asked, "How old is Arthur now?"

"He is thirteen; there is only a year between him and John."

"Has he begun to fit for college?"

"Yes, sir; he recites to our minister a part of the time, but he goes to school besides."

"Well, I think I shall remember my promises better in future. The fact is, I had got this boy so mixed up in my mind with my own little Arthur, that I was thinking it would be years before he'd need that money; and meanwhile it could accumulate. And now, to make all fair and square between us, you must make me one promise; and if you make and keep it, I'll overlook your hair-brained scamper down Broadway this afternoon."

Lucy smiled, and promised.

"Understand, then, that when I get ready— I am not now, but I shall be some time— I am to make you a present you'll neither refuse, nor give way, nor sell."

"I thought I wouldn't press her about that watch," he said afterwards, to Mrs. Whittier; "the poor child behaved very well about it, on the whole; and I like her all the better that she is not yet quite perfect. It was a pretty bold step to take. But the watch was her own; she had a right to do what she pleased with it. And if Miss Prigott ever finds it out, I'll lay a flattering unction to her soul that will make it young again. The truth is, it was a very unsuitable present. So showy and expensive an article, to a young girl fresh from the country, was ridiculous."

The Flower of the Family

"Do you think Lucy will be willing to spend the summer with us?" asked Mrs. Whittier.

"I don't know. Let me see; it is a year and a few months since she came. No; she ought to spend the summer vacation at home. She will not be happy without seeing them all; nor they without seeing her."

"If she goes home, I fear she'll not return."

"Oh, there's no danger of that. Such a passion for books I never saw before. Mr. Jackson says he never had such a pupil; she is going on very rapidly."

"But if she goes home, she will see how much she is wanted there; and I know just how it will be. She'll sit down and sew from morning till night, or drudge about house; and they'll tell her every little trouble they've had during her absence; and the end of it will be, she'll return, if she comes at all, entirely unfit for school, as she was when she came here."

"I wish she was my child!" said Mr. Whittier.

"So do I! It does seem sad to think of such a girl as she is, being buried in the country."

"She's going to make a beautiful woman."

"Better than that! A good and an accomplished one."

CHAPTER 20

Every Life has its Romance

LUCY FOLDED AND SEALED THE LETTER, in which the fruits of her watch lay snugly folded, with a beating heart. She longed to fly home, and be herself the bearer of the relief she knew the unconscious sheet of paper could carry, but not appreciate. Helen met her—half running, half dancing— with it in her hand, and was not much surprised to feel herself caught and kissed, after a glance at the radiant face that fairly shone with happiness.

"Always smiling," said she. "I do think you are the happiest creature I ever saw."

Lucy always liked to be called a happy person; and another kiss told Helen so.

"It is time for school," said Helen; "are you ready?"

"Just let me give this letter to uncle, first."

"He's gone. He went some time ago."

"Oh dear! Then my letter won't go by to-day's mail! Oh, how I wish I had mailed it on Saturday night!"

"Never mind. It will go just as safely to-morrow. Come; it is high time for school."

Lucy was greatly disappointed; she felt like crying almost, and a wild fancy shot across her mind relative to setting off homeward on foot. The loving heart could certainly reach home sooner than the mail; if alas! it need not travel in that slow, uncertain coach, a frail body! Horses could go faster than that; and so could steam.

"Mamma is calling you, Lucy," said Helen.

"Your uncle did not forget your letter, my dear," said Mrs. Whittier. "He is going to send for it in a few hours; and, in the

The Flower of the Family

meantime, I am to write to your mother, myself. Shall I tell you what about?"

"We shall be late at school, mamma," said Helen. "Lucy can hear just as well when we get home. Can't you, Lucy?"

"If you please, aunt," said Lucy, feeling herself almost carried off by Helen, who besides her dread of being late, had a strong desire that her mother's letter should go before its subject should be revealed.

On their return, the letters had gone— but, at the dinner-table, Lucy's curiosity was satisfied by her aunt.

"We have been thinking, dear Lucy, that you would wish to spend the summer vacation at home, and it is very natural you should. But your uncle and I talked it over last night, and again this morning; and we have decided to write to your mother, and ask her to come here and make us a visit, and then to allow us to take you with us, as we did last summer. The sea air is so good for you; and you have been studying so hard!"

Lucy reflected a little before she replied. She felt that it would do her mother a world of good for once to leave home and all its cares, and change scene and air; but would she consent to do it? If so, her own duty was plain; otherwise, it did seem very hard to give up seeing them all for another year.

"Dear aunt, how very kind you are! you think of everything," she said. "I wish mother could come here; I am sure you would like her. And she would enjoy being here. But it is so many, many years since she left home, even for one day! Not since I can remember."

"You are so aged," said her uncle.

"I was afraid to let you hear mamma's plan," said Helen. "I knew you wanted to see Arthur and Hatty, and all of them, so much."

Lucy made no answer. She had formed no definite plan about going home; but had rather, in her own mind, taken it for granted she was to go.

"Let us drop the subject for the present," said her aunt, observing her; "there are still two months before vacation, and it is not necessary to decide on anything at present."

Lucy found the subject not easily dropped. It clung to her wherever she went, and however she busied herself, especially on Saturdays and Sundays; those days in which home sickness weekly revenges itself for the partial respite it has given during the other five. She was, therefore, less sorry to find herself dragged by Miss Prigott from shop to shop, to help her examine carpets, tables, chairs, and even pictures; for thus one of her hard days was softened every week, since there was comfort in giving pleasure, irksome as was the labor involved in it.

"How worn-out you look!" cried Helen, as one day Lucy returned from such an expedition. "I wonder how you can let yourself be served so! This is the fourth Saturday you have been under her thumb."

"She has been very kind to me," said Lucy; "and I am glad to have an opportunity of gratifying her. You know aunt advised me to go. But I know no more about carpets and curtains than a kitten. To-day, though, I've seen beautiful things; pictures and writing-desks, and the funniest little nests of tables; and the moment I said I liked what I saw, Miss Prigott bought it, till I hardly dared open my mouth. One room, in particular, she says, is to be furnished exactly to my taste. She wants you to go with me on next Saturday to see the house."

"So she's really going to let us see it at last, is she? But I can't go on Saturday, for Mary Anna Milman is coming to spend the day: and she always comes early."

"Could not she go with us? I dare say she would like to go. Miss Prigott is to call for us in her carriage. I forgot to tell you, she's bought a new carriage and horses; and she wants your father to see them."

"Well; when I get married, I hope I sha'n't be left to build a house, and buy horses and carriages for my husband."

"Oh, I don't think she's going to be married."

"But, of course, she doesn't expect to live all alone in that large house. I mean to ask her, if I go on Saturday, and make her tell me. Dear me! who would want to live with her! Should you?"

"I'll tell you when she asks me," said Lucy, laughing.

"It is almost five weeks since I have heard from home," she said, after a pause.

"I thought you received letters soon after you and mamma wrote last."

The Flower of the Family

"Yes, I did; the last of that week. It is four, then, since I heard. But I thought mother would write as soon as she received aunt's letter, to say nothing of mine. I begin to be afraid some one is sick."

"No news is safe news," said Helen. "Of course they would write if anything was the matter. But here comes papa, with his hands full of letters."

"Two for Lucy!" he cried, coming cheerily in, "and one for Helen; and one for you, my dear," he added, as Mrs. Whittier entered, "which I've taken the liberty of opening and reading."

"From your sister, I suppose," said Mrs. Whittier; "and as you've read it, you may tell me what its contents are, for dinner is ready."

"The contents are too numerous to mention," he answered. "They have had sickness, or she would have written sooner."

"One of my letters is three weeks old," said Lucy. "It was written the very day they received mine. It went safely," she added, in a low voice, to her uncle, whose face asked the question.

"Who has been sick, dear?" asked her aunt.

"Three of the children have had the measles severely, Arthur says. The three youngest were all sick together. Poor mother must be all worn out."

"She says she cannot possibly decide at present whether she can come to see us. But that she is quite willing to let you remain, at all events."

"I didn't want her to be willing!" thought Lucy. But when, after dinner, she had time to read Arthur's letter, its cheerful, relieved tone revived her spirits. The eagerness with which he thanked her for the money she had sent home, showed her how much he had been embarrassed by the want of it. He said, too, that his uncle had written to their father about John, and had promised to find something for him to do in the fall, which would be more profitable than going to sea. He told her, too, what progress he had made in his studies, and how happy and grateful he was. "Nobody in the world has so much to be thankful for!" he said, as he closed his letter. Lucy thought she could say the same. And the next week passed away speedily; for happiness makes time travel fast, as everybody knows. On the following Saturday, Miss

The Flower of the Family

Prigott made her appearance, carriage and all; and Helen, Lucy, and Mary Anna were driven to see the house. They went in fine spirits; and everything in the house and about it was "splendid," or "lovely," or "delightful."

"Now, you shall see the rooms Lucy furnished," said Miss Prigott, throwing open the doors of two hitherto closed apartments.

One of these was a sleeping-room, simply furnished, but in perfect taste; and adjoining it was another, fitted as a little library. Books and pictures, and a tempting rosewood desk, made this room attractive.

"Why, here is the Madonna I liked so much!" said Helen. "I saw one at Mr. Ripley's, one day last fall. And oh, what a delightful desk! Places for everything! Room for such hosts of papers! And, Mary Anna, do look at these prints! But sit in this chair first. Isn't it nice! Oh, Miss Prigott! are these the rooms you are to occupy yourself?"

"No, my dear; they would not suit an old woman. They are for a young lady."

"What young lady did you say? " asked Helen, playfully.

"Oh, that is a secret. I have not told her name. But these two rooms and their contents are for her. She is fond of study, and I thought it would be pleasant for her to have a place where she could always be quiet; and then I decided to have pretty things about her, to make her cheerful. And she likes pictures; so I ordered some. Outlandish things they are; women holding babies on their laps, and all that, but people nowadays seem to fancy them."

"Why, those are Madonnas," said Helen. "But do look at Lucy! There she sits, as comfortable as you please, reading, as if her life depended on it. Lucy!"

Lucy looked up from her book, and smiled.

"This is a charming room!" said she.

"I hoped you would like it!" said Miss Prigott rubbing her hands. "And how do you think the carpet looks, now it is down?"

"Very nicely, indeed."

"And you think the rooms pleasant? I am very glad," Miss Prigott said again. "And now you may go. By next Saturday I

The Flower of the Family

hope to be quite settled and you must all come and spend the day. Bring your work, and do just as you would at home."

As they entered the carriage, Miss Prigott detained Lucy a moment, to give her a slip of paper. "You'll find the name of that young lady who is to be my daughter, on this paper," said she. "Don't let those girls see it just yet."

They drove off, and Mary Anna and Helen could talk of nothing but those mysterious rooms.

"She is going to marry a widower with a literary daughter, I am almost sure," said Helen.

"Mr. Stanley is a widower, and his daughter is a regular book-worm," said Mary Anna.

"Oh, but she is almost as old as Miss Prigott. She said a young lady."

Meanwhile Lucy peeped privately at the paper in her hand, and read there, to her astonishment, the words, "Sweet Lucy Grant." Her hand closed over it. She felt, for the moment, as if Miss Prigott's grasp thus clasped and crumpled her.

"Why, Lucy, are you faint?" cried Helen, "you look so pale!"

"No; I am not faint; and I don't *feel* pale."

"You don't now; but you certainly did when I spoke."

"Did you ever hear any one say that Miss Prigott had been insane?" asked Mary Anna.

"No; but everybody says she is odd: as odd as she can be. She is certainly to be pitied, for I'm sure she can't help it."

"My mother knows all about her," continued Mary Anna, "and I will tell you what she told me; but you must not repeat it. Lucy, was not your father's name Robert?"

"Yes; but what has that to do with Miss Prigott?'

"A great deal; as you will see. In the days of her youth, she knew him very well; and as she was so rich, some young men treated her with great attention, notwithstanding she was not very attractive otherwise. Your father was studying theology at that time, and she took a fancy to him, and began to send him presents anonymously. There was no end to the books and clothes she gave him. At first he would not use them, not knowing whence they came; but some of his friends at last persuaded him that this was wrong; so by degrees he appeared out in some of the things, and Miss Prigott was in ecstasies. It

The Flower of the Family

went on so for a year or two; but by that time she began to get tired of keeping her secret, and confided it to a friend, who confided it to somebody else, and soon after it reached your father's ears. He immediately went to Miss Prigott and insisted on knowing whether these reports were true; and it was said she offered herself to him on the spot. At any rate, he came from the interview looking as pale as possible; and she never was the same from that day. She always said he behaved honorably through the whole affair, and that she had no one but herself to blame."

"Soon after, she had a fever, and kept calling for him all the time. She was an orphan; and your father felt so much for her, and there was so much talk about the affair, that his health really suffered. He wanted to send back the books and other things; but he was advised not to do it, she was in such a sad, enfeebled state of mind."

Lucy remembered that her mother had said in one of her letters, "We wish you to do everything in your power for the gratification of Miss Prigott. We have special reasons for this wish: do not forget it." Mary Anna's story threw light upon many points in Miss Prigott's character, as well as on this remark; but it made the bit of paper she held in her hand burn like fire into her heart.

"I shall not respect poor Miss Prigott any the less for what you have told me," she said. "But I am not sure I ought to have let you tell it."

"Almost everybody knows she has had a 'disappointment,'" said Helen. "But I think it's quite interesting to know all about it."

"Don't you wish your father had married her?" asked Mary Anna. "You would have been as rich as could be by this time."

Helen laughed; but Lucy felt pained. It seemed to her a most amiable weakness in Miss Prigott to fall in love with her father. She was glad when they reached home, when she could reflect on all the incidents of the morning; and as soon as an opportunity offered, she went to her aunt.

"The girls have been giving me an account of their morning adventures," said Mrs. Whittier, "why did not you come with them?"

"I wanted to see you alone, aunt. Did they tell you about those rooms she has fitted up so nicely?"

"Yes; and that they are for some unknown young lady."

"Just as we were coming away, she put this paper into my hands, saying I should find the name of the young lady upon it."

Her aunt took the paper, and laughed heartily as she read the words, "Sweet Lucy Grant."

"What nonsense!" said she. "It is not possible she thinks you are going there to live with her! I never heard of such a thing!"

"But she has furnished those rooms exactly to my taste; everything there I had selected, not dreaming what was coming; and she seems to be so sure I am coming. Oh, aunt! it makes me wish I had never left home!"

"Why, how flushed and excited you are, my dear child! Do you suppose we would allow you to go and bury yourself alive in a tomb because somebody had been silly enough to build one for the purpose? And I do not really believe Miss Prigott expects you to do it. She only wanted to see what you would say."

Lucy half believed her aunt for the time, and went away relieved. But in the evening there came a long letter from Miss Prigott, in which, in the most pathetic manner, she described her long, lonely life, and told Lucy how happy she could now make its closing years; and conjured her to come and begin this work of mercy.

Poor Lucy cried herself sick over it. A romantic notion that she ought to sacrifice herself to Miss Prigott, who had suffered so much, whose life had been so cheerless and lonely, well-nigh carried off her judgment by storm. It was fortunate for her that in this emergency she was not left to act for herself.

Her uncle went to Miss Prigott at once, and settled the question; proposing, however, that Lucy should spend a few weeks in the pet rooms prepared for her, call them hers, and from time to time, as years passed, use them as such. With many tears, Miss Prigott yielded; declaring that from the outset she had wished, rather than expected, to secure Lucy for herself. Lucy went to her early on the following Monday, and devoted every leisure moment to her comfort and pleasure. They were some of the happiest weeks she had ever spent.

CHAPTER 21

A Not Agreeable Surprise

A FEW DAYS AFTER HER RETURN to her uncle's, Lucy received letters from home. She went to her own room to read them; Helen saw her kissing them all the way upstairs. She walked thoughtfully herself to her mother's room, where she found her busy with Charles, who was trying to impress upon her mind the expediency of the purchase of a certain horse for his special benefit.

"Lucy has letters from home, mamma," said Helen

"Is that the reason you look so forlorn?" asked Charles.

"I did not know I looked forlorn. I was thinking, however, that it is not likely Lucy will be contented to spend the summer with us. I long to know what her mother will say about it."

"I am afraid we are all getting selfish in regard to Lucy," said Mrs. Whittier.

"Do you think they miss her at home?"

"Oh, yes, of course they do. But as to the mere work, there's Rebecca, you know, who is older than Lucy. And then, where there are so many children, they help each other."

"But they can hardly miss her as we shall when she leaves us. I do love her so dearly! And it seems exactly as if I had always known her; if she were my own sister, I could not love her better. Oh, how dreadful it will be when she leaves us! I don't believe they miss her!" said Helen.

"Oh yes, they do!" cried Charles. "I have been there, and know all about it. It was nothing but Lucy, Lucy, from morning till night. Lucy must dress the baby, and Lucy must comb and brush all the heads— all the ten heads! and Lucy must see that the pot boiled, and Lucy must fit all the work for the other girls; and, in

The Flower of the Family

fact, Lucy was everywhere, and doing everything at once. I declare, it tires me to think of it! Rebecca was so slow and so dull! and Hatty! that Hatty was romping round, and making blunders, and looking at herself in the glass!"

"Oh, Charles!"

"It is true, every word; and you may ask father if it is not."

Helen sighed. "I believe it will break my heart if she leaves us," said she.

"Break your heart! Oh, Helen! what a face! I wish I could catch that expression, frame it, and hang it upon the wall," cried Charles.

"What expression?" asked Helen.

"Why, the expression of your face! Look here! This is the way you looked. Such a countenance! Now, for my part, I don't mean to let Lucy go home at all. There are ten left, and they don't need her."

"Mamma! I do wish Lucy would never go home!" said Helen. "I do want a sister so very much! and she is so happy here; and you and papa are so fond of her!"

Her mother smiled, and made a faint effort to be prudent, and not to reveal the secret plans of which Lucy had been so long the object. But it was of no use; almost before she knew it, she had said:

"Your father is very anxious to keep her with us, and we have written to your uncle about it; but I was not to tell you that."

Helen's lively imagination caught her up, and ran away with her, as these words fell from her mother's lips. In a twinkling of an eye she flew from the council of war held between her own and Lucy's parents, onward to that time when, young women grown, she and her beloved adopted sister should go hand-in-hand as ministering spirits to the needy, the neglected, and the heavy-laden to the end of their days. She was aroused from her reverie by Lucy's voice.

"Why, Lucy! you have been crying," she exclaimed.

"I ought to be ashamed of myself for that," replied Lucy, trying to smile away her tears. "But I was taken by surprise. Rebecca is going to be married."

"*Rebecca!*" repeated every one, in surprise and dismay.

"And must you go to the wedding?" asked Helen.

"Of course she will," said Charles, observing that Lucy seemed at a loss for an answer. "They can't get ready for such a great occasion without her."

"But will you be gone long, dear Lucy?" asked Helen, who dreaded even a short separation from her cousin.

Lucy looked down, and hesitated.

"If Rebecca leaves home, I shall be needed there," she said.

"You don't mean," cried Charles, "that you are going to take French leave of us? Just as we had all planned everything so nicely, and were to have you for our own sister! It is outrageous! Who under the sun wants to marry Rebecca? Why, I thought she was cut out for a nice little old maid, who would always stay at home, and take care of the rest."

"Oh, Charles!" whispered Helen, "you don't think what you are saying." And she drew Lucy away, in terror lest he should say something more.

"It is too bad!" cried Charles, the moment they were out of hearing. "Rebecca was meant for an old maid. She is ugly and dowdy and fussy, and now she is going to be married."

He looked around for his mother's sympathy, but she had vanished.

"Ah! I have been talking to the air, I declare! Well, it's all one! I've relieved my mind, at all events. And I know what I will do. I will write to Rebecca, and tell her she has mistaken her vocation; that she is ugly— however, that would not do. Nothing provokes a girl like telling her she is ugly. Indeed, nobody nowadays is more than plain. Well! perhaps father could do something about it. I'll just go and hunt him up, and see what he'll say."

While Charles thus consoled himself, Helen and Lucy read together the letter which had conveyed such unexpected tidings.

"Well!" said Lucy at last, "I have had a whole year at school with you! A whole happy year. And now I will go and take Rebecca's place in the family, and teach the children, and try to make things pleasant for mother. And, Helen, we will write to each other very often."

Helen sat in gloomy silence, and made no reply.

"And we will study together," continued Lucy. "I will study just what you do, and that will be so pleasant! Almost as pleasant as if we were near each other."

The Flower of the Family

Helen would not be comforted! She felt as if a great stone lay against her heart.

"We will read the same books, too," said Lucy. "And one of these days, when I get old, and stiff, and good for nothing, I'll come back to live with you."

"You won't have time to read, and you'll lose all you have learned. Oh, Lucy! I haven't any sister, and I thought I was to have you!"

"I ought to tell you then, dear Helen, that I could not have been so. I hoped to be able to go somewhere and teach, and so help educate my brothers. I am almost sure they won't be farmers. It is too hard work, unless there is a fortune to start with. A wearing, harassing, toilsome life! I felt as if I could not bear to see my brothers follow in poor father's footsteps."

"But if you taught school, you could not earn much."

"I thought I could help them along, one at a time. But it was not so to be: I had planned wrong."

"Rebecca is very young, to go and get married," said Helen, dolefully.

"She won't be married until October. Then she will be nearly twenty. She does not seem so old as that, because she has been sick a good deal. But I always thought John Wright would be carrying her off as soon as he could. Now, *I* shall be the old maid of the family, and you'll see what a nice, plump little one I'll be!"

Notwithstanding the playful tone in which Lucy spoke, Helen observed that her voice trembled. Looking up hastily, she perceived that the hopeful, cheerful manner was only assumed, and that she was in real distress.

Instantly forgetting her own grief, which now struck her as truly selfish, Helen strove by the tenderest expressions of sympathy to comfort and cheer Lucy.

"I will come and make you a long visit, whenever mamma will allow," said she. "Then I can take to you all the new books, and we will read them together. And who knows but all will come right again!"

"All *is* right, now," said Lucy, shaking off her depressions, and smiling once more like herself. "No one in this world can know what a disappointment this is to me, but I am sure it is right, and for the best!"

The Flower of the Family

Her aunt came in and kissed her tenderly.

"Oh, mamma! you have been crying, too!" cried Helen. "I could not imagine what made you run away and leave us so suddenly."

"You must not decide to leave us, until you have talked with your uncle, my dear Lucy," said her aunt. "I assure you that to lose you now will be the sorest trial we ever met with."

"What have I done, that they love me so?" thought Lucy. She felt grateful and humble, and that her lot was far from being one of unmixed trial and sorrow.

"Oh, here is papa!" cried Helen, "let us see what he says!"

"He says it won't do!" shouted Charles from the foot of the stairs.

"Why, Lucy!" said her uncle, "what is all this? Rebecca going to be married; you going to leave us? What have the two things to do with each other? You know you were to stay with us two years, at least; and you have been here little more than one. But set your hearts at rest, all of you; I shall write to Robert, and you will find he has no thought of taking Lucy home."

"But, uncle," said Lucy, "when Rebecca is gone, I shall be needed at home. Mother's health has been feeble for many years, and I know she has had a great deal of care thrown upon her by my absence Hatty is so young—"

"Is so selfish, you mean," interrupted Charles.

"Hatty is so young, and so full of spirits, and hates so to take care of children."

"Well, then, let the next one do that," said her uncle.

"Why, he is a boy!" said Lucy.

"Well, the next, then," said he.

"Oh, he is a boy, too! They are *all* boys after Hatty. And real boys, too," she added, laughing.

"I give you up, then, Lucy," said he sadly. "May God go with and bless you!"

"Why, father! did not you see them all when you were there?" asked Helen.

"Yes, I suppose I did; but I did not particularly notice whether they were boys or girls— why should I? But now, it seems, it is quite an important question."

The Flower of the Family

"Mamma!" cried Helen, suddenly growing cheerful again, "Lucy's mother will not let her stay at home! She will certainly send her back to us again. Mothers are never selfish, you know!"

With this consolatory thought, Helen sustained herself. She could not see those seven boys, of whom, like assorted needles, there were one or two of every size, from "ones," upward. She could not see the fourteen stockings, that every week a mother or a sister must mend; nor the jackets out at the elbow; nor the trowsers out at the knees. She could not conceive how often some of those little faces wanted washing; how much time it required every night to undress and get safely to bed, every morning to dress and get safely on their feet, these miniature men, who already by their helplessness and awkwardness proclaimed that they were not born to perform those works of indoor life which fall properly upon the sisters, mothers, and wives, for whom they are designed. But Lucy saw all these things, and more; and her heart turned itself homeward, resolutely and cheerfully.

CHAPTER 22

Shows the Clouds Dispersing

It was decided, after not a little discussion, that Lucy should not return home until the week of Rebecca's marriage. Lucy had no share in this plan; she would gladly have returned home at once, to help Rebecca as well as to see her before her departure. But her uncle would not listen to a word on the subject. The more sure he felt that, once home, she would not return, the more he was resolved to give her every possible pleasure before parting with her. Hasty preparations were therefore made for a journey, which was to commence in August, as soon as school closed. At Lucy's suggestion, Miss Prigott was invited to make one of the party; and Mrs. Lee, who was welcome everywhere, no sooner heard what was going on, than she invited herself. Everybody was busy; Mrs. Whittier planning for all the rest; Helen and Lucy with the last pressing labors of school; Miss Prigott flying round and getting into the way of each and all; and Mrs. Lee in conferences with Dr. Thornton, letter–writing abroad, and all manner of final arrangements.

When school closed, and Lucy went to take leave of Mr. Jackson, he expressed both astonishment and displeasure at the idea of her not returning; would not bid her good-bye; said he should write to her father and visit her uncle, and all sorts of extravagant things in her praise, none of which had much effect upon her, except to excite her gratitude.

"And now, Miss Lucy," said her uncle, as she came to the table, quite worn and tired after the leave-takings at school, "suppose you take the trouble to inquire where we are all going."

The Flower of the Family

"I did not know that I had not asked, uncle," she answered. "I have had so much to think of lately, that I have not had room in my head for journeys."

"And I suppose you care not a whit to know which way we are to go; north, east, south, or west?"

"Don't tease her, papa; please don't!" pleaded Helen. "Let me tell her; mayn't I? Oh, Lucy, you'll be so pleased! We're going to H __, to spend all the rest of the summer, and nearly the whole month of October. Only five miles from where you live! All of us, and Miss Prigott, and Mrs. Lee, and all her children! Papa has engaged rooms for us, or rather he wrote to your father to do so, and he has. Isn't it nice?"

"Now they'll see *my mother*!" was Lucy's first thought; "and Arthur! and all of them!"

"I knew you would be delighted!" continued Helen. "Papa would not let me tell you a moment sooner. And we can all go to Rebecca's wedding! And mamma has such hosts of things for her!"

Helen ran on, as fast as a nimble tongue could carry her, unfolding all the plans, and Lucy listened and applauded, while her uncle and aunt sat still and enjoyed her pleasure.

"Papa is to send the carriage, so we shall be able to come to see you very often, and have you to see us. And if he and mamma find H__ a pleasant place, perhaps they'll go there every summer!"

These anticipations of pleasure were not, however, to be realized. Mrs. Whittier was suddenly attacked with illness, which though not severe, rendered travelling unsafe; Helen would not be persuaded to leave her; and none of the party wished to do so. At almost the last moment it was arranged that Lucy should go home alone, and that the visit to H__ should be postponed to another season. Helen's anxiety about her mother sustained her through the leave-taking; but when Lucy bade farewell to her uncle, aunt, and cousins, Mrs. Lee and Miss Prigott, it seemed to them all, as they parted, that the ties of many years were broken. Not often is it thus in this world; yet there are cases where the affections seize upon a beloved object, and straightway it begins to seem that there never could have been a time when it was less dear, or the heart free from a sense of emptiness without it.

The Flower of the Family

Mrs. Whittier's illness proved somewhat obstinate, and all thought of going to the country this year was given up, unless a short trip to a quiet spot near home should be found desirable. She was confined to the sofa, and needed cheerful society, such as Helen usually afforded. But she did not afford it now. She felt as if one half herself at least had gone with Lucy, and her hopeful anticipations of a return in the fall began to cloud over. Her mother too gave her little encouragement. Helen saw that, however she desired Lucy's return, she did not really expect it. Indeed, there was but one point on which hope rested; it was that already seized by Helen's imagination: "Mothers are never selfish."

However true this may be, there is a limit to the strength of the most devoted mother; and the very qualities that rendered Lucy attractive abroad, made her doubly precious at home.

But this was Helen's first real trial. She had never known anything like it in her life. She went moping about, looking very dreary and desolate, and refusing to be comforted. Her mother therefore thought best to revive the favorite project so long deferred: the fitting out a great box of garments for the relief and pleasure of Lucy's mother. It had the desired effect; it made Helen forget herself, and leave off sighing and weeping, while it opened a channel into which her busy, loving heart could run and find peace. There was no end to the pleasure they all gained from this affair; even Charles enjoyed their consultations, and sat often with them in their councils. He was of use too, in selecting articles that would be of service to his cousins; for he had been among them, and knew something of their real wants. How vulgar to the uninitiated ear would a list of the contents of this box appear! How suggestive, to the wife and children of the Home Missionary, of privations long endured and patiently submitted to!

"You must contrive room for me to tuck in something," said Mr. Whittier, just as the last stout jacket had been coaxed into an incredibly small space.

"Oh, papa! you are too late!" cried Helen, triumphantly. "You can't even crowd in your love! Mamma and I have filled up every spare nook and corner with ours. Oh, I do wish you had come sooner to see all those nice jackets, from five years old

The Flower of the Family

upward! And those dear little plaid frocks for the baby! And those comical little shirts; all sizes: I never saw anything so funny! Mamma and I laughed till we cried, thinking how the children would look, hopping round trying on the things and dear Lucy helping them all, and never dreaming what there is for her, away down at the bottom of the box!"

"And what, pray, is that?" he asked, drawing Helen down to a seat upon his knee.

"Why, one of those little clocks, papa, that will be almost as useful as a watch; I don't know what you call it exactly, but it does not go by weights at all, and you can carry it in your travelling-bag, if necessary. Mamma thought of this, and we all think she will like it very much, as well as many other little things we have gathered among us."

"And so you won't let me send my budget in your box?" said her father.

"Indeed, papa, there is not room for anything more. But, let me see; if it is very small—"

Her father held between his finger and thumb a bit of paper, old and yellow, and uninviting to Helen's fancy.

"Oh, is that all?" said she. "Dear me! I thought you had been getting some splendid present!"

"Lucy does not want splendid things, my dear, and I assure you this little bit of paper is of some value."

Her mother came and looked over his shoulder and smiled.

"I knew you could not help doing that," said she. "I am *very* glad!"

Helen looked puzzled.

"It is an old note of your uncle's, my dear," explained her father, "and I intend to make Lucy a present of it."

"But what will she do with it, papa?"

"Throw it into the fire, I hope," he answered, enjoying Helen's bewildered air.

"My dear," said her mother, "that little bit of paper kept your father and uncle apart many years. The trouble began when they were young men, and before your father was a Christian. Uncle Robert was unfortunate; and never could pay what he owed us; and this debt has harassed him for years. Now you see, when this note is destroyed, there will be no debt; and poor Lucy, who has borne this yoke in her youth, will be forever at ease. It is but a trifle to your father; he can now afford to do it; and as for sending it in the box— that is just one of his jokes."

Helen threw her arms around her father's neck, and told him he was the very best man in the world, and, whether he believed himself such or not, he loved dearly to hear his darling child say so.

Not many days after the departure of the box Mary Anna Milman came to visit Helen.

"Now, do tell me," said she, as soon as she had seated herself, "about poor Lucy. I have so longed to hear all about it!"

"About what?" asked Helen: "her going home?"

"Yes. What could have induced her to leave you, and school, and all her comforts and pleasures here, to go home and nurse babies? It really is ridiculous! They all say so!"

"Was it ridiculous to love her mother?" asked Helen.

"Oh! of course not! But just as if some one could not have been got— some low person, good for nothing else— to go and take care of those children!"

"Oh, Mary Anna! some low person to take all the care of dear little children! To teach them, and—"

"Why, have not they a mother? I should think a mother would suffice as teacher, and anybody can wash children and put them to bed, I suppose."

"I don't know," said Helen, thoughtfully. "I have heard Lucy often speak of her mother's poor health as a hindrance in the way of her teaching. And she says a mother with such a family needs a daughter to lean on; to sympathize with her. She used to say no one could be more useful than a truly affectionate daughter."

"Well! she was a strange girl, to leave such a home as this!"

"Papa says he wishes there were more such girls in the world," said Helen.

"Your father said that! Why, I thought he wished beyond everything to keep Lucy here!"

"Yes, he did indeed wish to keep her, and so did we all. We loved her as if she had been always one of us. But we all feel that she did right in going; and that if she decides finally not to return, she will decide from a clear conviction of duty."

The Flower of the Family

"Well!" said Mary Anna, sighing, "I am sorry she has gone. I really did think I should catch some of her cheerful ways of looking at things, if I saw more of her. Seeing her always so serene, so unruffled, made me discontented with myself. I don't know how it is; but I am always in a ferment. You and Lucy always seem so happy!"

"Oh, don't class me with Lucy!" cried Helen. "I do not know any young person who deserves to be mentioned on the same day! I do think her the most faultless character I ever met with! Mamma thinks just as I do. She says Lucy has a peculiar charm and attraction about her— one that cannot be described, but which I am sure I felt from the outset. When I was with her, I seemed to be with almost an angel; there was something so pure and even heavenly in her air!"

"Heavenly! oh, Helen!"

"Yes, heavenly!" repeated Helen. "It was the result of the prayerful life she led. She prayed all the time, I do believe."

"And yet she always seemed so cheerful!" said Mary Anna.

"Why, that was the secret of her cheerfulness. I think she used to feel, when anything interrupted or delayed her seasons of devotion— only in a more intense degree— just as we feel when we long for communion with a beloved earthly friend. She said once that she had always a *'consciousness of God.'* "

Mary Anna's eyes filled with tears.

"I do not even so much as know what that means!" said she.

"It can be learned by every Christian," said Helen, very gently and timidly, for she felt that she was talking of mysteries into which many a saint has for years struggled vainly to look.

"It seems like presumption for *me* to think of such things," said Mary Anna.

"I said so myself to Lucy," replied Helen; "and she said it was a kind of presumption to which God called all His children. But I did not, at first, understand what she meant. Afterwards I began to see that I had been trying to be holy, not entirely in my own strength, but still wanting to have that come in and take its share in the work. Then I saw that I must renounce that, and let God do the whole. After this, as I reflected more and more on the grace and strength in Him, I saw that He had enough even for me, and that He was willing to give it to me. So, it no longer seemed like

The Flower of the Family

presumption for a Christian, even a poor, weak Christian, to strive and long after holiness. It seemed like *faith*."

Mary Anna only sighed, and looked perplexed.

"Oh, it is just as plain as daylight!" said Helen. "Lucy used to make it seem so to me; and I wish she were here now. But, Mary Anna! God will teach you Himself! I don't know anything. I keep going to Him and telling Him so; and then He teaches me. When I first became a Christian, if I found myself sinning, I always said to myself; 'Now, I know I am not a Christian!' and so I would sit crying and lamenting, and never had time to *go forward*. After Lucy came, I learned not to do so. When I fall, instead of lying on the ground, crying and wasting my time and strength in complaints, I just tell God how sorry I am, and beg Him to forgive me, and get right up and go on. Lucy told me to do so. And oh! how many times I have thanked her for it!"

Mary Anna caught this simple illustration and held it fast. She went home, already cheered and encouraged. There shone before her now a path in which, "looking unto Jesus," she longed to walk. Hitherto she had gone round and round in an endless circle of sins and sorrows, making no progress, and expecting no peace. To get to heaven at last, she hardly knew how, was all her aim. But to go there now, with Christ all along the way! This was to begin to live! Truly, the young Christian in that far-off, obscure home, had not, for Mary Anna, lived in vain! Not in vain had she made that almost "angel's visit," which to herself had ended in disappointment and pain, but to more than one was as the rising of the sun on a long-clouded wintry day!

CHAPTER 23

A Resolve

REBECCA WAS MARRIED, and had gone to her new home. The few guests who had been present on the occasion were likewise gone. The care-worn, weary mother sat down on one of the empty chairs, and would gladly have wept; but many sorrows had come and gone over her when she had not dared to steal time to shed tears, and now they were frozen up in her heart. She felt two warm, kind hands upon hers. They were Lucy's. "Dear mother," said she, "we shall be very happy, even if we do miss Rebecca."

"What! are you not to go back to your uncle?"

"And leave you with all these cares? No, indeed, mother!"

"Dear child! dear child!" cried her mother, folding her tenderly in her arms. "I thank you a thousand times; but I will never consent to this sacrifice!"

"I am here, and I will never leave you!" replied Lucy, firmly.

She felt tears dropping on her hands.

"Ah! I am so glad mother can shed tears again!" thought she.

She looked at the drooping figure, which was becoming prematurely bent, and at the gray hairs which had crept in among those raven locks she used to think so beautiful.

"I will never leave her again," she said softly to herself. And once more, when she rose from her knees that night, she repeated: "No, I will never leave her!"

"How glad I am you are going to stay at home!" cried Hatty, the next day. "I shall now have somebody to do my hair for me. It has looked like a fright ever since you went away."

So saying, Hatty placed brushes and combs in Lucy's hands, and threw herself down in a low chair, with a new book in her

The Flower of the Family

lap. Lucy sighed a little, but in a moment, resisting the thought which had occasioned the sigh, she said, pleasantly:

"I hope that is not the only reason you are glad to have me at home?"

"Oh, no! I have forty reasons," returned Hatty. "To tell the truth, I should not wonder if uncle should now invite me to take your place. Why should not he? He is rich, and can do it as well as not. And I should make a better use of my time than you did. I should see everything and everybody; and learn the fashions. And now I think of it; are you doing my hair in the latest style?"

"Oh, Hatty! what do we care for style?" asked Lucy. "I am sure I know nothing about it, at all events; I was busy with my lessons."

She felt pained by Hatty's thoughtlessness; perhaps the more so, that her strength was all summoned to one point, leaving other weak spots unguarded.

"I think in a year or two hence it would be of real service to you to go to uncle's," she said.

"A year or two hence! Why, my dear child, am I not as old now as you were when you went there with flying colors? And besides; you know very well that I came very near going in your stead, at that very time."

"What a pity you did not go!" whispered one of the boys, mischievously.

Hatty colored and kept silence for the space of, at least, two minutes.

Nothing but pride and an old bonnet, with an old faded ribbon, had decided the question. Her Uncle had invited her to accompany Lucy.

"A great deal depends on one's dress," said she to herself. "If I had had decent clothes, I should have gone, and should be there now."

She might more properly have said: "A great deal depends on one's self. If Lucy had been as vain as I, she never would have gone to visit city friends in just such garments as I disdained to wear!"

"Well, Lucy," said she, "I wonder at you, I must say. Judging from uncle's letters, they actually wanted to keep you there your whole life. And to think you should go and get homesick, and

The Flower of the Family

come driving back in such a hurry!" Twenty answers rose to Lucy's lips, but she did not give utterance to one. She thought within herself, "What matters it whether they do or do not know that it was not home-sickness that brought me here? God knows; and that is enough!"

Yet all day the remembrance of Hatty's last remark followed and grieved her. It does seem hard to be misunderstood by those one loves! And to have the great sacrifice she had made, counted as naught! Even laughed at as a ridiculous weakness! Poor Lucy felt as a little child does when it has had a fall and been bruised and wounded. She wanted to run right to her mother, put her head in her lap and cry. But a glance at the pale, worn face restrained her, and when she could break away from her labors, she went away to her own little room and 'told Jesus.' When she returned to the family, her face seemed to shine. Who has not thus seen the human face transfigured, whose happy lot has made him one of a household of Christians?

Attracted towards her, they knew not why, the little ones, who had looked shyly upon her hitherto, came and climbed into her lap, and patted her face with their soft, fat hands, calling her by those sweet, endearing names that everybody loves, but not everybody can win.

As they sat thus, Arthur came in from school.

"Oh, Lucy! are you really sitting down?" cried he. "I declare, I have hardly seen you off your feet, since you got home!"

He knelt down before her, and throwing his arms around her, gave her a real, joyous, boyish welcome home, that did her good.

"I am so glad you have come!" said he. "You don't know how I've missed you! None of them are like you, I think."

"Arthur, dear," said she, "have you been quite well since I left home?"

He looked up, quickly. She would not let her face express the anxiety she felt

"Oh, yes, pretty well, I reckon. Only this cough, more or less. But that's nothing." He went off whistling.

"Has Arthur coughed a great while, dear?" she asked, of one of the little boys.

"Yes— no!" said the child, watching her face, and instinctively shaping his answers to suit its varying expressions.

The Flower of the Family

Lucy sighed.

"I did not come home a moment too soon," thought she. "Mother has grown ten years older since I went away. And Arthur's cough! It almost kills me!"

Her eyes filled with tears, as she looked after him. He had grown very tall, but was thin, and looked delicate. Never had he looked to her so dear! As they sat together in the evening, she watched him, closely. His forehead had developed rapidly.

"What are you looking at?" he asked, a little abruptly, as he felt her examining him.

"At your forehead," she answered. "It has grown so! It is as wide and high as father's almost."

"How does home look to you, dear child?" asked her father.

"I was afraid to ask her that question," said her mother.

"It looks pleasant, father. Pleasanter than ever. My little room, too! I forgot to thank you for fitting it up so nicely."

"Arthur papered it, with Hatty's help," said her mother, "and John made the book-case. We are getting quite proud of John. And we got two boxes down at the shoemaker's, and covered them with chintz; they'll do for seats, and will hold your clothes, in part."

"And I buyed the tacks!" shouted Horace.

"Yes; Horace, dear little fellow, wanted to help on the cause, and he went and picked berries and sold them, all himself. He got sixpence for them; and to please him, I let him buy the little tacks with which we fastened on the chintz."

Lucy caught him up, and kissed him.

"How good it does seem to be at home," she said.

"Is New York as big as the world?" asked Horace.

They all laughed.

"Oh, it is bigger than that," said Hatty.

"Mother, I have not asked you yet about Mrs. Lee," said Lucy. "Did not you love her very much when you were at school together? She seems to love you dearly."

"We were intimate friends, though she was younger than the rest of *our set* as we used to call it. She was a very lovely girl, and had a fine mind. We corresponded a little after I was married; but I was full of care: you children took up my time and strength; and, by degrees, we wrote less regularly. But I love her just as well to-day as I did the day we parted, so many, many years ago. And only to think! the other day Dr. White was here, and I urged him, as I often have done, to tell me the name of the young man who ran over Arthur, and he told me it way Thornton— Edgar Thornton. And it occurred to me that he might be a younger brother of Mrs. Lee, for her father's name was Edgar."

"Then I have seen Dr. Thornton's brother, after all!" said Lucy. "Yes, it must be the very same. He must have thought it very stupid in me, not to remember! But how should I? I never had heard his name."

"Young ladies sometimes remember young gentlemen whose names they never heard," said her father, looking at her and smiling.

"I don't remember him," she answered, simply, and her father withdrew his questioning gaze, with a satisfied air, that said, "She is a child still. How could I doubt it?"

"Were you surprised when you heard our Becky was going to be married?" asked Hatty.

"Yes, indeed. I could hardly believe it. I know the boys used to joke about John Wright; but she never seemed to care anything about him. She seems still very young to be married."

Her mother sighed. "I never can realize that any of you grow older," said she. "When John Wright first spoke to me about Rebecca, I thought he was jesting. You know he is always full of fun."

"As full of fun as Rebecca is empty of it," said her father.

"He has a good farm," continued her mother, "and would not give me any peace till I would consent to their marriage. I hesitated on your account, dear; but it was of no use."

"She says I shall come and live with her," said one of the little boys.

"Unless *I* go," said Hatty.

Lucy looked at Hatty with surprise for a moment. "Oh, don't go, dear Hatty!" said she.

There was so earnest a tone in these words, that Hatty was struck by them.

"Oh, I was only jesting," said she. "But why shouldn't I go as well as you?"

The Flower of the Family

Lucy looked at Arthur; Hatty's eye followed hers, and rested upon him.

"I don't know what to make of you, Lucy," said she.

"Now, mother, I am going to be a real comfort to you," said Lucy, glad to change the subject, "I've had a long rest, and I've been to school; now I feel the better for it, and I want you to divide off a part of the work for me. Let me have all the care of the youngest children. I'll wash and dress and put them to bed; make their clothes and all that, and you'll then have time to take a little rest. Will you, dear mother?"

"You've always been a comfort to me, dear child," she answered.

"When I see how much there is to do, I wonder how I could stay away so. But I did not realize it then."

"It will be just so when we get to heaven," said Arthur, looking up from his book. "We sha'n't realize how much care and trouble and work people have; if we could, we shouldn't be happy; at least, I shouldn't."

There was silence after this remark. Arthur returned at once to his book; no one seemed particularly struck with what he had said. But to Lucy it had a voice unheard by the rest; just as his cough had. She put the little one down from her lap, and went quickly to her room— that same room where, a few years before, she had struggled with her terror and her grief on his account. All that forgotten anguish came back; it seemed to her that she *could not* live it over again.

"Oh, how thankful I am that I came home! That I can stay, and be with him; and if he is sick, take care of him!"

She heard him coming up to his room, and went out to meet him.

"You look pale, Lucy, dear," said he, stopping before her door. "Don't you feel well?"

"One thing is, I'm so glad to get home! so thankful! Dear Arthur, you don't know how hard it was not to see you for so long!"

"Yes; it was hard for me, too. Next to mother, I love you. I always have. And sometimes I think that when I am a man, and have a house of my own, you'll come and live with me; and then how we shall read and study together— you on one side of the fire, and I on the other, and a little table between us. I often lie awake at night, thinking it over!"

His face lighted and glowed, as he spoke.

"He doesn't look so sick as I thought he did," said Lucy to herself. "His eyes are very bright: I never saw such eyes; they're so large and dark, that they make him look pale and thin!"

So, for the moment, she comforted herself; not wanting to know the truth.

CHAPTER 24

A Relief

"OH MOTHER!" cried one of the children, hurrying in from school, not long after Lucy's return home, "there is a great big box down at the post-office, directed to you. And here's a letter for Lucy, too!"

While the mother suffered herself to be led off by the children, to make arrangements for the attainment of this wondrous box, Lucy eagerly opened her letter. It was from her uncle; and the old yellow note fell out and lay unnoticed upon her lap.

"I want this," said Horace, placing his hand upon it. Lucy read on, not observing the child.

"I'll put it in the fire!" he said, roguishly.

He had not lost his old trick of throwing things into the fire; and now proceeded towards it as fast as those little fat legs of his could carry him.

Closing her letter, Lucy looked up, saw the paper firmly grasped in the small hand, and hastened to rescue it. Hearing her steps behind him, Horace quickened his own; a moment, and the old yellow note was in the midst of the bright blaze; less than a moment, and there was nothing left but the logs of wood crackling and burning cheerfully away, and the minute fragment of ashes the paper had left to tell what had been there.

Lucy sat down and burst into tears.

"I'm sorry! I'm sorry!" cried Horace, not understanding her tears; and, climbing into her lap, he tried to unclasp the hands that hid her face.

She threw her arms around him, and kissed him over and over, while, with his little apron, he wiped away her tears.

"The box can't get in at the door!" shouted a merry voice.

"Oh, yes, it can, it is long and narrow!" cried another.

They all came tumbling in together, all those happy boys; and very soon the big box was opened, and then there was joy and confusion indeed! Never was there a happier group, as jackets were tried on, caps appropriated, and new city boots drawn forth and drawn on. Not one forgotten! Not one! And, in the midst of the uproar, Lucy drew her father aside and told him all about the bit of paper little Horace had destroyed, and the child repeated, "I'm sorry! I'm sorry! I won't do so again!"

"That note has lain upon me like a nightmare!" said her father, drawing a long, relieved sigh. "Yes, like a nightmare!"

"And you are free now!" cried Lucy, joyfully.

"You can't help it now. Horace has settled it for you!" and she caught the child and kissed him again, calling him a little rogue, and all sorts of pet names, till he began to think that throwing paper into the fire was a feat to be repeated on the first possible opportunity.

The good news soon reached the ears of the busy mother, who came to speak her gratitude, but could not. "This is too much!" was all she could say, and then she was glad to snatch up the baby and hide her face on his soft neck.

Lucy went now to help the children, who were almost wild with delight, as they looked farther and farther into the depths of the box. Hatty made herself useful in general and in particular, while she held fast under one arm a very special package addressed to herself, into which she had not time to look.

Lucy's quick eye soon perceived that Arthur had vanished from the noisy group. She went to look for him.

"I was tired a little," said he, apologetically, as she entered his room; "and, besides, I wanted to look at my new books. See, Lucy! all these books for me! Isn't it strange they should have sent just the very books I wanted most?"

"Yes, they are very beautiful!" said she. "But, dear Arthur, hadn't we all better be together just now?"

"How you always think of everything!" said he smiling, and following her.

"I thought they might not all understand your wanting to be by yourself when you are happy; that's all. I understand it myself, but perhaps Hatty and John—"

The Flower of the Family

"Oh, yes; I am very willing to come!" repeated Arthur. "But what have you been crying about?"

"Nothing new," said she, smiling. "Only at their kindness in doing so much for us all."

Arthur threw his arm around her, and they went down-stairs together. He saw with pride and pleasure that he was fast attaining Lucy's height, and that now they could easily walk in this position, of which brothers and sisters are so fond.

"I have grown an inch since you decided to stay at home!" said he.

"It is a dear, good home!" said Lucy. "I never wish to leave it, even for a better— if there is such a thing as a better in this world."

"It seems hard, too, for you to be tied down here when you might be enjoying yourself in school, and with Cousin Helen!" said Arthur.

"Oh, no; it doesn't seem hard! It seems *easy*!" returned she. With Arthur's loving arm around her, everything looked easy!

As they went down together, she began to explain to him about the note.

"Uncle once made me promise to accept a present from him," said she; "and I was neither to refuse, nor sell, nor give it away. So, of course, father could not help himself, if he would. Besides, Horace threw it into the fire; so that ends it."

"It wouldn't end it if father chose to make a new note; would it?"

"I don't know. I thought, when I saw it in the fire, that now father would be obliged to own himself out of debt. I don't know anything about business."

"Nor I, either. But I am pretty sure that the burning of the note need make no difference unless father chooses."

"But he can't choose! I promised uncle I would accept whatever he sent. Of course, I could not guess it was anything so important. But since I have learned to know and love uncle, and know how much money he gives away every month, I do not feel about this debt as I did before. And I don't think father does. I am sure he would not be willing to be dependent on uncle, or anybody else; but I can't see any harm in just this. It wasn't a very large sum."

The Flower of the Family

"I suppose it doesn't look very large to uncle; but it does to me; and if I live to be a man, I mean to pay it. I don't like to have people give us so much."

"People! You don't call uncle 'people,' do you? Oh, Arthur!"

He smiled.

"It is because you do not know him. Remember he is mother's own brother! You say you expect me to come and live with you one of these days; now, do you want me to pay for my board?"

He smiled again. "It seems different," said he. "I can't feel that Uncle Arthur is as near to mother as you are to me."

While this conversation was going on, another, of like nature, was proceeding between Mr. and Mrs. Grant. He was unwilling to accept this relinquishment of the old debt. Pride even urged him to leave it as an heir-loom to his children. There was no prospect that he would ever pay it himself.

"Your theory, that we must have trouble in some shape, troubles me to-day," said he. "Suppose, now, I consent to put my head out from under this yoke, do not you suppose some new trial will come hurrying in?"

"Perhaps so," she answered calmly. "But when God sends us new trials, He will send us new grace and patience. I'm sure patience with that debt was nearly worn threadbare."

"I've got so used to trouble, that I don't think I can get along without it. And no doubt God sees that I need it. But poverty is better than sickness and death."

"You can't choose for yourself which you will have. We have had the discipline of poverty a great many years. Perhaps it has done us all the good it can do. And so God is going to try something else. It may be prosperity; it may be affliction; but in either case, I know it will be just the best thing that could possibly befall us. It is no matter what happens, if we can feel that."

"I am not sure that I do feel it as you do; but I can be made to do so, when the time comes. The truth is, never, since we had children, have I been so proud of, so happy in ours, as since Lucy's return. How the child has improved! I can hardly keep my eyes off her face, it is so lovely! She is not in the very least spoiled. If anything, she is more childlike and simple than ever."

"But are you afraid anything is going to happen to her?"

The Flower of the Family

"No; only that I can see that the spot she occupies in my heart is a weak spot; one where I might be made to suffer as I never have suffered yet."

His wife looked up into his face, and smiled.

"What a mercy it is that you and I are so unlike! If I had as many gloomy fancies in a year as you have in a single day, I do not know what would become of us all."

"You've kept my head above water a good many years," he answered tenderly. "A'n't you almost tired of it?"

"It's worth living for!" she answered. "And now promise me! you'll write to my brother, accepting the release, won't you? or shall I?"

"If I accept it, I'll do it like a man," he replied. "I'll write myself."

She placed pen and paper before him. "It's best to strike when the iron is hot," she said. "By the way, have you ever asked Lucy about the money she sent home for Arthur?"

"No; we have had so much else to think of and talk about."

"Her uncle insisted on her having spending-money, as Helen did; and the dear child did not use a cent of it for herself. She must have seen a thousand things it would have been pleasant to buy. Books especially."

"We are rich in our children," said Mr. Grant, without looking up from his letter.

"I think this is going to be an easy winter," she continued. "There's no baby; and we are out of debt; and John and Arthur will both be provided for; and Lucy says she has clothes enough for herself and Hatty too. You know she won't need so many here as she did there. Every year there has been some special burden; usually a baby; but now I begin to see my way through."

She went back to the kitchen, where she found the children making merry with their new possessions.

The "baby," as they still called Willy, sat flat on the floor, in the midst of his treasures; and, with an air of ineffable satisfaction, consumed a stick of candy, while one hand grasped a stout wooden cart, whose wooden horses stood rampant under his inexperienced direction. Horace was near, arrayed in a new pair of trowsers; his hands were plunged into the depths of his pockets, where they jingled certain bright coins just discovered

The Flower of the Family

there. He looked still like a little king, as he used to do in his babyhood; and quite conscious of the dignity even majesty itself might be pardoned for seeking in new trowsers and real boots. His two elder brethren danced about him, similarly arrayed, while Tom went into silent raptures over his share of the spoils, and wondered what Fred Hays would say when he saw him come into meeting next Sunday! John was lost in thought; a complete set of tools had made him feel both rich and responsible. Such tools were not to be found every day. A boy who owned a treasure so valuable ought to be a sober industrious fellow, invent something remarkable, and immortalize himself! Every one was pleased. Every one had just what he or she wanted. Even Lucy went into raptures when she found the little simple clock, which she knew was of trifling expense, yet would be just as useful to herself as the most costly watch, as well as far more suitable in her circumstances. The combination of a great gift with a smaller one, is often happy. Thus the Grants, while weighed down under the sense of obligation, found it now. The box seemed to make the acceptance of the old note easier. The philosophy of this is simple. The smaller gift says: "Love and good-will were not exhausted in the greater favor. I come to prove it!"

Amid the joy and excitement of this day, Lucy's fears concerning Arthur were lulled to rest. He was in fine spirits during the whole evening; one of his cheeks was brilliant with apparent health, and the cough, as he sat by the fireside, sounded less ominous.

"It may be nothing more than such a cough as I had," she thought. But as she listened to it as she lay in bed, it struck her more painfully. She rose and went down as softly as possible, in search of some simple remedies that were always kept on hand, and in entering the kitchen for a candle, she awoke her mother.

"Is anything the matter?" she asked.

"Arthur coughs a good deal; I thought I would get something for him," she answered.

"He has said nothing about it," said the voice, now more anxiously.

"I think this will relieve him," said Lucy, as cheerfully as possible. "I'm so sorry you've waked up! I thought I could creep in softly without disturbing you."

"If he coughs badly, we must have Dr. White see about it," said her father.

"You know I got nicely over mine," said Lucy.

"Yes, she did," said her mother, as Lucy retired. "I dare say this is just such a cough as hers was."

Lucy crept up to Arthur: his candle was burning; he almost sat up in bed, there were so many pillows behind him. He looked up with his usual pleasant smile, and said, "Now you've caught me reading in bed!"

"It is one o'clock!" she answered.

"Yes, I dare say. But I sleep best towards morning. What's that?"

"Only a cough-mixture; come, take a teaspoonful."

"To please you, I will. Especially if you won't tell mother I read in bed!" he said, playfully. The smile and the jest did not deceive her this time. She went back to her room, and lay awake all night listening to the cough.

CHAPTER 25

A Shadow

"Oh Hatty! what spirits you are in!" said Lucy, as, arrayed in some of her sister's city garments, Hatty came dancing into her room early the next morning.

"There! isn't that a perfect fit?" said Hatty. "One would think the dress was made for me!"

"You may have it and welcome," replied Lucy. "I meant you should have some of my dresses. But, Hatty, how you do fly about!"

"Well, it is enough to make one fly, to see how cheerful father is looking. And I can tell you, such presents as came yesterday won't come every day in the year!"

"No, indeed, I hope not," said Lucy.

"Oh, Lucy! do put away that matronly air. It is not becoming to you at all. You and mother seem to think it a sin to smile."

"Oh, Hatty!"

"Well, you try to keep me from smiling, at any rate. Now, what harm is there in my 'flying about,' as you call it?"

"None, dear Hatty. It does me good to see you happy. Only sometimes I look forward to the time when you will have real troubles, and then I long so to give you something that is even better than mere good spirits— something to lean on when they fail."

"We should not borrow trouble," said Hatty.

"No; but there is no harm in borrowing sunshine, if it will make a gloomy future less gloomy. Indeed, dear Hatty, I hope your evil day is far off; and I would not alarm you now, if I could help it. But I must speak to some one, and I dare not excite mother's fears until I have consulted you. Ever since I came

The Flower of the Family

home, I have noticed how extravagantly fond you are of Arthur; as indeed we all are. He is certainly a remarkable boy!"

"That he is indeed!" returned Hatty. "His teacher says he is the finest boy in school. And you have not the least idea how he has appeared while you have been gone. So kind to all the children; so affectionate towards mother! She often has spoken of it, and said Arthur would be the stay and staff of her old age."

"I am sure he will be that to us all, if he lives to become a man," said Lucy. She paused and listened. From Arthur's little room she still heard that cough which through the long night had vibrated through every nerve of her heart.

"But I don't understand you!" said Hatty. "Is anything the matter with Arthur?"

"He seems changed; and looks ill, to me. And his cough—don't you notice that?"

"Oh, Lucy! I don't think he looks ill! What can have put that into your head? It is true he grows tall, fast; and that makes some difference in his strength."

"Don't be excited, Hatty dear," said Lucy, detecting beneath these careless, pettish words, real anxiety and alarm. "We must not forget that Arthur is in the hands of God, and that nothing can befall him without His consent. I shall be sorry I spoke to you about him, if you look so! I felt so afraid some terrible blow was coming! And you appeared so unprepared for it!"

"If Arthur dies, I hope I shall!" cried Hatty, passionately.

"I know you don't mean that! But I have given you great pain; needlessly, perhaps. But that cough! Listen, Hatty!"

Hatty listened. The cough, hitherto hardly noticed, now sounded painfully in her awakened ears.

"Lucy!" said she, "I'll tell you what I think about this world. I think it is a *hateful* place to live in! Just as you get to feeling contented and happy in it, some dreadful thing happens, and you don't care whether you live or die!"

"Well, dear Hatty," said Lucy, weeping, "and is not this the very reason why we want our happiness established on something which is not changeable? Something which cannot die, even?"

Poor Hatty could not answer. The shadow of her first real sorrow was stealing over that path which had seemed all

The Flower of the Family

sunshine. Everything hitherto had given way before her beauty, her health, her fine, joyous spirits. But now—

She rushed from the room to find her brother.

"He *shall* not die!" thought she.

She flew to Arthur's door: it was early, and, worn with the fatigue occasioned by his cough and a sleepless night, he had not yet risen.

"Come in!" he said, on hearing Hatty's knock.

She darted in, and threw herself into his arms, in a paroxysm of tears and sobs.

"What is the matter?" he asked, in great alarm.

"Oh, Arthur! dear Arthur! dear, darling Arthur! don't die! don't die!" she gasped.

"Who says I am going to die?" he asked, becoming very pale, and looking towards the little window in vain yearning for air. In her half frantic grief, she did not observe the look, but went on incoherently:

"Only just *live*, dear Arthur; you may be sick, if you've a mind, and you needn't even try to be well; and it's no matter if you don't even talk, if it hurts you! Only just live; only just promise you will!" She fell on her knees by the side of his bed, and, clasping her hands, looked imploringly up into his face. He looked down upon her with a smile she never forgot; the momentary surprise and alarm had subsided; he lay back upon his pillow, very pale, but serene, almost joyous.

"If it were not for you, and mother, and Lucy, I should be too happy!" he said, faintly. He coughed again; and the red life-blood gushed forth, staining the clasped, imploring hands, and the white sheets, and the pretty dress in which Hatty had decked herself. She ran shrieking to Lucy, who, on her knees, was wrestling for submission to the Will which was so full of mystery. In a moment she was at his side, had seen the pale, deluged figure, and, suppressing the agony that struggled not less fiercely in her heart than in Hatty's, she sought the simple remedy always at hand, and, for the moment, always available. Arthur was relieved; he smiled upon her, and pressed her hand, and would have spoken; but she would not allow him. Their father and mother now came hurriedly in. John, and Hatty, and the little children came on tiptoe, and holding their breath, behind their parents. How much anguish can be crowded into one small room! How much can lie in one heart, or hide under one calm smile!

Arthur greeted each with a glance of pleasure, which each strove vainly to return. His father allowed himself time for only one kiss upon the white forehead, and then went hastily out in search of Dr. White, who had not left his house, and was therefore speedily by Arthur's side. He said little, and prescribed little; entire rest, however, he enjoined strictly. Once more trembling hands arranged the "north room" for the sick boy; once more a fire burned on its cold hearth, and with gentleness and care he was carried thither. No one understood the occasion of his sudden illness, save Arthur and the self-upbraiding, miserable Hatty. She knew but too well that by her recklessness and precipitation she had hastened the evil day she sought only to arrest. How thankfully Lucy now recognized the good Providence by which she had been brought home! She was not now torn from Arthur's side by the pressure of other duties; she was granted the luxury of sitting by his side hour after hour, day after day; to watch every look, to dwell on every tone, to feel the thin fingers clasp her own with fervent affection; to see the pale face grow brighter at her approach, and the loving eye follow her every motion. With his failing life, her strong heart grew stronger; she felt that there was an Arm beneath and around her whose power she never could have learned save in the hour of sorrow. One evening, as he lay quietly with closed eyes and appeared to sleep, she sat down by his side, thinking over the past and arming herself for the future. All her disappointed hopes concerning him lay withered before her, and as she regarded them, a heavy sigh escaped her.

"Is that you, Lucy?" asked Arthur.

She started up and went to him.

"I thought you were asleep, dear," said she.

"No, I was looking at you. I was thinking how anxious you have been, ever since I can remember, first, to have me good; then, to see me wise. And now you need not feel grieved that I have not had the education you meant I should have. For I am going to a far better school than you even ever asked for me. Christ, Himself, will teach me. I shall learn of angels, and of

The Flower of the Family

apostles, and of those great and good men who are now saints in heaven. And I want you to know, because it will comfort you when I am gone, that you showed me the way there. You went first, and I followed. I did not think so very much of what my father and mother said. I thought they were old, and tired of life, and liked religion because it fell in with their matured tastes. But I could not think that of you. I knew, when you urged me to go to Christ, that He must be a friend for the young, too."

"I wouldn't talk any more now, dear Arthur," said Lucy, gently.

"No, it does me good. I want to hear you say that you are glad for me that I am going away from this world. And, Lucy, take care of poor mother. Comfort her when I am gone. And Hatty too; I think a great deal of her which I would tell you, if I were not so weak. You must lead them all to Jesus. Mother will help you; Jesus Himself will help you. Never mind if they don't learn anything else; I see how worthless the finest education would be to me now, if I had that and nothing else."

"I'm afraid to let you talk any more, dear Arthur," said Lucy: "I love to hear you; but I know it tires you?"

"No, it does me good. I want to say one thing more, because it may help to comfort you when I am gone. And I may not have another time, so good as this." He rested a few minutes in silence, then said, "I have been thinking of that day we went to the top of Mount Prospect, in H__ , together. You know I went first, and how tired I was, the sun was so hot, and the hill-side so steep. While I was going up, I kept pitying you, who were far behind, to think you had to climb all the hard, rough path, in the heat and over the stones. But when I got to the top and sat down there, and saw the beautiful view, that paid for all the trouble; then I left off feeling anxious about you. I said to myself, 'She'll soon be here; it isn't far; and she'll forget her fatigue when she sees what I see.' "

He paused again to rest. Lucy fanned him gently, and moistened his lips. After a time he began again:

"Just so it seems to me, when I look back now from the place I'm in. I should feel sorry— yes, I should be distressed to see you climbing up, and climbing up, and getting hurt in the rough places, and faint in the heat; but I look down, and it's only a little way; you're almost here; and when you get here, you won't even

The Flower of the Family

remember how you got here; you'll have enough to do looking at the beautiful view. You'll think you were only a minute in coming; you'll forget what hard work it was toiling up. Have I made it plain? do you understand? For I'm almost there; I sha'n't be able to say much more." He fell back, exhausted, upon his pillows.

Lucy went quickly out and called her mother. Arthur had fainted; it was long before they could restore him. When at last he opened his eyes, he smiled upon them and said, "I thought I was almost there!"

These were his last dying thoughts; he was never again able to converse, save in whispered sentences. Growing weaker every day, and not inclining to talk, he lay quietly listening to hymns and Bible words; sometimes making a single, child-like remark about going to Christ's school; and then relapsing into silence again. Poor Hatty, gentle and thoughtful now, hung over him night and day, secretly reproaching herself and bewailing her indiscretion; yet solaced by many a loving word and caress from the happy, dying boy.

At last, with a hand of his beloved Lucy in one of his, and that of Hatty in the other, Arthur entered fearlessly into the valley of the shadow of death; and they who had known his life, doubted not that when the sisterly grasp was detached from his, angels came and entered into their places, and guided him onward to a better country, and into the enjoyment of eternal felicity.

CHAPTER 26

The Broken Circle

ARTHUR WAS GONE, and his little room, wherein he had early given himself to God, remained as a Bethel for more than one of the weeping household. There his mother knelt often while her children slept, and sought consolation for herself and for them.

Lucy loved there to catch the spirit of her departed brother, and so nerve herself for the cheerful performance of the duties pressing upon her. And Hatty too would often steal to this little sanctuary, hide her face upon his pillow, and weep such tears as needed not to be repented of, while she breathed petitions which sorrow alone could have won from her hitherto thoughtless heart. Even the little boys felt heaven very near when they could creep noiselessly into dear Arthur's room, look at his well-arranged books, and recall holy words he had often spoken to them there. A quiet serenity settled down upon them all, and soon it might have seemed that everything went on as before. Alas! every bereaved heart knows it could not have been so! Death cannot enter a family circle and snatch thence the least of all its members, without leaving traces of his icy fingers on many a chilled hope, on many a silenced spring of action. Rivers of waters cannot wash away his footprints from the family hearthstone; ages of sunshine can never restore to it its original warmth!

To Arthur's parents this affliction was one of the last drops in a cup that years had been filling to its brim. Yet it was a new experience of life. Amid all their trials and cares, they had been spared the parting with their children. Up to this time the circle had remained unbroken; and whatever may be said to the contrary, before facts can prove it, a beloved object is not less

The Flower of the Family

missed and mourned from the full, than from the scanty household. Each takes his peculiar place in the affections of the rest, and death leaves that place vacant; no other object can perfectly fill the empty, aching spot. Who, of all that great family of children, could become Arthur? Not one!

To Hatty the death of Arthur was the first step in that process by which the great Refiner purified her unto Himself. Who is fit to live in this world or to die, and enter upon the next, who has not suffered? As well might the unripe grain be gathered in the harvest!

"The loving discipline of pain!" how good it is! how needful! The curtain which hides from the common eye the realities of life, was for Lucy rent in twain. She now saw with distinctness those truths whose vague forms she had dimly traced before, and the emptiness and nothingness of those things that once seemed full and substantial. Laying firmer hold on those truths that are as an anchor to the soul, she returned soberly, but at once, to the duties of life. For, changed as the world was to her, and that forever; deep and imperishable as was her grief, there was in her nothing morbid, nothing selfish. They who saw her smile light up the dark chamber of death, who marked her cheerful submission, her unshrinking faith, were taught lessons not too easily learned, yet not easy to forget. There had ever been peculiar love and sympathy between herself and Arthur, and his maturity of mind had lessened the distance years had placed between them. Very sorrowfully she wrote to her aunt, "If you and Helen had seen him, I should mourn him less!" Yet this was but one of those delusions with which the bereaved heart indulges itself: it must leave these tearful "*ifs*" ere it can find rest. The minute details of our afflictions are directed by Him who sends the sorrow with just these painful accompaniments. In time Lucy learned this, and saw that submission to the great sorrow involved submission to its peculiarities; for who that has suffered has not found in *his* lot something singular and unique?

The health of Mrs. Grant had been failing for some years. Her cheerful temper, combined with not a little power of endurance, kept her up when many would have fallen fainting by the wayside. But Arthur's sickness and death developed already existing disease, and gradually she was laid aside from her labors. She gave up one care after another, reluctantly, and after a struggle: at first she seemed to be about among them as much as ever; but, by degrees, her seat at the table became vacant; to-day she was not up in season for breakfast— to-morrow, both breakfast and dinner went silently through without her. Thus, in time, all the household care descended on Lucy; she became the "sister-mother." The books she had brought home with her, and which she had felt sure she could find a little time each day to study, lay untouched in her room. She rose early, toiled all day, went late to bed; the work was never *done*. For, however nicely it ended with the day, did it not begin again next morning, just as it did yesterday? But she carried no repining heart to her daily task. She felt that if their lives were all spared, there was nothing else to ask for but *grateful* hearts; and to her, at least, it came with the asking. This winter offered a strong contrast to the last. Then she was the admired, envied, advancing scholar, surrounded with luxuries, and free as the air she breathed. Now she lived almost unknown and unnoticed, in the retirement of an obscure country village, appreciated and understood only at home; a mere household laborer outwardly; bound with fetters that confined her to a tread-mill round of monotonous, over-recurring tasks. Very patiently she resigned herself to her lot; and every day's discipline, unconsciously to herself, mellowed and softened her character, making it more Christ-like, compassionate, and gentle. Thus was she taught to live as she prayed to live. Not merely by direct supplies of grace, but by temptations and trials, developing and strengthening the new life within, and forcing her to a closer union with the Author of that life.

She was not without solaces of another kind. The affection of her parents was like a living spring, and the satisfaction of making their last their best years, was very great. The children, too, enlivened and cheered her; she felt that they were better teachers than books. Then there were long, kind, loving letters from her aunt and Helen, and Mrs. Lee; sometimes, too, Miss Prigott's old-fashioned characters found their way to the village post-office, and thence to Lucy's heart. Since Arthur's death, Hatty had ceased from her restless, capricious mode of life; she patiently shared Lucy's labors, and proved herself most efficient and skillful.

The Flower of the Family

Meanwhile John secretly carried on a series of experiments in one corner of the wood-house, where he had made himself a workshop, on whose door appeared in large letters the words, "No admittance." He had "sowed his wild oats," he told Lucy, and would not distress her or his mother by going to sea. He thought he should invent something that would astonish her in due time; so, early in the morning, and at all other leisure moments, he might be heard, though not seen, busy at his work-bench. Now and then the cheerful whistle with which he enlivened these solitary hours would suddenly subside into a lower, sadder key, finally ceasing altogether. A remembrance of Arthur; an impulse to call him to look at his work; the image of the loving lost brother; these were getting the victory for the moment. But soon the boyish spirits would rise again; the whistle again came cheerily in at the opening doors, as Lucy moved about, busy with her work, and the new invention grew apace into actual form and shape.

He came to her one day with a flushed, triumphant face. "My machine works!" he cried; "it works, Lucy! Come out now and see!" She followed him, and he exhibited it to her; explaining its uses, enlarging on its capacities and beauties, till she caught his enthusiasm.

"You'll want money now to carry your scheme through," said she. "And I've got some for you; you shall have it all; I've been saving it for you. How glad I am!" She was hurrying away in search of the hoarded sum— that allowance forced upon her by her uncle, but still unappropriated.

"Thank you," said John, catching her by her dress, and bringing her back, "I don't need it. When uncle was here, he set me to blacking his boots one day, and he came out here when I was doing it, and saw a wind-mill and a lot of other things lying about. He examined them all, and especially that little steamboat: don't you remember I made one once?"

"Well; at the time I was so crazy to go to sea, and had got all ready to go, uncle wrote me a kind but very odd letter, saying he remembered that I had quite a mechanical genius, and that it ought to be the making of me. He sent a little money in the letter; enough, he said, to buy a few tools; and promised, if I would invent or make something useful, he would soon furnish me with

The Flower of the Family

a complete set of the finest tools New York afforded. He charged me, too, to study the mathematics diligently. I told nobody but Arthur a word about it; but I studied hard, as well as I could without help; and now you see the end of it! I mean the beginning: for the end will be, that you'll ride in your coach and six!"

"I never want to do that, or anything like it," said Lucy, smiling, "but I've no doubt you're going to make a great man, and throw us all into the shade!"

Not a month after this conversation, John was established by his uncle in the family of a Mr. Haskins, where he could pursue his mathematical education. Mr. Haskins had been a practical, scientific engineer; an accident had laid him aside from active duty, and he willingly instructed a few boys. The understanding between John and his uncle was, that after the first year he should pay his own way; and this, as the result proved, he was able to do with ease as well as pleasure. One care was thus lifted from the drooping shoulders of the anxious mother; Lucy's labors were also lightened, and the winter closed favorably for them all.

Early in the spring Rebecca came home to spend a few weeks. Her husband had taken it into his head, she said, to build a larger house; what for, nobody knew but himself; but there was no use reasoning about it. And theirs was to be pulled down, or dragged away, she did not know which. So she had come home and very glad she was to do so. At the time of Arthur's illness, John Wright was laid up with a broken leg, and Rebecca had not been able to leave him for any length of time; she was now, therefore, only too thankful to come to talk with them all about their beloved brother, and to tell Lucy many little, interesting things, known only to herself.

"I noticed his cough," said she, "and spoke to mother about it. But she thought it was like the one you had, and that it would pass away."

"I know you did, dear," replied her mother; "but I was so busy at that time, and beginning to be sick myself; and he seemed so well! I was perfectly infatuated; I can see that plainly. But God chose to have it so!"

"I did not ever think he would live long; at least, I never did after John spoke to me about it. But I wasn't ready for it, when it

The Flower of the Family

came! And it seemed hard to be away, and lose all his last words!" said Rebecca. "But now I am going to stay and help you all; and not make you cry. When I first came in, I missed Arthur so, that I couldn't talk about anything else."

She settled herself down among them, and the whole summer passed before the new house was habitable; so she remained and was a comfort and help to them all.

Her marriage had improved her not a little. She had been obliged to depend on herself as she never had done; her husband was cheerful and kind; there was only one thing wanting to complete her happiness. This was one of the children. She said it seemed strange to see no little folks about the house; that John said it was lonesome, and she must bring back one or two of her brothers with her.

"I should like to have Willy," said she; "but I suppose mother wouldn't spare him."

"Oh, no! he's my baby!" said his mother, laying her hand fondly on his little curly head.

"Horace would amuse John," said Rebecca.

"Oh, you can't have Horace!" cried all in a breath. "He is such a rogue, too; you could do nothing with him."

"The little ones would be too much trouble for you, dear," said her mother. "Tom had the promise of going; but he's our biggest boy, now; the girls need him. He's getting very useful, now. And you don't want him for that."

"No; besides, he's 'most too good to suit John. He wants to frolic with whoever he has; he tried me at first, but it was of no use. I couldn't."

The idea of grave, moderate, staid Rebecca, getting into a frolic, amused Hatty. She began to laugh as heartily as in olden times; but suddenly stopped, and burst into tears. "How can I laugh so, when Arthur is dead!" she cried.

"Do laugh, dear Hatty," said Lucy, tenderly; "we all know how you loved him. Nobody will think you have forgotten him! Dear Hatty! do smile once more, like yourself! I do think it would *rest* me, if you would!"

Hatty smiled through her tears; but it was not the old, sunny smile.

"No, I never can be what I was before!" said she. "But perhaps I shall be better! I'm sure I hope so!"

"We haven't decided yet who Rebecca shall have," said Lucy. "I think it should be Hatty. It will do her good; and if she chooses, she may take one of the children with her, if mother is willing. We'll have somebody come to wash and iron; I can do all the rest. And Hatty needs change and rest."

Her mother opposed this plan; she knew that Lucy could not bear all the household care alone.

"It is the will of God that I should sit here, almost helpless," said she. "If it were any will but His, I couldn't bear it."

"We shall get along nicely, mother," said Lucy. "I feel well, and able to do a great deal; I've got a little money to help us along when we get into hard places; and I'm going to use it, in making things easy and pleasant for you. I hear one of them coming now." She ran out, and soon returned with a comfortable, stuffed chair, in which she helped her mother to seat herself, and for which she had sent fifty miles.

"There!" she cried, "all the books in the world couldn't make me so happy as this chair does! Nor all the watches, either!" she added to herself.

CHAPTER 27

A New Home

THE ARRANGEMENTS MADE by Lucy's friends for the previous summer, were now executed. The whole party came to H__ , which was a pleasant mountainous region, and very soon had established themselves so agreeably there, as to resolve to make it their future summer resort. Lucy had now the pleasure of seeing the meeting between her mother and aunt; and was delighted to find them mutually attracted towards each other. It was also delightful to witness the renewal of the school-day friendship; to hear Mrs. Lee call her mother "Sarah," and to hear her mother, in return, address Mrs. Lee as "Hatty;" just as if long, long years had not passed since their last meeting.

"I must let you see your name-sake," said Mrs. Grant after the first greeting, and drawing Hatty towards Mrs. Lee. This was a pleasant surprise to Mrs. Lee, who needed, however, no proof that she had been beloved and remembered.

"I wish my brother had known this," said she, "when he was so unfortunate as to injure one of your sons. It would have made him feel that he knew you." Mrs. Lee was not aware that she was referring to the dear boy they all were mourning, but their silence suggested it to her. She hastened, therefore, to change the subject. Seeing her friends so often during this summer, was of great service to Mrs. Grant. She needed the gentle stimulus their society furnished; Lucy saw with delight that it seemed to reanimate her.

Helen was perfectly contented if she could only be near Lucy; by degrees she settled down among them as one of the family; Hatty charmed her; such good boys she never had seen; as for the bread and butter, there never was anything like it in the world.

The Flower of the Family

"I see there's no use in trying to carry you off," she said one day to Lucy. "They can't do without you. But if you'll let me, I'll come every summer; I shall read to you and improve your mind, while you make bread and butter, and all sorts of good things, to improve my color. And we'll have delightful times together!" So she followed Lucy one whole day, with a book in her hand; but at night she said, they must invent a new plan: for the children had each asked one hundred questions, that had to be answered one hundred times; and the pot had boiled over twice and put the fire out; and Lucy had got dreadfully tired, with mind and body on the stretch at once. Then she thought she would help about the work; so she insisted on dressing one of the children, whom she drove to such a state of desperation by the length of the process, that he told his brother in confidence, that if people were going to be a year in tying his shoes, he guessed he should have to learn to do it himself; also inquiring how *he* should feel, if a *girl* should button up one of her long ringlets in his jacket, so that they were fastened together like a yoke of oxen.

Rebecca, however, was at home; she smoothed away some of the difficulties, and made time for Lucy to devote to Helen. So the summer passed to the satisfaction of all, and when Mrs. Whittier and Mrs. Lee departed, it was in full expectation that the following summer would reunite the circle.

But with them, left also the transient flash of apparent health, with which Mrs. Grant had been borne through the summer. Her strength sank at once; she became helpless as a child, and needed constant attention day and night. Rebecca was summoned home by her husband, who was heartily tired of living alone; and the four little boys went with her, at her urgent request. Indeed, it was quite necessary that this relief should be furnished Lucy and Hatty; for their cares and anxieties were now very great. It was a long, hard, sorrowful winter: the smiles of the patient sufferer alone enlivened it; for, seeing her constant, ceaseless pain, they could not smile; they could only try to imitate her in her patience. It was on a quiet spring morning that the struggle ceased; and the face that had borne the impress of mortal agony for eight weary months, shone with the beauty of undisturbed repose. The tranquil, benign expression, put aside for a season only in the conflict with death, came back and was sealed upon

The Flower of the Family

the brow. They had not seen her look so like herself during the whole weary winter as now, when death restored what sickness had taken away. Who that looked upon that face, could doubt that "all was well?" Above all, who that had known the patient, Christian, cheerful life, could doubt it?

The mourning household went to lay her down by the side of Arthur. They thought they knew what sorrow meant, when they saw the earth cover him out of their sight. But it had a deeper meaning now, "for in all the world they could find but one mother."

Once more the old routine of domestic labor was taken up; the little motherless boys clung now to Lucy; to her they ran with their childish troubles; in her lap they hid their heads and cried, and wished mother would come back. And while her tears fell upon the bowed heads, she still had a smile for them, lest home should seem too dark and gloomy; and the cheering word for her father was not wanting, nor the loving one for Hatty.

Yet in all her life she never knew an affliction like this. Except as sin could bear more bitter fruit, she was now enduring the severest form of affliction: no earthly object had yet come between herself and her mother; and who has ever lost more than that he held dearest? It was finely said by an already bereaved mother, when informed of the sudden death of her only remaining child, "I see God means to have my whole heart; *and He shall!*" And so said Lucy now. From that hour when her mother was laid in the grave, God had her whole heart. She devoted herself, if possible, more entirely, too, to the little flock remaining.

The path of duty is comparatively easy when once made plain. There had been some conflicts in Lucy's mind as to hers. Mr. Jackson had twice written during her mother's illness, urging her return. He proposed that she should pursue her studies in his school for another year, and thus become qualified to take a prominent position as teacher there. She had felt that should her mother recover, it might be best for her to do this; Hatty, perhaps, could thus receive the education she needed, and much be done in behalf of the boys. But there was no question as to her proper course now; and she began at once to give herself to her family in love and labor, as to her life-work. The summer months

The Flower of the Family

brought her friends again to H__. They saw that she had planted herself in this country home, and that the best years of her youth must pass in the discharge of the merest household drudgeries; in the ceaseless care of those restless boys; the sacrifice of all her tastes. They suggested means of escape; devised plans among themselves; attempted to excite her father's ambition, and then his fears concerning her. But Lucy had decided for herself; and while she thanked her friends, she would not suffer them to move her. In vain they represented her choice as unworthy so noble, so refined a nature, fitted for the pleasures and the duties of a wider sphere; Lucy was satisfied with being unknown, with the "trivial round, the common task," with the sweet rewards of home-affection, and the approbation of a conscience at peace with God. What would be the worth of the highest honors of this world without these?

No idle time hung upon Lucy's busy hands. Hatty patiently shared all her labors; but she wished to give her such entire change of scene and rest as she had herself enjoyed. She did not hesitate to propose to her aunt to take Hatty home with her; and she was too eager to gratify her slightest wish, to make such a proposal improper.

"I longed to suggest it myself," was her aunt's reply; "but feared it would leave you too lonely, and with too much labor on your hands."

"It will do me more good to know that she is with you and Helen than I can possibly describe," said Lucy.

Hatty was not, at first, willing to go. She knew better than any other member of the family, save Lucy, just what there was to do. But Lucy was firm; she had resolved that this thing should be, and her strong will had great power in it. Two years ago, on her own return, she shrank from the thought of exposing Hatty to temptations for which she was then unprepared. But now the shield of sorrow was about the young heart; she felt that with God's grace it could protect her in the midst of dangers.

Hatty went: John had returned, after his mother's death, to Mr. Haskins. There were now left, for Lucy's love and care, four boys from seven to thirteen; the baby, Willy, still remained with Rebecca, who could not be induced to give him up. Of these four, Tom was the eldest; he was a noble little fellow, often getting into trouble, but always truthful, affectionate, and full of penitence after wrong-doing. To him Lucy now gave Arthur's little room, hitherto unoccupied; many of the books he loved, and the seat in the corner, so long left vacant. Tom was not equal, intellectually, to Arthur; he was small in stature, and fully aware of his inferiority in that respect. When his mother died, he thought he never should smile again; he wished he could die too, and have a little grave by her side, as Arthur had. He used to go and lie among the tall grass by her grave, and think how short and narrow a strip it would take for him; and if he were a good boy, how peacefully he should sleep there. But by degrees Lucy won his confidence; he began to honor and love her, and to tell her of his troubles at school, and how the boys laughed at him and called him "Tom Thumb." Lucy had intended to keep him at school a few years, and then, if advisable, send him to college. She hoped to be able to fit him for it herself by the time he left the school in which he was now placed, and which was of a very ordinary kind. But his mortification concerning his little stature, now first revealed, made her change this plan. She took him from school, made him bathe and take exercise, work on the farm, and amuse himself to his heart's content. He had never cared for books; his whole desire had been to play; but he had never had his fill of that, and of late he had moped about a good deal. The result of Lucy's experiment proved its wisdom. Tom gained health and strength and appetite; and years afterward, when a man, and six feet in height, to say nothing of the inches, he used to tell Lucy that she had *made* him.

Two years from the time he was taken from school, he began suddenly to grow tall; strong he had already become; at the same time he returned vigorously to his studies, and gained in a year what he had apparently lost in the two. Lucy worked hard to keep in advance of him; but she succeeded, and had the satisfaction of preparing him for college.

"Father," she said to him one evening, when he sat looking more than usually sad, "can you afford to send one of the boys to college?"

"Which of them?" he asked languidly; "the baby?"

Lucy laughed; "Tom is all ready," said she. "May he go?"

The languid air gave way before this unexpected news.

The Flower of the Family

"Lucy has fitted me for college!" said Tom triumphantly; "all herself! Can I go, father?"

"Yes, indeed, and Lucy too, if she will!" said her father, laying his hand on her head. "Dear child what should I do without her?"

"Can you really afford to let me go, father?" asked Tom again.

"Yes, easily. And to-morrow, if you choose."

Tom caught up Horace, and threw him into the air like a ball; he was half beside himself with joy. "You may hear me preach yet, father," said he.

"This looks like it, to be sure," said Lucy smiling.

Meanwhile the younger boys were not neglected: during the day they were all at school; but in the long winter evenings Lucy amused and taught them, and made them very happy. They never wanted to lose one of these evenings around the pine table, by going elsewhere; and after Hatty's return, one of them read aloud, while their sisters were at work; a plan of threefold value, inasmuch as it beguiled their father of the long evenings his failing eyesight made useless to him, entertained the busy needlewomen, and kept the boys employed and happy. Those who were not reading, knit: many years later, Horace exhibited to his wife a towel of his workmanship, with which he had bought an old Latin grammar.

Thus, year after year passed. The days of Lucy's youth went too; yet she remained still young. One temptation had disturbed the even surface of her life; and for a season, its very depths were stirred. It was put aside. Its history was never written. Thousands of hearts have thus suffered, and thus conquered. Dr. White had always prophesied that "that youngster" would come back. But if he came, he soon went, and Lucy remained outwardly the same.

Leaning upon her, her father passed serenely through his declining years, even unto death. Hatty went at last to a home of her own. The brothers ceased to be boys, and went forth into the world. Of all that great household, Lucy was left the only one alone. Even Helen's summer visits ceased at last. She, too, was a wife and a mother.

Among all the homes that now stretched forth friendly arms towards her, to which should Lucy go? She hesitated not long. In a wide, empty house, there dwelt still a little, old, faded woman;

older, more faded, more solitary than when, fifteen years ago, she offered a home to the young and beautiful girl. Thither Lucy went; not now so young, but to many eyes more beautiful. Miss Prigott's old heart rushed to meet her. Together they sat down at one fireside; talked over the years that had passed, and of the heavenly world yet unseen. Old age had been busy with the lonely, childless woman; but it had left the warm heart untouched. It glowed now with a happiness it had never known.

Years of domestic happiness had not stolen from Helen her school-day love. She welcomed Lucy with all her old tenderness; and found her the same Lucy with whom she had taken sweet counsel in her girlhood. Herself unchanged, save that from the enthusiastic dreamer, she had become the enthusiastic doer of all that is lovely and of good report, Helen applauded, rather than censured Lucy's choice of a home.

"You are making Miss Prigott's last days more than happy!" said she. "But remember, you are mine next!"

By widely differing paths, Lucy and Helen had arrived at nearly the same point.

God leads some of His children gently, and over a smooth and comparatively easy path; and to others He appoints the "winding way, both dark and rude." And while the same hand leads alike over the plain and through the intricate way, the favored pilgrim will not boast himself, neither will the wearied one repine.

In her own happy home, surrounded with every comfort this world can offer; blessed in husband, blessed in children, Helen still kept her eye fixed upon treasures that are invisible and eternal. If her leisure and her wealth were now almost without limit, so were her acts of benevolence, and her errands of mercy, and her "alms-deeds which she did."

"You are my own child, now!" Miss Prigott said fondly to Lucy, every day. At first it seemed only as an expression of affection; but there are not wanting those in every community who are faithless as to the existence, in this world, of pure benevolence. What could induce a beautiful, accomplished young woman like Lucy to come and live with a capricious, fretful, dying old woman, but the hope of ultimate gain?

These unjust suspicions assailed Lucy's ears; for a time disturbed her mind; but when, shortly after, Miss Prigott was found sleeping peacefully in her bed, that "last long sleep that knows no waking;" and it was found that, at Lucy's urgent entreaty, all her vast possessions had passed into the treasury of the Lord, busy tongues were silenced, and envious ones satisfied. True now to the playful promise of her youth, Lucy went to Helen, sat down, as of old, at her side, and there began to live over again the happy days they used to spend together.

Who that looked upon that radiant countenance on which the very peace of God had forever stamped itself, could venture to lament the discipline that had left such beautiful traces?

And here we would gladly leave her, had no more than one voice, exclaimed against it.

One of these voices, familiar to her youthful ear, made itself heard again in the depths of her heart. It whispered of years of long patience, fidelity, and devotion. It wooed her to all the refinements of the circle she was formed to grace; it gave her glimpses into a soul where she saw only noble aspirations and yearnings after God. At last, obeying its behests, she went whither it called her, found herself welcomed into a warm, manly heart; and there lived her last, which were also her best days! And thus was fulfilled the prophecy of Dr. Thornton!

~THE END~

"Daily Food for Christians"

In this story, Lucy receives a wonderful gift for her birthday. It is a devotional book called, "Daily Food for Christians." This is mentioned on pages 85 and 105. Lucy finds great comfort in reading her "Daily Food." This is a real book which was originally published by the American Tract Society in the early 1800's. It was a miniature book measuring about 2 inches by 3 inches in size. The subtitle describes its contents:

"Being a Promise and Another Scriptural Portion for Every Day in the Year Together with the Verse of a Hymn."

Mrs. Prentiss owned one of these devotional books. It was given to her, as a gift, in 1835 when she was 17 years old. Many years later, she wrote about her love for this devotional in a letter to a friend in 1868:

"I have had this little book thirty-three years, it has travelled with me wherever I have been, and it has been indeed my song in the house of my pilgrimage."

A new edition of this rare book is now available through The Legacy of Home Press. We have transcribed its contents into a larger, 5 inch by 8 inch edition, under the same title.

This book is available in both paperback and hardcover editions.

Paperback (5" x 8")   ISBN: 978-1-956616-06-4

Hardcover (5.5" x 8.5")   ISBN: 978-1-956616-07-1

Also Available:

The Legacy of Home Press edition of "Stepping Heavenward" by Mrs. Elizabeth Prentiss:

This edition is available in both hardcover and paperback.

Please visit our website to read about all the special features of this edition.

For more titles by The Legacy of Home Press, please visit us at:

https://thelegacyofhomepress.blogspot.com

Printed in Great Britain
by Amazon